I0565853

By the Author

Death Comes Darkly

Death Goes Overboard

Death Checks In

Death Takes A Bow

Death Overdue

Death's Prelude

Death Foretold

Visit us at www.boldstrokesbooks.com

Praise for David S. Pederson

Death's Prelude

"I highly recommend this story, introducing Heath and giving more insight to his past, as well as setting up the series nicely. The most fabulous thing though was seeing Heath blossom into the detective I met in *Death Overdue*, and I can't wait to read the next mystery he has to solve."—*LESBIreviewed*

Death Overdue

"Deftly drawn characters, brisk pacing, and an easy charm distinguish Pederson's winning follow-up to 2019's *Death Takes a Bow*. Pederson successfully evokes and shrewdly capitalizes upon the time in which his mystery takes place, using the era's prejudices and politics to heighten the story's stakes and more thoroughly invest readers in its outcome. Plausible suspects, persuasive red herrings, and cleverly placed clues keep the pages frantically flipping until the book's gratifying close."—*Mystery Scene*

"David S. Pederson never disappoints when it comes to twisted and suspenseful mysteries...I highly recommend the Detective Heath Barrington mystery series, and *Death Overdue* in particular is suspenseful and an absolute page-turner."—*QueeRomance Ink*

Lambda Literary Award Finalist *Death Takes a Bow*

"[T]here's also a lovely scene near the end of the book that puts into words the feelings that Alan and Heath share for one another, but can't openly share because of the time they live in and their jobs in law enforcement. All in all, an interesting murder/mystery and an apt depiction of the times."—*Gay Book Reviews*

"This is a mystery in its purest form...If you like murder mysteries and are particularly interested in the old-school type, you'll love this book!"—*Kinzie Things*

Lambda Literary Award Finalist *Death Checks In*

"David Pederson does a great job with this classic murder mystery set in 1947 and the attention to its details..."—*The Novel Approach*

"This noir whodunit is a worthwhile getaway with that old-black-and-white-movie feel that you know you love, and it's sweetly chaste, in a late-1940s way..."—*Outsmart Magazine*

"This is a classic murder mystery; an old-fashioned style mystery à la Agatha Christie..."—*Reviews by Amos Lassen*

Death Goes Overboard

"[A]uthor David S. Pederson has packed a lot in this novel. You don't normally find a soft-sided, poetry-writing mobster in a noir mystery, for instance, but he's here...this novel is both predictable and not, making it a nice diversion for a weekend or vacation."—*Washington Blade*

"Pederson takes a lot of the tropes of mysteries and utilizes them to the fullest, giving the story a knowable form. However, the unique characters and accurate portrayal of the struggles of gay relationships in 1940s America make this an enjoyable, thought-provoking read."—*Gay, Lesbian, Bisexual, and Transgender Round Table of the American Library Association*

DEATH FORETOLD

by

David S. Pederson

2021

ISBN 13: 978-1-63679-086-2

This Trade Paperback Original Is Published By
Bold Strokes Books, Inc.
P.O. Box 249
Valley Falls, NY 12185

First Edition: August 2021

CREDITS
EDITORS: JERRY L. WHEELER AND STACIA SEAMAN
PRODUCTION DESIGN: STACIA SEAMAN
COVER DESIGN BY SHERI (HINDSIGHTGRAPHICS@GMAIL.COM)

Acknowledgments

Thanks to my friend David Paris for his assistance with information concerning the Florentine Opera Company. He and my friend Derin Bjugstad are opera goers and a wealth of knowledge.

And thanks to Gloria Goodrich and her father, Gerald Goodrich, for their assistance in my research into life in Milwaukee in the 1940s, specifically police work and entertainment.

Their knowledge was a tremendous help, and any errors that may exist in the book are strictly my own.

The Blatz Hotel was a real place, but all the characters and events in my novel are fiction, and the interior descriptions are strictly from my imagination.

This book is dedicated to all the LGBTQ+ people in history who have fought and struggled, at first to remain hidden, and then to be seen and heard.

Special thanks to all my family, and to my friends who are my chosen family, and all my readers. Thank you!!!

And as always, thanks and all my love to my husband, Alan, the key to my lock.

Finally, thanks also to Jerry Wheeler, my editor with the most-est, and everyone at Bold Strokes Books who have helped me so much, especially Radclyffe, Carsen, Sandy, Cindy, Ruth, Stacia, and Sheri.

Chapter One

Afternoon, Friday, September 12, 1947

She glared up at me as I approached. If looks could kill, I'd be on a slab in the morgue. "Good afternoon, Miss Blake," I said cheerfully. The police chief's secretary was at her desk, going through some old case files. She was in her early to mid-thirties and wore her long, dark hair pulled back and up most of the time. She rarely smiled, at least not at me. I never could figure out why. I sometimes flattered myself by thinking maybe it was because we were both single, yet I'd never asked her out on a date in the three years she worked there. Or maybe she'd heard rumors about me, or maybe I just rubbed her the wrong way for one reason or another. Still, I continued to be friendly.

"He's expecting you."

"Yes, I know. You called me at my desk, remember?" I said, giving her one of my best smiles.

"Are you attempting to be funny?"

"No, just lightening the mood. Or trying to. I hope everything's hunky-dory."

"Hunky and dory, I'm sure, Detective Barrington."

"Plans for the weekend?"

"Not that it's any of your business, but I'm working both days for a few hours. The chief wants to catch up on a few things."

"Oh, that's too bad. About you having to work, I mean."

"I'm sure it breaks your heart. Your boss is waiting," she said, staring up at me, her eyes narrow and her red lips pursed.

I sighed. "Right, see you in the funny papers." I walked past her into the chief's small, cluttered office, closing the door behind me.

"You wanted to see me?"

"I did, Barrington. Have a seat." He was sucking on an unlit cigarette as he sat at his desk, his shirtsleeves rolled up to his elbows.

I pulled up a chair and sat down across from him, careful of the crease in my trousers.

"You're not working on anything at the moment, are you?" he said.

"No, I finished up that Martinelli case last week. Why?"

"Because the All-Seeing Almanzo is here in town this weekend. Ever hear of him?"

"Yes, actually. Almanzo Firestone, the spiritualist. I read in the newspaper a couple months ago that he was coming to Milwaukee. I have tickets to his show on Sunday afternoon. A friend of mine is a fan."

The chief's bushy caterpillar eyebrows shot up in surprise. "Firestone has lots of fans. Or lots of suckers who believe in all that stuff and are willing to pay good money to see him. Frankly, I thought all that spiritualism crap died out in the twenties and thirties."

"Well, this friend of mine is really a believer. There's a few of them still around."

"Apparently. You're a pretty cynical police detective, Barrington. I didn't think a man like you would be into all that hocus-pocus, crystal ball hooey."

"I try to be open-minded, but I'm mainly just going for support. Because of my friend."

"A friend, eh?" The chief leaned back into his chair and broke out in a grin, the unlit cigarette dangling precariously from his lips. "Oh, I think I see what you're up to. Your friend is a female, isn't she? Must be this Ellen I've heard the fellows talk about, and you're trying to butter her bread, so to speak, by attending something she wants to see even if you have no interest."

"Well, uh, no, not exactly, Chief. Not this time, anyway. I'm just doing a buddy a favor, is all. He doesn't have a car, and he lives on the other side of town. He'd have to take a bus and transfer to a streetcar just to get to the theater if I didn't drive him." I didn't really want to have to explain to the chief that my friend was police officer Alan

Keyes, and I certainly couldn't tell him Alan was my boyfriend. Not if I wanted to keep my job, and Alan's, too.

"Oh. Nice of you to help a buddy out like that, I suppose."

"He's done a few favors for me," I said, which was true enough. "And I figure the show might be entertaining."

"Good for a laugh or two, anyway. Well, this Almanzo character is hosting a reception tonight at the Blatz Hotel for members of the press and local dignitaries, trying to drum up some publicity, I imagine, and I want you there."

"At the reception? What for, Chief?"

"Reports have come over the wire from the Gary and Kansas City police departments, the last two cities he toured. Complaints about possible fraud. Typical stuff for these spiritualist types. Besides the Sunday matinee you and your buddy are attending, this All-Seeing fellow is also putting on a performance tomorrow evening, and I want to know if the complaints are justified before he skips town Monday morning."

"Most likely they are."

The chief leaned forward again and rested his hairy forearms on the paper-covered desk. "Most likely."

"Yes, but it's my understanding the victims in these types of cases don't typically complain," I said. "They get to talk to their dear departed, or they believe they do, they pay their money, and they go away happy. I'm surprised this Almanzo has gotten complaints."

"He must not be as convincing as some of the other shysters. The complaints were mostly from people who felt he wasn't on the level. That's why I want you at this reception. Get up close to him undercover and feel him out. I want you to arrange for a private performance with him before he leaves town, too."

"Private performance? In what way?"

"You know, a séance, a palm reading, card reading, whatever it is he does to bilk people out of their hard-earned money. Apparently he sets up these private performances with suckers before and after his public shows. See if you can catch him in the act when it's just you and him."

"Sure, I see. Pretend I'm a follower."

"That's right. You'll be posing as a member of the press at the reception, but I also want you to convince him you're a believer. Maybe your friend can give you some tips. Might be smart to take him along tonight if he's really that big a spiritualism fan."

"He is, and I'm sure he'd like that."

"Good. Just be discreet. Don't tip your hand. You'll be a reporter from WBSM radio. See Miss Blake for your credentials and phony business cards. I had to pull a few strings to get a couple of invites to the reception. I was thinking it would be you and a date, but if this friend of yours is really into all this ghost stuff, that might be better."

"I'll call him right away. I'm pretty certain he's free tonight."

"Okay. Ask Miss Blake for additional credentials for your friend, then, though if he's with you he may not need them. There wasn't time to put your name on the phony business cards, so you can both use them. The reception starts at eight."

"Right, I'll be there. We'll both be there."

"Good. Go easy on the booze at this thing, though. I want you sharp and alert. And don't forget to turn in your expenses, but don't go overboard, either. Spelling turned in an expense report last month for valet parking, champagne cocktails, and a steak dinner at the Circus Room in the Hotel Wisconsin when he was investigating a smuggling ring. I put him on a simple vandalism case and a strict budget this month."

"I'll be thrifty, don't worry."

"Glad to hear it. Keep me posted, Barrington. I expect a full report," he said, spitting out the wet cigarette into the wastebasket and taking another from the silver case on his desk.

"I will, of course. Still trying to quit smoking?"

He sighed heavily and stared at the unlit cigarette, turning it over and over in his fingers. "Yes. The things we do for our womenfolk."

"Yeah, but I guess they're worth it."

"Some are. Speaking of that, this Ellen I've heard the guys talk about, she's someone you're dating, is that right?"

I swallowed a couple of times. "Uh, yeah, nothing serious, though. Just a nice girl." I had made up Ellen to take suspicion off me and Alan, but the lie seemed to be growing bigger.

"Still, I'm glad to hear it. Bring her by the station sometime. I'd like to meet her. I'll talk you up, help you butter her bread and get in good with her."

"Sure, Chief, will do, thanks."

"You're welcome. You know, the wife and I sometimes have the detectives and their wives or girlfriends over for dinner to the house. If you and this Ellen hit it off, you could be included."

"That would be nice. I'll let you know how things work out."

"Do that. And you're dismissed for now."

"Yes, sir." I left his office, got the credentials and fake business cards from Miss Blake, and telephoned Alan about the reception that evening. As I figured, he was delighted. I told him we could eat at my place beforehand to save time.

CHAPTER TWO

Evening, Friday, September 12, 1947

"Thanks for dinner," Alan said, sitting back in his chair with a satisfied grin. *The Jack Benny Show* was playing on the console radio in the living room of my apartment, but we weren't really listening to the program.

"My pleasure. Though franks and beans aren't all that difficult."

"Everything was delicious. You even managed some good old Pabst Blue Ribbon, ice cold. You're a good cook."

I laughed. "I opened a tin of beans, heated them in a pan on the stove, boiled water for the frankfurters, and took the beer out of the icebox. Not exactly the work of a gourmet chef."

"Well, I thought it was top notch, cutie pie. And speaking of pie, what do you have in mind for dessert?"

"I have a craving for something tall, dark, and delicious," I said, winking at him.

"You are an evil man, Heath Barrington," he said, blushing adorably.

"Not evil, just mischievous."

"And playful and incorrigible. I must say I like that in a man."

"I'm glad to hear it."

"It's true. But I was thinking along the lines of pie or cake or something. You know me and my sweet tooth."

"I do indeed. I suppose we can save the other for another time, all things considered."

"Yes, especially since we have to go to the reception tonight and we're running short on time."

"Okay, handsome. I think there's a couple of doughnuts in the bread box, so help yourself."

"Chocolate?"

"Just plain, but they go good with coffee. I put a pot on earlier."

"Great, join me in a doughnut and a cup?"

"Sure."

"Coming right up," Alan said, getting to his feet and moving into the kitchen. "How does Grant Riker like being a detective, by the way?" he said over his shoulder as he poured two cups of coffee. "Has to be a change from being a police officer."

"Yeah, a big change. I guess he likes it well enough," I said. I was still seated at the dining table, watching him through the doorway. I enjoyed the way he moved, the way he stood, the way he looked. "I haven't had much of a chance to talk to him about it yet. He's a natural, though. Smart, inquisitive, tough, and he has a photographic memory. I think he'll do well."

"Sounds like you," Alan said, bringing the two cups of hot, black coffee into the dining room. "You've got more moxie than Carter's got little liver pills."

"Eh, I'm not so sure. Sometimes I don't feel so smart. And don't get me started on my memory some days."

"You just have a lot on your mind, that's all. Want a plate with your doughnut?"

"Yes, please."

Alan retrieved two doughnuts from the breadbox, put one of them on a small plate, and then stepped back into the small dining area. "Here ya go," he said, handing me the plate. "You might want to dunk that, they seem kind of hard."

"Thanks," I said, picking up my coffee cup and the doughnut.

"You're too rough on yourself, Heath," he said, standing next to the table, his own cup in his right hand, his doughnut in his left.

I looked up into his startling blue eyes. "Maybe. Riker doesn't lack for confidence, that's for sure. He oozes it, and that's something any detective needs. Certainly the extra money is a plus for a family man, too."

"Yeah, that's right. He has a wife and a kid. Harder to support a family on a policeman's wages."

"You ever think about becoming a detective?" I said, setting my cup down and taking a bite of the doughnut. Alan was right, they were a bit stale.

"Me? I don't have a wife and kids to support, remember?"

I smiled. "And that is a good thing. I don't sleep with married men as a rule. But you would be a good detective."

"Maybe someday, if I get the chance. But as I recall, you like me in my uniform," he said with a devilish grin.

"I like you out of your uniform, too, Officer," I said, grinning back at him and winking once more.

"Sweet talker."

"It's all true. I really like having you around here in general."

"I like being here with you, too."

"I hate having to sneak you in and out, though, or pretending you slept on the sofa in the living room when you spend the night."

"We do what we have to. It's the way it is," Alan said, moving slightly so he could lean against the arched doorway between the living room and dining area, still holding his cup with one hand while he dunked his doughnut with the other.

"True, but you know, Mrs. Murphy told me about a two-bedroom opening up on the second floor the first of November for fifty-two dollars a month, heat included. Mr. and Mrs. Mattern are moving to West Allis to be closer to their daughter. With the housing shortage, there's a waiting list for bigger apartments, but since I already live here, I think Mr. McNulty would let me have it."

"You thinking about getting a bigger place?"

"Yeah, but I'd need someone to share it with. A roommate."

"I'm no detective, but you're leaving clues that aren't too hard to figure out, even for a simple policeman like me."

"There's nothing simple about you, handsome. So, what do you say?"

He stood upright and arched his back, stretching. "Move in with you? Gee."

"If we got a two-bedroom it would seem like we're just roomies, you see? Plus moving in together would save us both money. We'd split the rent, the groceries, the utilities, and you're over here all the time anyway."

Alan chuckled. "Heath Barrington, last of the red-hot romantics."

"I'm sorry. I guess I'm not saying this very well."

He looked thoughtful. "Well, you're direct and to the point, at least."

"I usually am. So what do you think?"

"Gee, I don't know. I'd feel kinda guilty if there's a long wait for a two-bedroom and we just jumped to the head of the line."

"I know, but there's a long wait for one bedrooms, also, and if you and I took a two bedroom, there'd be two one-bedrooms available instead of just one two-bedroom."

"I guess that's logical, if a tad confusing, but I have a lease at my current place through the end of the year."

"I can carry the two-bedroom until your lease is up, I don't mind. I've got some extra money set aside."

He took another swallow of his coffee and finished his doughnut. "Let me give it some thought."

"Okay, but I really hope you say yes. It just makes sense, logically speaking."

He walked over and touched the back of my neck, giving it a gentle squeeze. "You're something, Heath Barrington. Thanks for letting me do my laundry downstairs again, by the way. The washer's still on the fritz in my building, and I'm out of clean underwear. I want to look my best tonight. I'm going to put on my best bib and tucker."

"You always look your best, and I highly doubt anyone at the reception is going to be seeing you in your underwear. At least I hope not."

"You know what I mean, wise guy."

"Yeah, I do. It's unfortunate your building only has the one washing machine, but if you lived here you wouldn't have that problem. There's multiple machines down in the basement. No waiting, even if one breaks down."

"Another romantic reason for moving."

"Hey, I've got lots of them. So, besides clean underwear, you're all set for tonight?"

"Absolutely. I still can't believe we're going to a private reception with the All-Seeing Almanzo. I almost dropped the phone when you called to tell me today."

"I'm glad you're looking forward to it. I figured you would be."

"You know it! I wonder if we'll actually get a chance to talk to him?"

"That's why the chief wants us there, though he doesn't exactly know it's you who's going with me, so keep that quiet if you can. I just said I was taking a friend who believes in spiritualism."

"I understand. Like I said, we do what we have to do."

"And don't forget, we'll be posing as reporters for WBSM radio."

"Okay, but I'm not sure I'll be very convincing, Heath. I don't know the first thing about being a reporter."

"Hey, this is your chance to see what it's like to be an undercover detective. Don't worry, I'll do most of the talking. If Firestone asks, just say you're new to the radio station and you're learning from me."

"I guess I can do that."

"I know you can. Think of it as playing a part, like acting when you were in that play. And don't forget your press badge and the business cards I gave you."

"I put the cards in my wallet and the press badge in my suit coat pocket. Are we using aliases?"

"No. Less chance of a slip-up if you're just Alan and I'm just Heath."

"What if Mr. Firestone calls that telephone number on the phony business card looking for one of us afterward?"

"It rings to a special line on the central police switchboard. The operator knows to answer it as WBSM radio for the next few days until the investigation is complete. We use the same number for most undercover operations and clue in the switchboard operator each time on how to answer."

"Smart thinking," Alan said. "How are you going to go about investigating him, by the way?"

"The chief wants me to see if I can arrange a private séance or something. I've thought about creating a late, great, wealthy Uncle Horace I want him to summon for me."

"Too bad you don't really have a late, great, wealthy Uncle Horace. If you did, maybe we could both retire," Alan said, glancing at his wristwatch. "Jumping Jehoshaphat, it's already a quarter after six, I better go check on my laundry. It should be done by now, and I want to get it hung up to dry before it gets too late."

"Okay. We should leave by seven thirty at the latest."

"Right, I'll be back in a jiffy." He left his now empty coffee cup and a few doughnut crumbs on the dining room table and walked through the living room out into the hall of the building, closing the door behind him. After he left, I swept up the crumbs, took the two coffee cups and the other dishes into the kitchen, and washed them up in the sink, along with the pot, pan, and other scant utensils I had used to make dinner. Just as I was drying the last plate, I heard the hall door open and close.

"Laundry finished?" I called out from the kitchen.

"Yes, all hung up to dry. Should be good to go before we have to leave. I can get everything folded and back in my hamper and then we can put it in the back seat of your car. You can drop me home after the reception."

"Good. Though you don't have to head home tonight if you don't want to. You could stay until morning."

"You know I'd love to do that, but I promised Mrs. Halifax I'd walk her dog later. She's visiting her sick brother in Sheboygan. Besides, I'm staying over here tomorrow night. Two nights in a row would raise suspicion. Like you said, you can't have the neighbors talking."

"Okay," I said with a sigh. I hung up the dish towel and walked into the dining room. "But once again, if we had a two-bedroom, we wouldn't have to worry about what the neighbors think."

Alan laughed. "You sound like a broken record."

I noticed he was carrying an old, small wooden box in his arms as he came toward me. He was peering down into it with a gleeful expression on his face, like a little boy who'd just gotten a puppy for Christmas.

"What's in there?" I said.

"Take a look!" He placed it carefully on the dining room table so I could see and then took a seat next to it.

"What on earth? Rats? You brought me rats? Where did they come from?" I said, exasperated and surprised. Two brownish-gray furry little creatures were scurrying about frantically, pawing at the sides, and squeaking, their whiskers twitching, their long tails flicking back and forth.

"Mice, to be precise, not rats. Rats are much larger. I noticed Mrs. Ferguson's cat had these two cornered in the basement when I went down to check on my laundry. The poor little things were terrified."

I stared at Alan, his face now full of concern and care. "I can imagine they would be. So, you rescued them, of course. Frankly, I'm surprised they got cornered. I thought Oscar was too fat and sassy to chase mice."

"Obviously not," Alan said, looking back at me. "Though I think he didn't know what to do with them once he caught them. Still, he was very proud of himself." He glanced back down into the box. "I locked Oscar out of the laundry room, then found this old box in the storeroom. I set it down and the mice scurried right in, like they knew I was there to help. I think they're kinda cute."

I looked at the little mice again. "In a rodent sort of way. They certainly are frantic."

"Yes. Reminds me of myomancy."

"You mean Milo Clancy? One of the sergeants down at the station?"

Alan laughed. "Sergeant Clancy does have whiskers like a mouse, but no, I meant myomancy, a method of divination using mice or rats. The All-Seeing Almanzo uses it sometimes."

I rolled my eyes. "I should have known. The All-Seeing indeed."

"I know you're a skeptic, but I must say I'm excited to see him in person. And I really do appreciate you inviting me to his reception tonight, even if it is only because you're investigating him."

"My pleasure. The chief thinks you being a legitimate fan might help me get close to Firestone. Though at first, he thought you were a lady friend I was interested in. I'm going to have to be careful about that. I've told a few of the fellows I'm seeing a girl named Ellen."

"Oh?"

"Yeah, seemed like a good lie at the time, but now some of them are asking to see a picture of her and wondering when I'll bring her around, including the chief."

"Jeepers, how does that saying go? Oh, what a tangled web we weave…"

"When first we practice to deceive. I know. I'll have to figure something out, maybe hire an actress to play the part and then, sadly, she'll break it off with me and shatter my heart. But maybe not until after she and I get invited to the chief's house for dinner."

"That seems a bit extreme," Alan said.

"It's how it must be. Ellen will end it, and I'll be so heartbroken, I won't be able to date again for a long time. That should keep the gossip down for a while."

"Hey, maybe you'll meet an actress that could play Ellen when we go to see the All-Seeing Almanzo's matinee on Sunday at the theater. Thanks again for getting tickets to that, by the way."

"You're welcome. Fortunately, tickets weren't too hard to come by and not all that expensive. And don't forget our deal."

"I know, I know. I said I'd go with you to the opera tomorrow night if you go with me to the matinee on Sunday."

"A deal's a deal. Don't forget the opera is black tie."

"I remember. It will be nice to have a chance to wear my tuxedo again."

"Same here. Want me to pick you up? I have to go into the station tomorrow, but I should be finished by noon. We can do dinner beforehand some place downtown."

"Dinner would be nice, but why don't I meet you here, say about six o'clock? No need for you to go out of your way to pick me up."

"Okay, if you're sure. And I think you'll like the opera, Alan, really, if you give it a chance."

"Maybe. And I think you'll enjoy seeing the All-Seeing Almanzo."

"Doubtful," I said. "So, he uses mice in his act?"

Alan looked up at me again. "It's not an act, it's a demonstration of his abilities. And no, I don't believe he uses myomancy on the stage, but he's written about it. Quite fascinating."

"I'm sure. You've actually read one of his books?"

"He's only written the one, and yes, I have. I borrowed it from the library. There's a whole chapter on myomancy and how mice can predict catastrophes and bad omens by their movements and sounds."

"I can't even imagine what the other chapters are on. Lizards foretelling our love lives by how they flick their tongues? Owls divining our future by how they hoot or the shape of what they regurgitate?"

Alan shook his head. "Ever the skeptic."

"Can't help it, sorry. But I'm glad you're up on all this. Like I said before, the chief thinks your knowledge will come in handy tonight, and so do I."

"I'll do my best."

"And that's good enough for me. Do you still have that library book that Firestone wrote?"

"No, I returned it, why?"

"I was just thinking it wouldn't hurt for me to study up a bit. Maybe I'll swing by the State Street library tomorrow morning and see what all I can find on spiritualism and the occult. I want to go into the station for a while, too."

"There's a lot of information on the subject. It can be overwhelming," Alan said. "There's one whole shelf devoted just to fortune telling."

"I'm sure. So, what are you going to do with these two fortune-tellers, anyway?" I said, pointing into the box but keeping my finger at a safe distance from the little rodents.

We both stared back into the wooden crate once more. I noticed at least one of the rodents had relieved himself, staining the floor of the box. "I don't know, exactly. I suppose I should take them over to the park and release them," he said, getting to his feet. "They should be safe there."

"Good idea. The farther from here, the better."

"Okay." Alan picked up the crate, and the mice went even more frantic, clawing and scratching at the sides. "You know, their peculiar cries like that are supposedly an indication of forthcoming evil or trouble, according to Firestone's book."

"So you've said. But evil is always present, Alan, and trouble is always just around the corner. You should know that as a police officer."

"Yes, that's true, but I can't help but think these two are trying to tell me something in particular."

"If they're trying to tell you anything, it should be a huge thank you for saving them from being Oscar's dinner. Now get them out of here. I need to shave and start getting dressed, and so do you."

"All right, we're going! I'll be back to get changed just as soon as I release Moe and Myrtle."

"Oh great, now you've named them."

Alan grinned. "You know me and animals."

"I do. I must admit it's one of the things I adore about you." I leaned over the box and kissed him lightly. "Better hurry up, though. It's nearly dark. And don't get bit."

"I'll be careful, I promise."

I was just putting on my suit coat and straightening my tie when the telephone rang. I turned off the radio and picked up the phone on the third ring, wondering if it was the station. Or worse, if it was Alan telling me he was at the doctor's office after getting bitten by a rabid rat.

"Hello?"

"Oh good, you're home."

"Hi, Mom. Yes, but I'm getting ready to go out."

"Of course you are. It's a Friday night, and it seems you're always out gallivanting. You've been doing that quite a bit lately. Taking Verbina to the theater, having tea with her, going to the movies. Who knows what all you do? I'm the last to know, it seems."

"I'm having tea with Aunt Verbina this Tuesday afternoon, actually."

"Oh, really? At the Pfister Hotel again, I suppose." She made that annoying clicking sound with her teeth.

"That's right. Auntie and I have tea there once a month, more or less. You know that."

"And how often do you see your mother?"

"I try to stop by two or three times a month. You *also* know that."

"Yes, you *try* to, but last month you only visited once. Your father misses you, you know. Would it kill you to come over at least once a week and to telephone once in a while?"

"I'm sorry. I've just been really busy. I'll see what I can do, Mother, I promise."

"Good. So, what are you doing tonight?"

"I have a reception to go to at the Blatz Hotel for work."

"That doesn't sound like work."

I sighed. "Well, it is. I can't really talk about it, though."

"Hmm. Well, I plan on baking an apple pie tomorrow. Mr. Archer gave me a whole bushel basket full of apples from his tree. Why don't you come for supper? I'm making roast chicken and red potatoes and carrots, and we can have the apple pie for dessert. I'll have your father make some vanilla ice cream."

"That sounds really nice, Mom, but I can't tomorrow. I'm going to the opera."

"The opera? Again? I don't understand where you get that from. What's wrong with a good old-fashioned play?"

"An opera is a play, of sorts. Only with music and singing."

"And expensive, I bet. Your father and I paid a dollar and a half each to see Fay Bainter in *Our Town* last fall, and I thought that was too much. I can't even imagine what they charge to see these highfalutin operas. You should save your money. And don't go buying things on credit, Heath. It's no good. If you can't pay cash, you don't need it. That's always been our philosophy, your father's and mine. We even paid cash for this house, at least a healthy down payment, anyway. We paid off the mortgage four years ago."

"Yes, you've told me that many times. You and Dad lived in a two-room apartment above the Woolworth's on Wisconsin Avenue until I was almost four years old. You made all your own clothes and lived on stew and creamed chipped beef made with dried and salted meat."

"Yes, all because we were saving money so we could buy a nice house for the three of us. Even during the Depression, we never went hungry and always had a roof over our heads and clean clothes on our backs."

"Yes, and I truly appreciate that. Funny you should mention saving money, Mom, because I'm thinking of getting a roommate."

"A roommate? In your little apartment? Whatever for?"

"To save money. And there's a two-bedroom coming available in my building the first of November."

"Well, that makes sense. But you could move back home if you're having trouble financially, dear. Your room is just sitting there, and you could stay here rent free."

"I know, you've told me *that* many times, too. My room is almost exactly as I left it. My glee club pennants are even still up on the wall."

"It's your room, Heathcliff. Whenever you want to come back, it's waiting for you."

"That's sweet, Mom, really. But I don't think that's going to happen."

More teeth clicking. "What's wrong with your father and me and our nice little house?"

I sighed. "Nothing. Nothing at all. I love you both very much. But I'm over thirty, as you often remind me. I think I'm a little old to move back in with my parents. And didn't you tell me once that you'd thought of turning my old room into a sewing room?"

"I can sew at the dining room table, like I always have. And you said you're having trouble financially, dear. Regular home-cooked meals would do you good. You're too thin."

"I didn't say I was having trouble financially, I just said I could save some money by getting a roommate. Besides, you're always saying I spend too much time alone."

"You *do* spend too much time by yourself, at least when you're not out gallivanting. But a roommate? That doesn't sound like you, dear."

"I just think it makes sense, that's all."

Rapid teeth clicking now. "Well, I did hear Ronald Schwartz has been talking about moving downtown. He'd make a good roommate. His mother tells me he's very tidy."

"Who?"

"You know him. Virginia Schwartz's boy. Ginny and I play canasta on Tuesday afternoons. Ronald is your age, and he's been working at the power company. He doesn't have a car, so he has to rely on the bus and it's been rather challenging, I've heard, going back and forth."

"Ronnie Schwartz. I remember him now. He used to steal my lunch in grammar school and sit on me on the playground at recess until I turned blue."

"No one's perfect, dear. And people change. Grammar school was a long time ago."

"*Some* people change, and not always for the better. Anyway, I'm thinking about asking Alan Keyes, my friend from the police department. We get along pretty well, he's about my age, and we could both save some money by sharing a space."

"You spend a fair amount of time with this Mr. Keyes. I should like to meet him some time."

"You will if we get a place together."

"Hmm. Is he seeing anyone?"

"You mean does he have a steady girl? I don't think so, no. But if he does, I'll ask her if she has a friend or a sister. Or the sister of a friend."

"That's always a good way to meet someone, Heath. You won't find nice girls in taverns or the theaters. Taverns aren't the place for a sensitive young man like yourself to meet a sincere, sweet young thing. No, much better to be introduced by a mutual friend. That's how I met your father, you know."

"Yes, I know. Your finishing school classmate, Ethel Kinney, introduced you to her brother's friend."

"That's right, and look how well we turned out. Speaking of meeting people through mutual friends, dear, I've heard Ronnie Schwartz's little sister is still single."

"I'm not surprised. She used to beat me up too."

"Well, I'm sure she wouldn't do that anymore. She's really a lovely girl, with very nice teeth. She'd make a beautiful bride."

"Mom…"

"You're over thirty, Heath. It's high time you settled down, you know. You could save money by getting married just as easily as taking on a roommate."

"I know, you've mentioned that a few times, too. Look, I've got to go, Mom. Say hi to Dad for me, okay?"

"All right, dear, but do let me know when you can come for supper again soon."

"I will. Bye."

"Bye, dear. Maybe next weekend, okay? Don't forget to eat well in the meantime."

"Right, gotta go, bye." I hung up before she could get another word in.

"Who was that?" Alan said as he came in from the hall, carrying the now empty box.

"My mom. Didn't get bitten by Max and Mitzie?"

"Moe and Myrtle, and no, I didn't. They have been happily relocated to the park. I watched them scamper away to a hiding place under a log."

"Lucky for them, and for me, that you have a big heart."

"Aww, pshaw." He looked me up and down. "Gee, you look spiffy. I always like you in that gray suit with the lavender tie."

"Thanks, that's why I wore it. You'd better hurry and get changed, though. We have to leave soon."

"I'll just run down to the basement and grab my laundry."

I looked at my pocket watch. "It's a few minutes after seven already."

"I'll be quick. And you can fold my clothes and put them in my hamper while I clean up and change. It will save time."

I looked at him suspiciously. "You hate folding clothes. Why do I feel like you dawdled in the park with those rodents on purpose just to get me to do that for you?"

Alan grinned. "You know me so well." He opened the door to the hall. "I'll be back faster than you can say jackrabbit, Mr. Barrington!"

CHAPTER THREE

Night, Friday, September 12, 1947

True to my word to the chief to be budget conscious, I parked on the street three blocks from the hotel rather than use the valet, even though a light rain had started falling and the wind had picked up off the lake.

We left my car at the curb and walked briskly up the sidewalk side by side.

"Gee, Heath, I would have paid for the valet," Alan said as he pulled his suit coat tighter about him and his hat down lower on his head. "And we're already late."

"Because you took almost an hour to get your laundry, clean up, and shave."

"Sorry, but I wanted to look my best."

"Your worst is most people's best, my friend. Besides, it's just a little rain, and the wind's not too bad," I said. "It's rather invigorating."

But I was glad when we reached the main entrance on Wells Street at half past eight. We were both damp and chilled, and it felt good to get indoors. The doorman informed us the reception was on the second floor, in the Braun Room. We took the stairs up and walked down the corridor to the coat check, where a pretty young girl who must have been all of eighteen or nineteen smiled at us. "Good evening, gentlemen. May I check your hats?"

"Yes, please," I said, handing mine to her as Alan did the same. "How much?"

"It's complimentary, sir," she replied, but I noticed she nodded ever so subtly to a tip jar off to the side.

"Don't worry, I can take care of the tip," Alan said. He pulled two dimes from his pocket and dropped them in the jar.

"Gee, thanks," she said, handing us our claim tickets. "Are you here for the reception?"

"That's right, for the All-Seeing Almanzo," I said.

"Just down the hall on the right, through the double doors."

"Thank you, miss," Alan said.

"My pleasure. You, uh, didn't bring your wife?" she said, looking rather dreamily at Alan.

"No, miss. I'm not married."

"Steady girl?"

Alan shook his head. "Not at the moment."

Her smile got bigger. "Gee, that's swell! I mean, I see. The reception ends at ten, and I get off duty at ten thirty."

"Well, be careful going home tonight, it's raining and rather windy out. The temperature's dropped a fair amount," Alan said.

She made a pouty face I supposed some men found adorable. "Yes, I noticed your hats were rather wet. This weather's going to mess my hair and my new shoes. I take the streetcar, you know. I'll get soaking wet unless someone would be kind enough to drive me. I don't live all that far."

"I'm afraid we likely won't be staying until the end of the reception," I said. "But I hope you get home safely."

She glanced briefly at me and then back at Alan. "Oh, that's too bad. I'm here most weekends if you're ever in the neighborhood. My name's Sally. Miss Sally Pfluger."

"How do you do? I'm Alan Keyes."

"Nice to meet you, Miss Pfluger, but I'm afraid we must go now," I said, taking Alan by the elbow and guiding him away and down the hall.

"Good night," Alan said over his shoulder.

"See you later, Mr. Keyes."

As soon as we were out of Sally's earshot I said to him, "You, my friend, have the curse of being too good looking."

"Aw, she was just being friendly and hoping for a ride home since it's raining and all."

"Uh-huh, sure." I glanced toward the double doors on our right as we approached. "Looks like this is the place."

A bored-looking waiter with a tray of champagne glasses was standing just inside. "Good evening, gentlemen. Members of the press?"

"Yes, that's right, WBSM radio," I said as we showed him our press badges.

"Welcome," he said. "The champagne is complimentary, courtesy of Mr. Firestone, but it's a cash bar."

"Thanks," Alan said. We each took a glass from his tray, stepped in, and surveyed the small meeting room.

"Sparsely attended," I said, looking around. "Can't be more than fifteen or twenty people here at most."

"Yeah, not exactly the crowd I was expecting. But it's early yet. It just started half an hour ago."

"Still, it's just for members of the press and local dignitaries. It's not like it's open to all of his fans. That would certainly be a sight to see, I'm sure."

Alan gave me a disapproving look. "What kind of crowd do you think that would be? Kooks and weirdos? Dim-witted blokes and loony ladies? Spiritualism is real, Heath. Just because you don't understand something doesn't mean it's fake, and it doesn't mean that everyone who believes in it is off center."

"You're right, of course. I'm sorry. But you must admit a lot of people involved in this spiritualism gig take advantage. And they use that advantage to make money at other people's expense."

"I suppose that's true. But even if Almanzo is making money off people, even if he is fraudulent, that doesn't mean all of spiritualism is a hoax."

"Okay, I apologize, you're right again. Let's just see how the evening progresses. Come on, we need to find the All-Seeing Almanzo."

We mixed and mingled a bit, moving amongst the reporters and photographers in attendance, along with a few aldermen and members of the city council who most likely only came for the free champagne. Fortunately, I didn't recognize anyone who could blow our cover.

"There he is. Over there by the bar," Alan said. "The attractive, dark-haired one in the black suit and green tie. He looks just like his picture on the back of his book, right down to that eye thingy."

"A monocle," I said, finishing my watered-down champagne. "I think it's time for a refill."

"I'll follow you, Heath, but no more champagne for me. That stuff goes right to my head."

"It's mostly water, I think, but okay. Want a soda pop or something?"

"No, thanks, I'm fine for now."

"All right."

We wandered over to the bar, and I ordered another champagne while managing to maneuver close to our target. With my fresh glass in hand, I bumped into him ever so gently, causing him to spill a little bit of the drink he was holding.

"Oh, excuse me," I said.

Almanzo turned and glared at me, wiping a few drops of liquid off the sleeve of his suit coat. "Really, do be careful, sir. This is an expensive suit, tailor made." He looked me up and down. "Not all of us wear off the rack, you know."

"I apologize. I'm terribly sorry. You're the All-Seeing Almanzo, aren't you? Gosh, when we came here tonight, I was hoping I'd get a chance to talk to you," I said, trying to feign as much enthusiasm as I could.

"Yes, well, you got your wish, then, didn't you? Are you a member of the press or a city official?"

"Press, sir. WBSM radio—all the hits, all the time, so don't touch that dial. That's our slogan, you know," I said.

"How droll."

"Yes, well, our advertising department thinks it's quite catchy."

"So is a cold. How did you get assigned to cover my reception?"

"I volunteered, sir. I think you're really something. May I buy you a drink to make up for my clumsiness?"

"You may, at the very least. Glenfiddich, not the schlock they serve the masses," he said, depositing his now empty glass on a passing waiter's tray.

"Right." I knew a glass of Glenfiddich in a place like this would run me at least ninety-five cents plus tip, but it couldn't be helped. Hopefully, the chief would understand when I turned in my expense report. I moved down the bar and got the bartender's attention.

"One Glenfiddich, please," I said. "For Mr. Firestone."

The bartender, a handsome lad, looked mildly surprised. "Mr. Firestone's been drinking rail scotch all night."

I sighed. "Well, since I'm paying for this one, I guess he wants the good stuff."

"Your money, mister. Neat or on the rocks?"

"How has he been drinking his others?"

"On the rocks."

"Then make it that way, I guess."

"Yes, sir, coming right up." He moved away from me, and I made my way back to Mr. Firestone while I waited. The All-Seeing Almanzo was staring intently at Alan.

"By the way, Mr. Firestone, I'm Heath Barrington, and this is my friend, Alan Keyes. He's an even bigger fan of yours than I am," I said.

"Admirer, Heath," Alan said. "And yes, sir, I am."

"Oh, how lovely. At least you have a few redeeming qualities, Mr. Barrington. You two are friends, you say?"

"Yes, we work together, at the radio station. I gave Alan a lift here since he doesn't have a car."

"I see. Married?"

"No, sir. We're both single," Alan said, "though Heath has a girl he's been seeing."

"But not you, dear boy?"

"No, sir. Not yet, anyway."

"Interesting. You're reporters, then?" Firestone said. "I don't see any cameras."

"Well, we are in radio, you see," I said with a smile as I handed him one of the business cards Miss Blake had given me.

He put it in his pocket without looking at it. "They say television is the wave of the future. That radio is dying, on its way out."

"I wouldn't bet on that, Mr. Firestone. I've heard television is just a passing fancy."

"If you did bet on that, Mr. Barrington, you'd lose. Television is here to stay."

"You would know, I suppose. Isn't that your business, seeing into the future and all that?"

"I'm more into the past, the spirit world and such, though there are ways and methods of divining the future, of course, and I have been known to delve into that on occasion."

"Fascinating. And what do you see when you do divine the future?" I said.

"It's often cloudy, but right now I see that my drink is nearly ready," he said, looking over my shoulder at the bar.

"Oh, right. Excuse me." I paid for his drink along with a modest tip for the bartender. "Here's your scotch, Mr. Firestone," I said. "Glenfiddich, just like you asked for."

He glanced at the glass and waved it away. "Ice? Why are there ice cubes in Glenfiddich? That's an insult to the whiskey. I put up with it in the rail scotch they serve because that stuff is almost undrinkable otherwise, but Glenfiddich requires two drops of water, no more. Have them remake it."

I resisted the urge to roll my eyes as I looked at the two lonely ice cubes floating in the liquid. "Sorry," I said. "My mistake." I turned back to the bar and motioned for the bartender again. This was going to require another tip, probably not so modest.

"So, you're an admirer of mine, Mr. Keyes? How lovely. In addition to working for the radio station, you follow spiritualism?" I heard Firestone say over my shoulder.

"Yes, sir. I even read your book."

"Really? How delightful. I'd be happy to autograph it for you if you want to bring it by later."

"Gee, that would be nice, but I got it from the library."

"Oh, that's too bad. But do tell, what was your favorite part?"

"Oh gosh, it's hard to pick just one, Mr. Firestone. Your chapter on myomancy was quite fascinating, though. I happened upon two mice just this evening, as a matter of fact, in the basement of my friend's building. I released them into the wild, but they were quite frantic."

"To the untrained, the noises and movements of mice and rats are meaningless, but to one who knows, such as I, they can predict deep, dark things."

"Yes, yes, I know. It's all very interesting," Alan said sincerely. "I wish you'd been there to see and study them."

"So do I."

"Also your chapter on stercomancy was so fascinating. Who knew one could divine the future by studying seeds in bird excrement?"

I turned and handed Almanzo his new drink. "Here you are, Mr. Firestone, Glenfiddich with two drops of water, no ice."

"Good. Ice dilutes the high-quality scotch, you know," he said, never taking his eyes off Alan. "But the water droplets open up the flavor just enough. So, always two drops but no more."

"You're welcome," I said dryly, but he didn't seem to notice. "Did I hear you say something about divining the future by studying seeds in bird excrement?"

He looked at me briefly. "It's called stercomancy. It's not something I study regularly, but it can be useful in certain situations."

"I can't even imagine what those situations may be."

"I'm sure you can't. You look rather dull." He turned back to look at Alan again. "Your friend here has an aura about him, did you know that, Mr. Bennett?"

"Barrington. And yes, I've often thought so."

"He does. I can see it, I can feel it," he said, looking Alan up and down now, from head to toe.

"Really?" Alan said.

"Yes, dear boy. Quite so." He looked back at me for just a moment. "Here, hold my drink." He didn't wait for a reply before he handed me back his glass. I held his in my left hand and my own in my right as I wondered what he was going to do next. He removed his monocle, letting it dangle from a gold chain attached to his suit coat, and turned back to Alan.

"Now then," he said, putting both of his hands on Alan's temples and closing his own eyes. "Let me see. Hmm. Oh, interesting, very interesting."

"What?" Alan said.

"Shh," he said, placing an index finger on Alan's lips. "I must concentrate." He moved his hands down Alan's face, onto his neck and then to his shoulders where he stopped, moving his hands in deep, circular motions, his eyes still closed. Alan looked a tad uncomfortable.

"Relax, Mr. Keyes. Calm yourself, take deep breaths." He took his hands off Alan's shoulders and moved them slowly down his arms, squeezing here and there. "My, my, you're quite strong, aren't you?"

"Um, I guess so, sir," Alan said. I could tell he was embarrassed as people around us stopped to watch and see what was going on.

"Please, call me Almanzo." Firestone opened his eyes and removed his hands from Alan's body, somewhat reluctantly it seemed to me. He put his monocle back into place and chewed thoughtfully at the back of his left thumb. "There's definitely something special about you. Mm, yes, indeed. Have you ever had your fortune told? Your past lives investigated?"

"Golly, I didn't know I even had any past lives."

"But you *have*, I can sense it. I should like to do a private session with you—complimentary, of course—to delve into the depths of your soul."

"A private session? Complimentary? Gee whiz, Mr. Firestone, that would be swell. That's awfully nice of you."

"Almanzo, please, and yes, I think so, too. That it would be swell, I mean." His smile was now rather lustful, his voice low. "The power of the body can tell us much. Unclothed, naked, raw, and exposed."

"Naked and exposed?" Alan said, his face turning an interesting shade of red.

"Yes, of course. Baring your soul is the only way to divine the truth, you see. All completely natural, without inhibitions and restrictions."

"How about you divine me, Mr. Firestone?" I said, interrupting his flow.

"What? You?" he said, turning once more to me. "You don't seem very interesting, as I said before."

"I suppose I'm not, but it's just that my Uncle Horace suddenly passed away, and it's been most distressing. We were quite close. One of the reasons I volunteered to cover your reception is because I was hoping to speak with you about it."

"Hm, sudden death, you say?"

"Yes, a heart attack. Just last week."

"My, my. I suppose we may be able to contact your uncle, at least briefly."

"Gee, that would be wonderful."

"Yes, I'm sure. Of course my research into the spirit world is ongoing and requires an extensive amount of time and money, but let's see what we can do. I believe I have an opening on Sunday afternoon, after my matinee performance. Two dollars, in the sitting room of my suite."

"Okay, sign me up. My uncle was fairly wealthy, and I'm supposed to inherit a hefty sum, but it doesn't make up for losing him, of course.

It would be a wonderous thing indeed if I could speak to him one last time."

"Inherit a hefty sum, you say? You're more interesting than you first appeared, I must admit," Mr. Firestone said.

"Um, thanks. Will you be conducting a séance, then?"

"Hm, no. I think I shall be using my crystal balls with you."

"Balls? You use more than one?"

"Oh, yes, absolutely. One to see into the past, one to divine the future, and one to contact the departed. They travel with me everywhere, in a special case. Of course, my balls aren't useful in every situation. I may hold a séance with you, perhaps, in the future, on a return trip, provided I have enough funding. As I mentioned, my research is extensive and expensive."

"I'm sure it is, Mr. Firestone. If my uncle's inheritance is substantial enough, maybe I can assist with that."

His eyebrows went up a tad. "Oh, my, that would be most generous of you. Are you attending one of my public demonstrations as well?"

"Yes, the Sunday matinee. Mr. Keyes and I will both be there."

"Oh good, there's a bright spot. Now then, Alan, you don't mind if I call you by your given name, do you? What about a private session for you? As I said, completely complimentary. I could squeeze you in tomorrow afternoon before the evening performance. My wife will most likely be in our suite at that time, come to think of it. Perhaps I could arrange a small, private room here at the hotel instead, for just the two of us."

"Your wife?" I said, surprised.

He flicked his left hand dismissively. "Yes, Muriel. She's around here somewhere, or maybe she's gone up to the suite. She hates these events," Firestone said, never taking his eyes off Alan. "Now then, Alan, about that private session for tomorrow…"

"Golly, Mr. Firestone…"

"Almanzo, please."

"Almanzo. I'm terribly flattered. I uh, think that would be really interesting, but I'm afraid I'm busy tomorrow afternoon and evening. I'm going to the opera."

"Oh, that's too bad. You don't look like the opera type."

"Well, I'm going with Heath, here, as his guest."

"I see. Well, how about sometime on Sunday, then? We leave town on Monday, so it will have to be soon."

"Gee, uh, I don't think so, I'm sorry. But I am looking forward to the matinee performance on Sunday, and all."

I cleared my throat. "As am I, and *our* private session afterward, Mr. Firestone. I assume we'll be keeping our clothes on for that."

He looked at me again, annoyed. "You assume correctly, Mr. Barrett."

"Barrington."

"Bennett, Barrett, Barrington, whatever. Your session will be three dollars in advance, payable just before we begin."

"You said before it was two dollars."

"Did I? Oh well, inflation, you know. Bring something that belonged to your uncle, if you can. An article of clothing, a pipe, something like that. I find it helps. Oh, and a photograph of him, as recent as possible. Now, I must go mingle. I promised a newspaper reporter a brief interview. If you'll excuse me."

"Of course. Here's your drink back," I said. "I'll see you Sunday after the show."

"Performance. A demonstration of my abilities, not a show." He took the glass and downed a good portion of it as he stared at Alan once more. "Bring your friend here along. Perhaps if you do, I can offer you a discount and a signed copy of my book."

"I'm sure," I said.

"So am I. Inquire at the front desk after the performance. They'll announce you," Firestone said, and then he turned and walked away.

"Well, he was sure something," Alan said.

"Yes he was. And he certainly liked you."

"It was embarrassing. I mean, talking about being naked, raw and exposed, and all that. It made me kinda uncomfortable."

"It made me kind of uncomfortable, too. I wonder what his wife thinks of all that."

"Yeah, gee."

"Want to stick around for a while yet?" I said.

"No, I think I'm ready to go. I'm a bit tired."

"Okay, I'll drive you home. I believe we're done here, anyway."

We retrieved our hats from the hat check girl, who flirted with

Alan once more and tucked her home telephone number inside his hatband.

Downstairs in the lobby, we could see that the rain had increased to a downpour.

"Let me go get the car while you wait here," I said.

"I can walk with you, Heath, I don't mind."

"Naw, you stay inside where it's warm and dry. It was my idea to park a couple blocks away. I'll pull up. Back in a flash."

I dashed out into the rain and hurried to my car, wishing I'd brought my rubber overshoes and umbrella. Alan was standing beneath the awning as I pulled up to the hotel just a few minutes later.

"Going my way, mister?" he said, looking in at me with a goofy grin as he opened the passenger door of my car.

"Always, sailor," I said. "And all the way."

He climbed in. I put the car in gear, turned the windshield wipers on high, and drove off.

"Thanks for getting the car, Heath. Looks like you got pretty wet."

"I'll dry. And it's the least I could do for a handsome bloke like you. Sally's going to be awfully disappointed when you don't call her, you know," I said.

"The hat check girl? I do feel kinda sorry for her. It's really raining hard now."

"I have a feeling she'll find some eligible bachelor to take her home tonight."

"I suppose so."

"And if not, I noticed an umbrella and a lady's raincoat tucked in the corner of the coat check room next to what looked like her handbag and hat."

"Oh, that's good. I'm glad she's prepared, and I'm glad I've got a handsome eligible bachelor taking me home tonight," Alan said.

I smiled then, glancing over at him briefly. "Sweet talker. No wonder everyone finds you so irresistible."

CHAPTER FOUR

Early morning, Saturday, September 13, 1947

I had a quick breakfast consisting of a boiled egg, toast with blackberry jam, and hot, black coffee as I read the morning *Sentinel*. When I was finished, I did the dishes, left a note for the milkman, and brushed my teeth before getting dressed. I put on my navy blue suit, straightened my cream-colored tie, and then walked out into the living room, looking around at the furniture, the artwork, and my simple belongings. Everything was the same as it had always been, and yet my apartment seemed somehow empty now.

I'd been alone a long time before Alan came along, and I'd never minded it much. But now it bothered me quite a bit when he wasn't nearby, and I felt lonely. My consolation this morning, though, was knowing he would be spending the night at my place tonight, and it lifted my spirits considerably. I smiled, put on my hat, and whistled a gay tune as I left my place and headed downstairs to my car. It was parked on Prospect Avenue beneath the great grandmother elm tree, whose leaves were just beginning to turn an autumnal yellowish brown. The rain had stopped, but the temperature had dropped considerably overnight, and I could see my breath in short, billowy puffs each time I exhaled. I drove quickly to the State Street library, arriving just after opening at nine.

As I entered, that familiar scent of musty, woody old leather, ancient pages, and reams of paper filled my nostrils. As I half expected, Evelyn Caldwell, the head librarian who was involved in my last case, was at the circulation desk, flipping through a golf magazine and sipping a cup of coffee. She looked up at me as I approached, my shoes squeaking against the tile floor. She was solidly built—not fat, just tough, muscular, and fierce looking, in a fresh-scrubbed, naturally attractive way.

"Well, if it isn't Detective Barrington." She was dressed in a plain brown, long-sleeved dress, belted at the waist, with a high white collar. Her short, chocolate brown hair, streaked with wisps of silver, was combed straight back, and her face was unadorned with makeup of any kind.

"Hello, Miss Caldwell. Nice to see you. How's Mrs. Crow?"

"Miss Armstrong is as well as can be expected."

"Miss Armstrong?"

"She reverted to her maiden name. So, who's been murdered this time?"

"What? Oh, no one I know of. I'm investigating potential fraud is all, and I was hoping to do some research on spiritualism, the occult, and all that."

"*Potential* fraud? Is that a crime now? So glad my tax dollars are hard at work paying your salary."

"And I'm so glad my tax dollars are hard at work paying you to read magazines and drink coffee."

"Touché," she said. "That means you made a good or clever point or retort."

"Thanks, I'm familiar with the word."

"Also used in fencing when one is hit by one's opponent."

"Yes, of course. I took fencing in college for a while."

"Why am I not surprised? And tennis, I imagine."

"Yes, actually. How about you? Were you on the women's boxing team?"

"Funny man. No, I wasn't, but I could knock you flat on the mat. I throw a wicked corkscrew punch."

"Of that I have no doubt. I probably wouldn't last three rounds with you."

"Probably not two. This must be some potential fraud you're investigating to bring you in this early, and on a Saturday."

"Just making sure you get your money's worth out of your tax dollars, Miss Caldwell. Now, where would I find books and information on spiritualism?"

"Are you familiar with the card catalog, Mr. Barrington? It's just over there, by the entrance to the reading room."

"Yes, I am familiar with it, but I'm in a bit of a hurry. Perhaps you could just show me."

"You mean, do your work for you."

"Actually, I think part of *your* work is to assist the customer, isn't it? It's what *my* tax dollars are paying for."

"I *am* assisting you by directing you to the card catalog. This is a self-service library and I have other things to do."

"Like drink coffee and read magazines?"

"My day is just getting started, and I'll have you know the publisher of this new magazine," she said, pointing to the *Golf World* magazine in front of her, "sent it to me on approval for consideration, so I was reviewing its contents to see if it's worthy of adding to our periodicals."

"All right, fair enough. Do you at least have some paper and a pencil I might use to jot down the call numbers of the books I'm interested in?"

"There are some in the little wooden boxes on top of the catalog."

"I see. And where would I begin? Under *S* for spiritualism, or *A* for afterlife? And is it fiction or nonfiction?"

She let out a large breath and closed the golf magazine. "Clearly you're rather helpless. Typical man. Very well, this way, then," she said, stepping out from behind the desk and leading me toward the stacks in the rear of the building.

"Are you this hostile with all your customers, Miss Caldwell? Or just the men?"

"Just the annoying ones, and the annoying ones are usually men."

"Why do I get the feeling you'd like to be a man?"

She glared at me sideways as we walked. "That is a terrible thing to say, Mr. Barrington. You're right in that men have certain privileges in life, certain things open to them that are not open to women, but I aim to change that. If I may quote Eleanor Roosevelt, "'I have never wanted to be a man. I have often wanted to be more effective as a woman, but I have never felt that trousers would do the trick.'"

"Okay, touché, as you say. And for what it's worth, I agree with you."

"Then you're less of a man than you appear, and I mean that in the nicest possible way."

"Thanks."

"You're welcome." She stopped short and pointed to a bookshelf. "Here's the section you want—the spirit world, the occult, reincarnation, fortune telling, black magic, and the afterlife."

"I'm looking for books on spiritualism in particular. Oh, and one written by an Almanzo Firestone."

"Hmm, Firestone. Let me see," she said, looking up, down, and across the shelves. "Here it is, *Spiritualism, Séances, and the Afterlife*, by Almanzo Firestone." She pulled it off the shelf and handed it to me. "And may I suggest *A Victorian Guide to the Study of Spiritualism*," she said, adding that one on top of Firestone's. "Would you be interested in *Ghosts, Spirits, and Specters*? You may find it helpful."

"Sure, if you think it merits reading."

"Depends on what you're hoping to find, but it can't hurt. Here." She plunked it down on top of the other two. "Anything else?"

"I think these will do nicely, Miss Caldwell, thank you. I truly appreciate your knowledge and assistance. You're an asset to this library."

I think she was taken aback by my sincerity. "How funny you are, Mr. Barrington. Not like a typical man, not at all. I sensed that about you the first time we met, and it appears I was right. Walk with me to the circulation desk so I can check these out for you."

"Well, who wants to be typical?" I said, walking beside her.

"Indeed. And indeed you're not. In fact, I'd say you're atypical. The greatest compliment I could give you is to say you have female attributes."

Now it was my turn to be taken aback as I set the books down on the counter of the circulation desk. "Well, I wouldn't say that."

"I would. I assume you have a library card?"

"Oh, uh, gee, I did once. But I think it expired."

She sighed, drumming her short, unpainted fingernails atop one of the books. "Nice to know you stay well read and up to date. When was the last time you were in a library as a patron?"

"Well, it's been a while, but I enjoy reading, I do. It's just that I've been busy recently. Work, you know."

"Of course. A man's work is never done, unless it's done by a woman."

"Who said that?"

"I did, and it's true. I'll let you have these on your word, Detective, but if you don't return them by Friday, I will hunt you down and stamp you but good, so that you will wear the word 'overdue' on your forehead until the ink wears off. Understand?"

"Yes, ma'am. Don't worry. I'll get them back to you on time and in good condition."

"Somehow I know you will, Slug."

"Slug?"

"I'm referring to banana slugs, of course, and I mean that as a compliment, too."

"Your compliments could use some work, Miss Caldwell."

"Read up on banana slugs sometime. They're born with both male and female genitalia."

"Really? I wasn't aware of that. How do they, uh, reproduce?"

"When they find a mate of similar size, each impregnates the other. It's far more civilized than what humans do, in my opinion."

"Fascinating. But our civilization is based on certain beliefs, certain expectations."

"You mean like men are the breadwinners and the protectors, and the women are docile and care giving?"

"Well, yes. Generally that's how it's always been."

"Gender roles are learned behavior, nothing more."

"I think that's true, but you must admit that men are generally larger and stronger."

"Yes, generally. But we're no longer a cave-dwelling people, Mr. Barrington. Women don't need to depend on men to club their dinner. Besides, the race doesn't always go to the largest and strongest, but sometimes to the smallest and swiftest."

"Somehow, Miss Caldwell, I think if you were a cave dweller, you'd club your own food."

"Of course I would. One should never depend on anyone else for one's own survival."

"Perhaps you're right."

"Of course I am. But the best solution would be if humans were like banana slugs, all both male *and* female. There would be far less problems in the world because there would be no great sexual divide, you see?"

"I do see. Thank you, Miss Caldwell, from one slug to another."

She raised her eyebrows ever so slightly and nodded. "For what?"

"For helping me and for fighting the fight."

"Just making sure you get what you pay for with your tax dollars, Detective. Now, do me a favor and make sure I get what I pay for. And don't forget, those are due on Friday."

"Right," I said. "Give my best to Mrs. Crow. Miss Armstrong, I mean." I picked up the books and headed back out to my car, turning it in the direction of the station, a smile on my face once more.

CHAPTER FIVE

Morning, Saturday, September 13, 1947

It was a quarter to ten as I climbed the stairs to the detectives' room. I expected to be the only one there, but then I saw Grant Riker, the newest addition to the team of detectives. He had been assigned Alvin Green's old desk, and he looked slightly uncomfortable sitting there, all alone, as if he felt he didn't belong. I set the library books down on top of my desk, hung up my hat and suit coat, and made a pot of coffee in the break room. When it was finished, I poured myself a cup and sauntered over to him. He looked quite dashing in a medium gray double-breasted suit with a wide orange and red tie, which stood out against his crisp white shirt. His fedora hung on a rack nearby.

"Morning," I said.

He gave me a half smile, looking a bit tired. "Morning, Heath."

"What are you doing here on a Saturday?"

"I was here at a quarter of eight. You know what they say about the early bird," he said. The eagerness of the new detective is something I remembered well.

"And you know what they say about the early worm."

He cocked his head. "What's that?"

"The early worm gets eaten by the early bird."

Riker chuckled. "Any more of that coffee?"

"Sure, I made a full pot. I'll get you some. How do you take it?"

"A little cream, one sugar."

"Got it, be right back," I said, setting my cup down on his desk.

I returned shortly, hoping I'd gotten the proportion of cream right. "Here ya go, Detective," I said, placing the coffee on the top of his desk next to mine.

"Thanks," he said. He picked it up and took a sip, and then glanced up at me and nodded. "Perfect."

"Glad to hear it. So why *are* you here on a Saturday morning? You're too new to be on call."

He shrugged. "Just wanted to get a jump on things, I guess. Still trying to get the lay of the land, so I thought I'd come in for a few hours. Maybe make a good impression on the boss."

"The chief doesn't usually come in on the weekends, and even during the week he doesn't get here until about nine thirty or ten. Nine at the earliest."

"Yeah, well, I couldn't sleep, so I figured I might as well be here as at home. Besides, I heard the chief *was* working this weekend, for a few hours, anyway. Have a seat if you like."

"Thanks. Yeah, I heard that, too. Him and Miss Blake." I made myself relatively comfortable in the beat-up wooden armchair next to his desk and picked up my coffee cup once more.

"So, what are *you* doing here on a weekend?" Riker said.

"Just working on some research for a case. I don't plan on staying more than a couple hours," I said. "So, now that you've been a detective a whole week, how does it feel?"

He unbuttoned his suit coat and leaned back in the chair, his hands on the back of his head. "Okay. Different. Strange."

I laughed. "Sounds about right. I almost didn't recognize you when you came in that first day, out of uniform and all."

"Which uniform would that be? My steward's outfit from the stint on the boat or my policeman's uniform?"

"Both, now that you mention it. You wear a uniform well. But you look good in your suit, too," I said, glad we were alone and could speak relatively freely.

"Thanks, but I feel like a fish out of water sitting at this desk. I'm not sure what I'm supposed to do exactly. So far this morning I've organized all the desk drawers and played two games of solitaire with a deck of cards I found on top of the filing cabinet. I feel like I don't fit in with the other guys."

I smiled as I took a sip of my coffee. "I understand. I've been there, remember? I started out as a flatfoot walking a beat, and when I finally made detective, I thought I'd never figure out what to do. Fortunately, Hank Stein took me under his wing in the beginning, but of course he's retired now. Isn't Detective Spelling supposed to be helping you?"

"Yeah, but I don't think he's too keen on it. He's on call this weekend, which is one of the reasons I came in this morning, just in case something came up and he needed a hand. But frankly, I think he's annoyed at having to spend time breaking me in, and he doesn't want my help in any way."

"Sounds like him. What's the chief got you two working on?"

"I'm supposed to be helping him with a vandalism case, but I don't think he cares for me much, and honestly, I don't know how to help."

"You're intelligent, savvy, and have an amazing photographic memory, and you'll make an excellent detective. You'll probably run circles around Spelling eventually."

"Swell, that will definitely win him over."

I smiled. "You know what I mean. Just give it time. He'll come around, don't you worry."

"I suppose. What about you? What case are you doing research for?"

"I'm investigating some hokey spiritualist who's in town, Almanzo the All-Seeing."

"Ugh, what a name. All-Seeing indeed. I'm sure he can at least see who's an easy mark and relieve them of their hard-earned money before they know what hit them."

"That's what the chief wants me to find out. Is he just a showman, a smoke-and-mirrors entertainer, or is he taking advantage of people? He sells tickets to his performances, but he also does one-on-one presentations, séances, and such. For a fee, of course."

"Of course. Probably a small fee to get them hooked. Then when the lights are low, the sucker's Great Auntie Betty comes a-knocking, or something like that. And at the end, the spiritualist asks the sucker for a tidy contribution for their continued research, if you can call it that."

"That's pretty much it to a T, Riker. This Almanzo fellow is pretty well known, I guess. He travels around the country putting on these shows, or demonstrations, as he calls them. There were some complaints from the last two places he was in."

"What kind of complaints?"

"Accusations against him of fraud and deception. Almanzo left town before the complaints could be fully investigated, which is why the chief wants me to check him out in cooperation with the Kansas City and Gary detective divisions."

"Sounds more interesting then Spelling's vandalism case."

"We'll see. Believe it or not, Alan's actually a fan of this All-Seeing Almanzo."

"No kidding?"

"I kind of wish I was. He believes in all that hooey. Spiritualism, fortune telling, horoscopes, you name it. When he heard this guy was coming to town, he wanted us to go see him. He came with me to a reception at the Blatz Hotel last night that this Almanzo character put on for members of the press. We went undercover."

"Oh? How did that go?"

"The chief is the one who got me in there as part of my investigation. He wanted me to size Almanzo up, find out if he's on the up-and-up, and also set up a private appointment with him to get my palm read, though it turns out he doesn't do that, at least not with me. He's more into crystal balls, studying seeds in bird droppings, and stuff like that."

"Bird droppings? You're pulling my leg."

"Nope, I'm totally serious. He even studies the movements and sounds of mice and rats, and supposedly divines the future from it."

"Wow, he sounds like a first class nut."

"Yeah, but it turns out lots of people believe in that sort of thing, and who knows? Maybe there's something to it. Anyway, I'm seeing him in his hotel suite tomorrow afternoon, right after his matinee, for a private consultation with him and his crystal balls to see if he can contact my dear departed Uncle Horace. That will set the department back three bucks."

Riker chuckled. "Three bucks for a consultation with a crystal ball? Maybe I'm in the wrong profession."

"You and me both. Plus, like you said, once it's over, he'll probably hit me up for a hefty contribution. He mentioned his expensive research a couple of times, at least."

"That will be an interesting line item on your expense report. How are you going to expose him as a fraud, anyway?"

"Well, I don't really have an Uncle Horace, so I suppose if he succeeds in contacting him, that will be proof right there. I'm supposed to bring a pipe or something that belonged to him, along with a recent photograph, and I'm sure he'll ask me all kinds of questions before we begin that will help him conjure up the old boy."

"Well, I can't wait to hear what he sees in his balls for you and what he has to say."

"I'll be sure and let you know."

"Please do. So, what's this Firestone like, anyway?"

"He's arrogant, obnoxious, conceited, and rude. But the one thing he likes, so to speak, is Alan."

"Oh? In what way?"

"In every way." I lowered my voice, even though we were still the only two there at the moment. "He offered a *complimentary* session to him tonight, in a small, private room at the hotel. He said something about the human body and being naked and raw."

"Geez, seriously?"

"Yes. Alan said no, thankfully."

"I would, too. So, you think this Firestone is…you know?"

I nodded. "He certainly gave us that impression. He couldn't take his eyes off Alan, and he kept touching him."

"Where?"

"In public. Firestone is a tad flamboyant," I said. "Being a little eccentric probably makes him seem even more alluring to his followers."

"How did Alan react to all this attention?"

"He was embarrassed by the whole thing."

"I would imagine. Are you sure this Almanzo character wasn't just being friendly to a fan?"

"Apparently he doesn't have fans, only admirers. And he was definitely doing a good job of admiring Alan, rubbing his hands up and down his arms, squeezing his shoulders, gazing at him like a schoolboy."

"Jeepers. That seems rather blatant."

"I think the All-Seeing Almanzo had already had a few scotches by that time and was probably feeling uninhibited."

"But behavior like that in a public place could get him into all kinds of trouble if he's not careful."

"And how. But like I said, his admirers didn't seem to notice or mind too much, and the press keeps those kinds of secrets pretty well when it comes to celebrities. Plus he's married, and his wife was there someplace. It will be interesting to see how tomorrow goes. I've got three fat library books on spiritualism to read in the meantime, including one this Almanzo wrote."

"Say, maybe you could mix a little business with pleasure. Get tickets to his show and have the station reimburse you. You'd just be doing more research."

"Not a bad idea, actually, except I already got tickets. I ordered them over a month ago, when the performance was first announced, long before the chief asked me to investigate this character. Alan really wants to see him in person and has been looking forward to it ever since it was advertised in the paper he was coming to town."

"Mr. Keyes impresses me. I didn't think he would have been able to convince you to sit through something like that if it wasn't for work."

"Actually I used it as a negotiating tool."

"How so?"

"I've been wanting to get Alan to the opera. I told him if he went with me to that, I'd go with him to see the All-Seeing Almanzo. As it happens, the opera is tonight."

"You're a clever man, Heath Barrington."

"A fair trade is all. And now that I'm investigating this guy, more or less, part of it is work. I want to see him in action, see what he's all about."

"I think you and I *know* what he's all about. He's all about making money."

"And trying to make time with Alan. He gives me the creeps."

"Understandable," Riker said. "So, what opera are you seeing tonight?"

"Mozart's *The Marriage of Figaro*. The Florentine is putting it on at the Pabst Theater."

"Never heard of it. Never heard of most of that longhair stuff. Can't say I care much for it," Riker said.

"Alan's not all that excited either, but I think he'll enjoy himself. I hope so, anyway. *The Marriage of Figaro* is pretty easy to follow, even if you can't understand the language. The famous bass Ezio Pinza is the lead."

Riker shook his head. "Is that someone I'm supposed to know?"

"He's in town from New York, the greatest operatic bass baritone around, they say. Over twenty years with the Metropolitan Opera."

"Oh, well then, I stand corrected."

I smiled. "So, opera's not your cup of tea, that's okay. I'm not a huge fan of this 'Choo Choo Ch'boogie' stuff that you seem to like, but I try to keep my mind open."

"The only time I went to the opera, I couldn't keep my *eyes* open."

"You look like you can barely keep your eyes open right now."

He stifled a yawn, sat upright in his chair, and took another sip of coffee. "Ugh, sorry, excuse me. Mary Jane was up all night with the kid, which kept me up."

"Sorry to hear it."

"Thanks. It's been rough on both of us. She was none too happy being a policeman's wife. When I got shot, she went crazy. Even begged me to quit, to resign right then and there. But what would I do, you know?"

"I think I do know."

"Yeah, well, Mary Jane's a little happier now that I'm in the detective division, but she still doesn't like it. She was none too happy I had to buy a new suit and all, too, when she's been making do with her old house dresses."

"Maybe you can pick her up something pretty with your first paycheck."

"Yeah, that's what I was thinking. But she thinks even being a detective is too dangerous, and she doesn't like the hours I keep. She was not happy I came in to work this morning."

"It's not easy being a policeman's or a detective's wife."

"As she frequently reminds me. We're going through a hard time right now. She's talked about taking little Jane Marie and moving back to Des Moines to stay with her mother for a while."

"Just because of your work? Or is it something else?"

Riker gave me a look through bloodshot eyes. "What do you mean?"

"You know what I mean, I'm sure. Do you think she has an inkling about your other activities, so to speak?"

He frowned at me. "I keep my private life private, Detective. She doesn't know."

"Are you sure? Women can sometimes sense these things, I've heard."

"Women's intuition? I thought you didn't believe in that stuff."

"I don't, but I'm telling you women always seem to know. Several years ago, my dad promised my mom he'd quit playing poker with some fellows from the post office, but he'd occasionally sneak in a game on his lunch hour in the back room. Don't ask me how, but Mom knew, and she gave him hell."

"Maybe so, but I'm cautious and very discreet. Besides, it's not like I'm out meeting men every day. The occasional chap at the gym or steam bath, but even then, it's rare nowadays."

"Best to keep it that way if you ask me, or stop it altogether. You can't be too careful. As I told you before, find your path and be true to it, whatever that may be."

"Easy for you to say, Heath."

"Not so much. In fact, it's harder for me as I get older. People are always wondering why I don't date, why I'm not married. And they're always trying to fix me up with some pretty young thing, even my mother. *Especially* my mother."

"Handsome confirmed bachelors of a certain age do raise a fair amount of suspicion. I'm willing to bet part of why this Almanzo character can get away with acting the way he does is because he's married, which gives him an air of respectability, rightly or wrongly. It's just the way it is."

"I suppose so, but I wouldn't be happy living my life like that, not being honest with myself or anyone else."

"I'm happy. Happy enough. And so is Mary Jane."

"Right, that's good then, I'm glad, I guess. Let's do lunch sometime, my treat."

He smiled. "I'd like that, Heath, and thanks."

"For what?"

"For believing in me. For encouraging me. For listening and caring, and for not judging me too harshly."

"Judging you?"

"You know, because I do live my life like that."

"It's your life. But just remember it's Mary Jane's life, too."

He nodded thoughtfully. "Yeah. Well, thanks, just the same."

I touched his shoulder gently as I got to my feet. "Always, my friend. But think about that."

"I will, I promise."

CHAPTER SIX

Early evening, Saturday, September 13, 1947

I got home at a quarter past six and found Alan already waiting for me on the front stoop of the building, dressed in the tuxedo I had bought for him in Chicago a few months earlier. A small brown leather satchel was at his feet, which were encased in well-polished, black cap toe shoes.

"Holy moly, will you look at you?" I said as I came up the walk.

"What?"

"Just that never have I ever seen a more dapper-looking gentleman in all my life."

"Aw, quit," Alan said, smiling.

"Totally true. I'm sorry I'm a bit late. After I left the station, I stopped and got a haircut and shave, then I had lunch downtown and did some shopping."

"It's fine. I was visiting with your downstairs neighbor, Mrs. Murphy. She wanted to know where I was going all dressed up like this, in my glad rags."

"And you said?"

"To the opera with you, of course. But I also told her we had to swing by and pick up our dates yet."

"Good thinking. Mrs. Murphy is a nice lady, but we don't want her getting the right idea, so to speak."

"Yeah, I figured. She wanted to know if I was serious about this girl I'm supposedly taking tonight, because apparently there's a Miss

McBain who lives here. Her fiancé was killed in the war, and Mrs. Murphy thinks she'd be perfect for me."

I rolled my eyes. "Oh my. Yes, she's tried to fix me up with her, too. She's all alone, you know, and such a sweet young thing."

Alan laughed. "That's exactly what she said to me, but I told her I was pretty serious about my sweetheart, which is the truth."

"Well, your sweetheart's pretty serious about you, too."

"I'm glad to hear it. I feel kinda sorry for this Miss McBain, though."

"Yeah, I know. Eligible men are in short supply these days, after the war. But she'll find someone soon enough, I'm sure, especially with Mrs. Murphy in her corner."

"She is quite a matchmaker, it seems."

"Yes, and determined." I studied Alan, standing there on the stoop in the twilight, leaning against the door frame, arms crossed, his dark, wavy hair slicked back. "I can see why Mrs. Murphy would try to set you up with Miss McBain, though. You have the curse, like I said last night."

"The curse?"

"Of being too good looking. You wear that tuxedo well, you know."

"Thank you, kind sir. Compliments of you, I must say."

"But you're missing one thing."

Alan looked down at himself and then back up at me. "I am? What?"

"An opera scarf. White silk."

"Oh, well, I'll have to get one, I suppose."

I reached into my inside suit coat pocket and pulled out a tissue-wrapped package. "You just did," I said, handing it to him. "It's partly why I was a tad late. I stopped at Boston Store and Gimbels to find just the right one."

He smiled, his face beaming. "For me? Gee, Heath, you shouldn't have. Why? It's not my birthday."

"Because," I said.

He unwrapped the tissue and removed the scarf, draping it around his neck. "It's beautiful, and so soft. Do I wear it like this?"

I adjusted it slightly. "Yes, perfect."

"Gosh, thanks, but you really shouldn't have." He looked ever so pleased and happy.

"I should have and I did. You're worth it. That look on your face is all the reason I needed. Besides, it was on sale. Like it?"

"I do. I really do. I feel so elegant."

"Good, I'm glad. Ready for tonight, then?"

"Yes, sir. Like I always say, if you're waiting for me, you're wasting your time."

"Let me get upstairs, put on my tuxedo, and give my shoes a quick shine, and then we should be ready to go. Since I was a bit late getting home, I think we'll have to settle for grabbing a quick bite at Art's Diner, if that's okay with you."

"Sure, if you're buying, though I think we might be a tad overdressed for Art's. Maybe we should have a light dinner afterward instead, perhaps at the Circle Room."

"That sounds like a lovely idea, and that way we won't be so rushed. What's in the satchel?"

Alan glanced down at the bag by his feet. "A few things for when we get back from the opera, and some fresh clothes for tomorrow. That is, if you still want me to stay over."

"Silly boy. I want you to stay over tonight and forever. I should get you a key so I won't keep you waiting out in the cold. In fact, I've got a spare building key upstairs. I'll get it for you."

"Thanks. It has gotten a bit chilly, but I'm fine, really. Maybe if we get that two-bedroom."

My spirits lifted even more. "So you've been thinking about it?"

He nodded. "Yeah. I'm still not sure, but I'm thinking about it. I said I would."

"Excellent. It just makes sense, you know? You wouldn't have to pack an overnight bag, we'd both save money, people wouldn't wonder…"

"Yeah, so you've said. But right now you'd better get upstairs to change, shine your shoes, and freshen up. It's nearly six thirty."

"All right, handsome, I'm going. Do you want to wait here or come up?"

"I'll come up. I need to use your bathroom, you can get me that building key, and I can leave my bag in your bedroom."

"Okay, let's go." I unlocked the front door and held it open for him.

"Have anything to snack on to tide me over until dinner?" Alan said as we started up the two flights of stairs to the third floor.

"I think I have a few apples. We can each have one, which should keep our stomachs quiet during the opera and won't spoil our appetites."

"Good idea. I'll slice them up while you change."

We made it to the Pabst Theater by seven thirty, and to the Circle Room in the hotel LaSalle for a late dinner afterward by ten, finally getting back to my place at just a few minutes before midnight, both of us exhausted but happy.

CHAPTER SEVEN

Morning, Sunday, September 14, 1947

I awoke slowly, noticing my bed was empty. I placed my hand where Alan had been, and it was still warm. I sat up slowly, pulling the covers up to my chest as I wondered where he could have gone. It was just past dawn, and the room was chilly. I got slowly out of bed, shivering in the cold as my bare feet hit the wood floor, and I walked to the window, noting the gloom of an overcast, gray morning as I raised the shade.

I wondered if I should slip my robe on over my white boxers and go start a pot of coffee, or if perhaps Alan had already done that. Then I heard a slightly off-key singing coming from the bathroom. I couldn't help but smile as I realized it was Alan in the shower. It took just a moment for me to recognize it as "Voi che sapete," one of the songs Ezio Pinza had done in *The Marriage of Figaro*. I was still smiling when Alan emerged from the bathroom, dripping wet and wrapped in one of my white bath towels. He stepped into the bedroom, leaving damp footprints on the hardwood floor.

"What?" he said, looking at me quizzically. "Did I wake you?"

"No, not really. I think the chill woke me, and the absence of you."

"It is a cold morning. Hasn't your landlord turned the heat on yet?"

"Yes, but it doesn't seem to be working too well." I put my hand atop the radiator, but it was just slightly warm. "I'll have to call Mr. McNulty and have him look at it."

"Good idea. So, what are you smiling about?"

"You. I noticed you were singing one of the songs from last night in the shower."

He smiled impishly. "Oh, that. Well, it's a catchy tune."

"It is. And you did it well."

"I can't remember all the words, so I made some of it up and hummed the rest."

"You put Ezio Pinza to shame."

Alan laughed. "Thanks, but I don't think he has anything to worry about from me."

"Still, I'm glad you had a good time at the opera."

He cocked his head. "It wasn't awful. Better than I had expected."

"A glowing recommendation if I ever heard one. Would you go again?"

"I'd go to the moon again if you asked me."

Now it was my turn to laugh. "You haven't been to the moon even once, so how could you go again?"

"Aw, you know what I mean. I just enjoy spending time with you. And I like experiencing things you like, even stuff like the opera."

I walked over to him and kissed him gently, wrapping my arms around his waist. "I like that, too. So, you would go again?"

"I would. But first we get to see the All-Seeing Almanzo today, which I'm really looking forward to. The demonstration is at one, so do you want to have lunch somewhere first? My treat this time. I've got the whole day off."

"Now, that is a tempting offer, but I'm afraid I have to go into the station for a bit this morning and probably won't be back in time for lunch."

Alan cocked his head in that adorable puppy way of his. "Again? Why? You detectives are supposed to be Monday through Friday men."

"Ideally, yes, unless we're on call, but I haven't yet finished going through those books from the library, including the one book he wrote, and I want to cross-reference them with some stuff in the files of similar cases. I want to have some idea of what this spiritualism stuff is all about before we see him in action and before my private consultation. It might help me catch him in the act, so to speak."

He frowned ever so slightly. "I know you said the chief has you investigating him, but I really don't see why."

"I already told you why. There have been some complaints against him in the last two cities he toured, and the chief wants to make sure that doesn't happen here, that's all. It's my job to investigate him, Alan. Let's see what I find out at the station this morning, how the matinee goes, and what I find out at my private crystal ball reading, okay?"

Alan pouted like an adorable little boy. "I suppose, though I still think you'll find he's on the level."

I smiled and touched his cheek. "Perhaps. Anyway, I'd better get cleaned up and dressed and get down to the station."

"Okay. I'll put the coffee on and make us some breakfast while you're cleaning up, and then I can putter around here, if that's okay with you. I still have a clean suit and shirt in your closet I can wear to the performance, and I brought fresh underwear and socks with me last night."

"Sure, that's fine, putter away. You can do the breakfast dishes and press our tuxedos while I'm gone."

"And rifle through your underwear drawer," he said with a devilish grin.

"Be my guest," I said, laughing lightly. "Just be sure and fold it neatly when you're done. Sorry about lunch, but we can go out for dinner again later, if you want."

"I'd like that. What time will you be back from the station?"

"I'll try to pick you up by noon at the latest. Best to have a sandwich before. I think I have some bread in the breadbox and some cheese in the icebox. I'll grab something quick downtown."

"Okay, fair enough." He glanced down at the damp towel clinging to his waist. "I suppose I'd better get dressed now."

I looked him up and down, and then over at the clock on my nightstand. "Well, it's only a quarter of seven. I don't technically have to be in at any certain time since it's Sunday, and I could even skip breakfast, depending..."

"Oh, I see," he said, a twinkle in his eyes. He walked over to the window and pulled down the shade as the towel fell in a heap to the floor.

CHAPTER EIGHT

Morning, Sunday, September 14, 1947

I made it in to the station just after nine. I sat at my desk, reviewing the books I'd gotten from the library for the third time, a smile on my face in spite of the dry material before me. I was softly humming "Voi che sapete" and daydreaming about our earlier morning rendezvous, when the telephone on my desk rang harshly, shattering my mood.

"Barrington," I said, picking up the receiver and blinking several times.

"It's Miss Blake," the chief's secretary said in that familiar, harsh voice. She was direct and no nonsense, as always. Her first name, I believe, was Clara, but no one I knew ever called her that, not even the chief.

"Good morning, Miss Blake. How did you know I was here?"

"The chief saw you come in and told me to call you."

"Oh, so he's working today, too?"

"Brilliant detective work, Mr. Barrington."

"I guess that was a pretty stupid question."

"Considering I told you on Friday we'd both be working the weekend, and the fact that I just told you he saw you come in this morning, I'd say it was a very stupid question."

"Right you are, sorry. What can I do for you?"

"Your boss wants to see you in his office right away. And by right away, I mean five minutes ago. Got it?"

"Got it, thanks." I replaced the receiver and got quickly to my feet.

I slipped on my suit coat and straightened my tie as I walked briskly to his office, wondering what was up.

"Go right in," Miss Blake said as I approached his office door. "He's expecting you."

"So you said." I gave her my best smile, but she didn't seem to notice or care.

The chief was seated behind his oversized oak desk as I entered, a frown on his jowly face. He appeared deep in thought. His bushy eyebrows were moving up and down rather comically, like two wooly caterpillars dancing the jitterbug.

I closed the door behind me and cleared my throat. "You wanted to see me, Chief?" I moved in front of his desk, which took up a good portion of his office, and waited, shifting my weight from one foot to the other.

He looked up at me and leaned back in his chair, which creaked loudly. He crossed his hands over his stomach and drummed his thumbs against his chest. "Yes. What brings you in on a Sunday morning?"

"Just some more research on spiritualism for the Firestone case."

"Right. About that. I'm glad you're here, actually. I was going to have Miss Blake call you at home before I saw you come in."

"Oh, what for?"

"Because something's come up I thought you might be interested in. A dead body was found in an alley downtown this morning by some trash collectors. A wallet was found on him, and his wife made a positive ID a short while ago. I just got off the phone with the morgue."

"Gee, that doesn't sound good, but I'm not on call this weekend, Chief. Spelling is. Shouldn't you be telling him this?"

"Normally, yes, but the dead man is Almanzo Firestone. The All-Seeing Almanzo."

"You're kidding! He's dead?" I couldn't believe my ears. Death and murder happened all the time, especially in my line of work, but I was startled by this news.

"Dead as the proverbial doornail. Murdered, in fact. Shot twice, apparently sometime last night. No witnesses that we know of, no suspects, and no apparent motive as of yet."

I whistled low. "Holy cow."

"Yeah, and that's not all. He was apparently caught with his pants down, literally. Since you were investigating him anyway, I want you on the case. I know he was a huckster, but a popular one and rather famous in some circles, so keep it as quiet as you can. Try to keep the seamy details out of the papers."

"Sure, I understand, Chief."

"Good. Some fellow from one of the radio stations was already nosing around the morgue, and one of the *Sentinel* reporters just rang up, but we only gave them the basic information at this point."

"They don't waste time."

"No, they don't. I had Miss Blake type up the preliminary report from the officers who responded and were first on the scene. Here, look it over." He sat upright and picked up a file folder from atop his messy desk.

I glanced at it briefly, skimming it. "It says here nothing appears to have been missing. His watch and wallet, with cash still in it, were on his person."

"Correct. Rules out robbery, most likely."

"Interesting." I read a bit farther down to where the description of the victim was listed. "And I see what you mean about being caught with his pants down." I looked up at the chief, who was staring at me.

"Yes. Rather embarrassing."

"I'd say. Quite unusual," I said. "When did it happen?"

"Still waiting on the autopsy results to narrow down the time of death. He had a show last night at six, and it ended a little before eight, so sometime after that. The garbage men found his body around five this morning. He was supposed to have a matinee performance today at one."

"Yes, I know. I was going to go to it as a part of my investigation. And per your request, I'd set up a private consultation with him afterward for a crystal ball reading."

"That's right, I remember you mentioning that. The show will be canceled, I'm sure. The wife just left the morgue after identifying him. I had a black-and-white drive her back to the Blatz Hotel where she and Firestone were staying."

"Anyone else traveling with him?"

"I'm sure there was, but you'll have to check with the Blatz. Ask for the general manager, Elmer Suskind. Use my name, we go back a few years. He's a good man, honest. If you need anything from him or the hotel staff, I'm sure he'll give you his full cooperation. I'll have Miss Blake telephone him and let him know to expect you, as I'm sure you'll want to speak to the wife, at least. Keep me apprised of any developments. Any questions?"

"No sir, not that I can think of right now."

"Okay. Oh, and I asked the lab to send up the crime scene photos to your desk as soon as they're ready, along with the autopsy report when Fletcher finishes it."

"Always a good place to start. I'll get right on this."

"I know you will. You're dismissed, then."

"Yes, sir," I said. I tucked the folder under my arm and left his office, still stunned by the news.

Back at my desk, I picked up my telephone receiver. "Outside line, please." When I heard a dial tone, I dialed my home phone number, letting it ring once, and then hanging up. I repeated that, and then the third time I let it ring. It was my signal to Alan to let him know it was me calling and not my mother or someone else, and so it was safe for him to answer. He picked up on the second ring.

"Hello?"

"Hi there, it's me. I'm at my desk at the station."

"Hello," Alan said, cautious and aware someone from the police switchboard could be listening in. It wasn't likely, but we had to be ever vigilant.

"I've just had some jarring news. Almanzo Firestone was killed last night near the hotel."

"What? On the level? No joke?"

"I wish I was joking, but he's dead all right. Murdered. The chief's assigned me to the case, since I was investigating him already anyway."

"I can't believe it. I mean, we just saw him Friday night."

"I know. I was pretty surprised myself."

"You say he was murdered? Wowzer. So, they don't know who did it, or why?"

"Not yet, no. No known suspects, witnesses, or motives at this point."

"Holy chocolate cow."

"Yeah. So, naturally the matinee is off."

"I suppose so, geez. Crazy. Will you get your money back for the tickets?"

"I imagine they'll be refunding everyone. I'll try and stop by the box office later. Sorry to spring this on you over the phone, but I felt I had to let you know as soon as possible. I'm going to be here longer than I thought today because of all this. I need to start working on the case right away."

"Sure, Heath, I understand. Will you be back in time for dinner?"

"Hard to say, really. At this point, I don't even know where to begin or how long it will take. Best if you head home to your place. I'll call you later."

"Okay. Thanks for letting me know."

"Sure, of course. Keep the news under your hat for now, by the way. It's kind of on a need-to-know basis."

"Of course, I understand. Mum's the word. And you'll figure it out, you always do."

"Thanks for the vote of confidence."

"Always. Bye."

"Bye."

I hung up and set the books on spiritualism I had been perusing earlier aside, focusing now on the typed report from the two responding officers, making notes as I went. When I finished, I placed a call to the Blatz Hotel and asked to speak to Mr. Elmer Suskind, the general manager. Fortunately he was in and available, and he took my call when I mentioned the chief. Not surprisingly, Miss Blake had already telephoned. He cooperated fully, just as the chief had said he would, and gave me the names of everyone who had been traveling with Firestone and staying at the hotel with him. I had just hung up the receiver when I noticed Riker striding over to me.

"Hello," I said, looking up at him. "Back again? Didn't anyone tell you detectives get the weekend off?"

"Yeah, I know. I dropped Mary Jane and the baby off at church. She hates it when I don't go with her, but I just wasn't in the mood for a sermon today, so I thought I'd swing by here for a while. Spelling mentioned yesterday that he'd be here today. I guess he has some leads he wanted to follow up on this morning."

"I haven't seen him yet, and I've been here since around nine."

"Apparently, he got in at eight. Not sure what he's up to, but he doesn't seem to want my help, as usual. He left just before you got here, but I figured I'd stick around for a bit just in case. I've been talking to the desk sergeant, filing, and killing time."

"And you were here a good part of the day yesterday, too," I said. "And as I recall, your wife wasn't too happy about that."

"No, that's true, she wasn't."

"And yet here you are once more, when you don't need to be. Are you the eager new dick or are you avoiding spending time with your wife and baby?"

Riker looked slightly annoyed. "Like I said, I was just trying to be useful to Spelling, but that seems to be a waste of time. Why are you here again?"

"I wanted to have another look at those books on spiritualism I got from the library, but the case has taken an unexpected turn."

"Yeah, I heard. I'd wondered if you had. I thought maybe that's what brought you in on a Sunday morning."

"What did you hear?"

"That the spiritual guy was murdered last night, the Amazing Almanzo or whatever his name is. The guy you were investigating."

"The All-Seeing Almanzo, also known as Almanzo Firestone. How did you hear about it?"

"I've got a buddy at the morgue. He rang me up a few minutes ago."

"Better than a buddy *in* the morgue, I guess. The chief just filled me in on what happened. Unbelievable. I guess the All-Seeing Almanzo didn't see that coming."

"I guess not." Riker dropped down into the creaky wooden chair next to my desk and leaned in closer to me. "I heard some garbage men found him."

"Yes, early this morning, five a.m. They called the police, of course, and the responding officers figured out where he was staying from a receipt in his wallet. Two officers went over to the hotel to see if he had been traveling with anyone. The clerk told them he was sharing the room with his wife, so they woke her up, gave her the bad news, and took her to the morgue to make a positive ID."

"Wowzer, talk about a rude awakening. What do you think the story is? Robbery? My buddy didn't have too much information other than he was shot."

"Robbery doesn't seem likely in this case, as he had his wallet and watch still on him."

"Nothing missing from the wallet?"

"According to the report, he had seven dollars inside. A five and two ones, along with an identification card, a photo of a woman—presumably his wife, as her name was written on the back—and a receipt from the hotel, as I mentioned before."

"Maybe someone held him up, but this Almanzo refused to hand over the wallet, so he shot him and fled."

"It's certainly possible, though you'd think the robber would take the wallet before fleeing."

"Unless he panicked."

"Which would be natural, I suppose."

"My buddy said the body was found in an alley."

"Your buddy likes to talk, but yeah, that's correct. He was apparently shot sometime last night, after his evening performance at the theater."

"What would he be doing in a dirty old alley late at night?"

"Good question," I said. "What would anyone without ill intent be doing in a dirty, dark alley late at night?"

"Though it does sound rather spooky and mysterious. Right up a spiritualist's alley, so to speak."

"Yes, so to speak."

"Whereabouts is this alley?" Riker said.

"Just up the street from the Blatz Hotel, where Firestone and his entourage were staying."

"The Blatz is kitty-corner from City Hall and not far from the theater. A lot of actors, performers, and singers stay there."

"And spiritualists, it seems."

"Right. Well, my money is still on a robbery. Firestone may have been out for a walk, a fellow approaches, maybe asks for a light. The man pulls a gun and forces Firestone into the alley. He demands Firestone's wallet. When Firestone refuses, maybe even yells for help, the robber shoots him and flees in panic."

"Good theory, but there's something else in the report that doesn't really jive with a robbery."

Riker raised his eyebrows. "What?"

"You mean your buddy at the morgue didn't tell you?"

"Very funny. Just spill it."

"Firestone was found dead with his pants and underwear pulled down around his ankles."

Riker whistled. "Jeepers, now that's something you don't hear every day."

"Definitely not. We're doing our best to keep the part about his trousers being down out of the headlines. Almanzo the All-Seeing being gunned down less than a block from his hotel is bad enough for Milwaukee as it is."

"Sure, I understand. Hmm. I can't see a robber making him drop his pants."

"Doesn't seem likely."

"So, what was the motive?"

"That remains to be seen, and it won't be easy, I think. According to the report, there were no known witnesses, though of course someone may have seen or heard something. That's what I need to find out."

"Have you talked to his entourage? The people traveling with him?"

I smiled. "Already thinking like a detective, Riker. No, not yet, but I intend to. I just got off the phone with the general manager of the hotel, who gave me the rundown." I glanced briefly at my notes. "There's his wife, Muriel Firestone, his assistant and apparent protégé, Lorenzo Ricci, and his agent, a Clive Goodacre. I'll need to get over there and talk to each of them and remind them not to leave town just yet. I asked the general manager to be sure they don't check out."

"You think they'd try to? I mean, Firestone was just murdered. Wouldn't they want to stay and find out what happened?"

"Most likely, but you never know. To flee would certainly point toward guilt, so they will probably stay put."

"You think one of them did it?"

"Not necessarily, but even if they did or didn't, they certainly wouldn't want us to think they did."

"I've got a lot to learn about this detective stuff, it seems."

I smiled. "You'll get the hang of it, I have no doubt."

"Thanks. So, how will you begin the investigation?"

"It's already begun. I read the preliminary police report. Right now I'm waiting on the crime scene photos and the autopsy," I said, turning in my chair to face him. "Once I get a look at those, I'll know better what my next step may be."

Grant Riker looked past my shoulder. "I don't think you'll have long to wait. Officer Jordan is heading this way with a large envelope."

I turned back around as Jordan approached, his hand outstretched, holding the envelope. "Photographs, do not bend" was printed in large block letters on the outside of it.

"I was told to deliver these to you, Detective. The chief said you wanted them right away."

"I do indeed. Thanks, Jordan. That was quick work. That will be all for now."

"Yes, sir." He nodded at Riker and then went back downstairs.

"Have a few minutes to look at these with me, Grant?" I said.

"A few minutes? I have all day. Spelling left without me, remember? He got a solid lead on the vandalism case and said he could handle it better on his own. He gave me some filing to do, since I was here, which I finished in about ten minutes. That's about all I've done since I was assigned to him. File his paperwork, type his reports, get his coffee…"

"Well, Spelling's loss is my gain. But don't you have to pick up Mary Jane from church?"

"Naw, Mr. and Mrs. Krupky said they'd drive her home when I told her I wanted to come into the station for a bit. They live just up the street from us, nice folks. I'll give Mary Jane a call later."

"Okay, come on then, might as well make the most of your time here. Let's go into the briefing room and examine these photographs. We can spread them out on the table and see them better."

"Lead on, Heath," he said, getting to his feet.

I stood also, tucking the manila envelope under my arm as we crossed to the briefing room. I flicked on the overhead light and closed the door behind us. It was a small space, with a large rectangular table in the center. On either side of it were wooden chairs for each of the detectives, and an armchair for the chief at the head. Next to the chief's chair was a small metal side chair for Miss Blake. On the wall to the right was a map of the city of Milwaukee, with thumbtacks in certain locations. On the wall to the left was a bulletin board with a few Wanted posters pinned to it. A dusty, well-used chalkboard stood to the side. There was a solitary window on the opposite wall from the door, its venetian blinds coated with a thin layer of dust, and the glass was dirty and smudged.

"All right, let's have a look at the crime scene pictures," I said as I opened the manila envelope and spread them out on the table beneath the bright light. They were grisly, even in glossy black and white.

"So, that's the Amazing Almanzo," Riker said, staring down.

"The All-Seeing Almanzo. And yes, that's him, or what's left of him, anyway. I recognize him from the reception Friday night."

"Not what I expected, really. But not a bad-looking chap. Looks to be in his late forties."

"Yeah, that's what I would guess."

"Hmm. Looks like two shots, one to his left side and one to his left shoulder."

"So, he wasn't shot straight on."

"No. And it looks like he must have fallen into the trash can to his right, then to the ground. You can see the trash can is tipped over, and he appears to be lying on some of the trash."

I picked up the photo he was pointing at and studied it. "Good eye. Yes, I agree."

"What street is the alley off of?"

"According to the report, it opens off Wells, just a little east of the Blatz, across Water street."

"And the Blatz is on the corner of Wells and Water."

"That's right. The body was found close to the Wells Street entrance to the alley."

"Okay." Riker walked over to the chalkboard and picked up a piece of chalk, drawing out a rough outline of Wells and Water streets, the location of the hotel on the corner, and the approximate location of the alley. "If Firestone entered from Wells Street and stopped about three to five yards in, he'd be in shadows."

"Yes, far enough from the streetlights, most likely."

"But still more visible than he probably realized," Riker said.

"Probably. I'm thinking someone shot him from the sidewalk."

"Makes sense. Firestone probably stopped just inside the alley and turned. His back was to the wall, which would expose his left side to the street. When his pants were down, the shots were fired, causing him to fall away from the street into the trash cans, like so." Riker sketched a stick figure falling into what I assumed were supposed to be trash cans.

"But why did he drop his pants?" I said.

"Maybe he had to relieve himself, and the alley was convenient."

"Many men have done that at one time or another, myself included. But most men don't drop their pants and underwear all the way down. Plus, if your theory is correct, he was facing away from the wall when he was shot. Most men relieving themselves would face toward the wall."

"Speaking from experience, I would say that's true," Riker said.

"And the bigger question, *why* did someone shoot him?"

"Does make one wonder." Riker put the chalk down, turned back to the table, and picked up one of the other photos, holding it close. "Is that a carnation in his lapel?"

"Yeah, a bit wilted from the looks of it," I said, glancing over Riker's shoulder. "According to the police report, Firestone was wearing a navy suit with a baby blue tie, and a green carnation in his lapel. He also had a monocle attached to a chain leading from his other lapel. You can just see the chain in this picture here. He's probably lying on the monocle," I said, pointing to another one of the 8x10s with my finger. "The report says it was broken and cracked."

"A monocle? Jeepers, I've never seen a real person wear one of those before."

"Me neither, but he was wearing it Friday night, and in nearly all of his publicity photos. Doesn't seem very comfortable or practical. But then this Almanzo was all about showmanship, it seems, and a monocle would make him stand out."

"Yes. And a green carnation in his lapel. Hmm."

"What?"

"Nothing. Just curious," Riker said, setting the one photo down and picking up another, which showed a close-up of Almanzo's upper torso. He studied it carefully.

"About what?" I said. "The green carnation? I don't see anything too unusual about that."

He looked at me, then dropped the photo back on the table. He seemed embarrassed, but I couldn't imagine why. "You're right, forget it."

I set the photo I was holding back down and turned to him. "I'm investigating a murder, Riker. No detail, no thought, is unimportant."

"It's probably nothing. Guys wear carnations all the time. Like you said, nothing too unusual about that."

"I suppose some men wear them all the time, though green ones don't seem very typical."

"No, they're definitely not. I wonder."

"What? You're thinking something, I can tell, Grant. Spill it. Tell me what it is."

"Well, it's curious, that's all. I was just wondering about the green carnation, and how he was found in that alley by the Blatz Hotel, with his pants and underwear down around his ankles. It's not typical by any means."

"I agree with you there. But what does the carnation have to do with anything?"

"It's just that there's a little flower shop near the Blatz called Birdy's, been there for years. It's run by a smarmy little man named Leslie Birdwell. He keeps late hours for a flower shop."

"Okay. So, what about this flower shop, besides the fact he keeps late hours?"

"It's been in business a long time, like I said." He looked around the briefing room. "Can anyone hear us in here?"

"No, not with the door shut and the window closed. It's the one place we can go in the station when we need to concentrate without outside interference. Why?"

He slid a finger in between his neck and his collar, then wiped his brow with his handkerchief before stuffing it back into his pocket. "A long time ago, before I was married, before I was on the force, hell, before I was even in the Navy, I had heard about Birdy's. It was a place to make a fast buck, you know?"

"You worked there?"

"In a manner of speaking, yeah, sort of. Mr. Birdwell runs a side operation selling carnations to men who are looking for, shall we say, an evening's distraction."

Slowly the light dawned on me. "Oh, I see. He was fronting a prostitution ring, is that it?"

"Yeah, though it sounds bad when you say it like that."

"Not sure how else to say it, Riker. I don't understand the carnation angle, though. What do carnations have to do with prostitution?"

"Well, the way it worked was, men would go in to the shop and they would buy a carnation. A green carnation if they were interested in male company, red if they wanted a female. Then Mr. Birdwell would make a phone call to one of his boys or girls and say he has a floral delivery for them to make. The chosen boy or girl would then meet the gentleman with the carnation in the alley, the one Firestone was found in, it sounds like. They could then either go to a hotel room or something or take care of it right then and there, depending."

"Depending on what?"

"On what the client wanted. Sometimes it was just quick and easy, and it was simpler to do it right there, in the shadows and darkness of the alley. Other times they wanted something more, or it was during the day, and for that a room and more privacy was required."

"Sounds risky, for both parties."

"I suppose so."

"How did Birdwell know just by a man buying a carnation that he wanted more than just a carnation?"

"The customer was supposed to say, 'I want a green—or red—carnation, young and fresh off the stem.' 'Young and fresh off the stem' was the code word, or phrase to be more accurate, though it may have changed since then."

"Fascinating. And this Mr. Birdwell charged a hefty amount for those carnations, I imagine."

"Five dollars apiece. At least, that's what he used to charge. He kept three, and the boy or girl got a dollar and a half or two dollars, depending on if the client was referred by someone or not. He paid them direct, always cash. That way, if the cops ever caught one of the boys or girls, it was all on the up-and-up, according to him. The client never paid directly for sex, you see? All they did was buy a carnation. And the boy or girl was just making floral deliveries if they ever said anything. Nothing could be proven against Birdwell."

"Nice and tidy. And how did you fit into this operation?"

His face turned crimson and beaded with sweat. He turned away and stared down again at the array of photographs on the table, shuffling them about absentmindedly with his fingertips. His voice was soft and quavering when at last he spoke. "Well, gee, I was young, you know? I had just turned eighteen, and I needed the money badly."

"Oh."

"Yeah."

"So, you were one of those boys in the alley. Young and fresh off the stem."

"I'm not proud of it, Heath. I had to support myself, and that seemed safer than robbing a bank."

"I'll give you that. But what about a regular job?"

He glanced up at me, his face still red and sweaty. "It was 1935, the height of the Depression. Jobs were scarce. I did manage to land a part-time job at Marshall Field's thanks to the personnel manager taking a liking to me, if you know what I mean, but it wasn't enough to pay my bills."

"Okay, the Depression was hard on everyone. But what about your parents? Your family?"

He snorted. "There's a laugh. My mother died when I was just a kid. I don't even remember her. My dad was a drunk."

I felt a lump in my throat. "I'm sorry, Riker. Did he hit you?"

He shook his head. "No, he was actually a funny drunk, a laugh a minute. He loved me, but he didn't love himself. He drank himself to death when I was fifteen. I went to live with my aunt after that, but she was glad to get rid of me when I turned eighteen. I got that job at Field's and took a room at a boardinghouse. That in turn led me to Birdwell. One of the other tenants of the boardinghouse worked there, and he put in a good word for me."

"So, you became one of Birdwell's boys on call. One of his delivery boys, so to speak."

"Yeah. I was a pretty good-looking guy, if I do say so myself, and he was eager to sign me on. I suppose you're shocked."

I looked into his beautiful eyes and touched his arm gently, giving it a soft squeeze. "Not shocked. Not really. It sounds like you did what you needed to do to take care of yourself, though I still think there must have been other ways."

"I'm not proud of it, but it was easy money, and good money. Where else could I make a buck and a half, sometimes even two bucks, for fifteen minutes or less of work? And sometimes the men even tipped me. So, I did it until I enlisted in December of '41, right after Pearl

Harbor. When I got out, I went to school for a while on the GI Bill and worked as a steward on one of those lake cruisers, like on that one case we were on. I found I wasn't cut out for school, though, and didn't like being a steward, so I joined the police force and married Mary Jane. And now, at age thirty, I finally made detective. The rest of my past life is all ancient history, and I'd like to keep it that way."

I looked again at this handsome man standing next to me, so bright, so full of life, so full of surprises. I could tell he was ashamed, trembling, afraid. "And you never reported this little flower shop to the vice squad once you became a police officer?"

"The vice squad?"

"You know, that office downstairs that covers things like gambling, narcotics, illegal sales of booze, and prostitution?"

Riker bristled, arching his back. "I don't need a lecture, Heath. I'm just trying to help. And I'm confiding my darkest secrets to you, damn it. I hope I can trust you."

I squeezed his arm once more, this time a little more firmly. "I'm sorry, I know you're scared. It took a great deal of courage for you to tell me all this. Please know you can trust me, just like I can trust you to keep my secrets, but what that Birdwell fellow is doing is against the law, Grant. He's taking advantage of young men and women who are probably in dire straits."

He dropped his chin to his chest and sighed deeply. "I know, I know. Believe me, I know. But maybe he's *not* doing that anymore. Maybe he's just selling flowers."

"Possible but not likely. He's not going to stop a cash cow like that unless he's forced to."

Riker looked up and over at me again. "I suppose you're right. But how can I report it without bringing suspicion on myself?"

"There are ways, but we'll deal with that later. We have to put a stop to his enterprise."

"Yes, I guess so. I suppose I should have said something a long time ago."

"Easy for me to say, but yes, you should have. It must be done, and it will be done. Is that okay?"

He nodded slowly. "Yes, that's okay. It has to be done."

"Good. So, you're thinking Firestone might have been a customer of this flower shop?"

"Yeah, I think he could have been, given he was wearing a green carnation and he was in that alley late at night with his pants down. It all adds up. He left the hotel, stopped by the flower shop and bought his green carnation, and headed toward the alley."

"And he was all over Alan at the reception Friday night, so a green carnation, as opposed to a red one, makes sense."

"Yes, I remember you saying how he kept running his hands up and down Alan's arms."

I shuddered at the memory. "Yeah, gave me the creeps. How do men find out about the flower shop anyway? Certainly Mr. Birdwell doesn't advertise that little side business in the newspaper."

"Back then when I was involved, it was through word of mouth, as well as the concierges at some of the major downtown hotels, like the Blatz, and probably still is. If a guest inquired, the concierge would direct him to Birdy's and give him the code phrase. The concierge got a cut of the action, of course, for the referral. Fifty cents for each one, which is why sometimes we only got a buck and half. I don't think the hotel managers ever knew."

"Nice and tidy indeed. I think we need to pay a visit to Birdy's and see what a little Bird can tell us."

"Us? I'm supposed to be working with Spelling, remember?"

I grimaced. "Yeah, doing his filing and making his coffee. What's next, washing and waxing his car? Let me talk to the chief and see if I can get you reassigned to me. I do my own filing and get my own coffee."

"Gee, I'd appreciate that, Heath, truly. Thanks."

"No thanks necessary. You'd be a big help to me. You're a bright man, and I could use you on this case. Not to mention you have inside information."

"Let's keep that to ourselves, okay?"

"Of course. Mum's the word, Detective. And Riker? Thanks for trusting me with your secrets. I won't let you down."

Chapter Nine

Morning, Sunday, September 14, 1947

After we left the briefing room, I stopped at my desk and made a call to Miss Blake, asking to see the chief. A short while later I was back in his office, standing before him once again. His eyebrows had settled down, but he still looked troubled.

"Solve the case already, Barrington?" he said, a wry smile on his lips. He was fiddling with an unlit cigarette again.

"No, not yet, Chief. How's it going with not smoking?"

"Hmm? Oh, yeah. The wife, you know. She doesn't like it."

"Yeah, so you said. I hear it's a hard habit to break."

He stared down at the cigarette between the fingers of his left hand. In his right, he held his silver lighter. "It is. And having to be here on a Saturday and a Sunday, even if just for a few hours, doesn't help. I'm hoping Miss Blake and I can get out of here soon. She gets overtime, you know, and I have to be conscious of the budget."

"I understand. I'll try to be brief."

"Do that. My wife wants me home for lunch. So, what can I do for you?"

"Grant Riker and I had a look at the crime scene photos from the Firestone case."

He looked mildly surprised. "Riker? He's assigned to Spelling."

"I know, but Spelling left him behind with nothing to do but some filing while he went out on his vandalism case, so I asked Riker to have a look at the photos with me. Frankly he had some good insights, and I think I could really use his help on this case."

The chief scowled now, his bushy eyebrows forming an M as they came together above his nose. "Ugh, Spelling. You'd think *he* was never a new detective, never had anyone take *him* under his wing. To be honest, I appreciate you wanting to help the new guy."

"I'm glad to do it. Riker has a quick mind and a photographic memory. I think he'll be an asset to me. That is, if you don't mind reassigning him."

"Sure, glad to. Anything that will get Spelling to shut up," the chief said. "He was none too happy to have to hold Riker's hand and has been complaining about it constantly. I'll talk to Spelling and let him know about the change. I'm sure he'll be thrilled. Tell the desk sergeant I want to see Spelling when he gets back."

"Will do, Chief. And thanks."

"You're welcome." He twirled the unlit cigarette about in his hand. "Sometimes I curse Green for resigning and making me go through breaking in a new guy again. Get Riker up to speed pronto, will ya?"

"I will, don't worry, sir." I left him scowling behind his desk, now sucking on the unlit cigarette like a pacifier. I wasn't sure, but I thought I heard the click of his lighter just as I closed his office door. Riker was back at his own desk in the detective's room, studying a book intently and finishing a Chicken Dinner candy bar, which despite its unusual name was just chocolate with crisp, crunchy peanuts.

"What are you so engrossed in?" I said, walking up to him. "Besides that candy bar, I mean."

He closed the book and set it down onto the desk, rubbing his eyes. He looked bored as he read the title aloud to me from the cover. "*Rules and Regulations of the Police Department of the City of Milwaukee, Detective Division.* I'm up to the section on the *Special Collections Room and the Procurement and Storage Thereof.*"

"The evidence room is actually pretty fascinating if you ever get a chance to go down there. But that there is dull material indeed. You were already tired. I'm surprised you're still awake after reading that."

"Just barely, but there was nothing else to do, and I thought it would be a good idea to study up some more. What did the chief say?"

I grinned. "You're all mine, partner. You have been officially relieved of filing and coffee duty effective immediately, and no more dull reading until further notice."

Riker grinned back at me, his mood noticeably improved. "That's the best news I've heard all day, thanks. I really appreciate it." He tossed the candy wrapper in the trash bin and wiped a bit of chocolate from his mouth.

"You're welcome. But I didn't do it out of kindness or pity. I can use your eyes, your memory, and your mind."

"Like you said, I'm all yours. Now what?"

"Now we get to work. We have a murder to solve, Detective."

"I'm ready, willing, and able." He picked up the book once more and set it on the cabinet behind his desk with a thunk. "By the way, the coroner's assistant left an envelope on your desk while you were gone."

"Excellent. That will be the autopsy report, no doubt. Let's have a look." We went back to my desk, and I opened the envelope, removing the contents. I scanned the results and glanced at the photos from the autopsy. They were even more gruesome than the ones from the crime scene.

Riker looked a tad white as he studied the photographs. "Those are pretty grisly," he said.

"Yeah. I couldn't do Fletcher's job, but he loves it. He's a first-rate coroner, one of the best." I set the pictures aside and studied the report more closely. "Fletch puts the time of death somewhere between nine and midnight last night. Two bullets, one in Firestone's left side beneath the rib cage and the other in his left shoulder, both from the same small caliber handgun. He didn't die immediately, but the loss of blood was significant. Bruises on the right side of the body are indicative of him striking the trash can as he fell and knocked it over, as you rightly assumed earlier."

"Just made sense."

"Yes. Hmm, shot sometime between nine and midnight last night. I think a visit to the Blatz Hotel and a chat with Firestone's entourage is in order."

"To find out where they all were last night during the time of the murder."

"Exactly. Or more precisely, where they say they were and where they say they weren't. You sure your wife doesn't mind you being gone all day today?"

"I actually haven't called her yet, but I will, maybe from the hotel."

CHAPTER TEN

Early afternoon, Sunday, September 14, 1947

Riker and I grabbed our hats and suit coats and went downstairs, stopping only briefly at the sergeant's desk to sign out and leave a message for Spelling to check in with the chief. Then we headed out to my car in the bright afternoon sunshine, our hats pulled low to shield our eyes. It was a short drive to the Blatz, an imposing, five-story red brick building located on the southwest corner of Water and Wells. Built in the mid-1800s, it had a mansard roof and a gothic tower. I found a parking spot near the Pabst Theater, not far from where I had parked on Friday night. A rusty sign affixed to a light pole stated it was a one-hour parking zone from 10 a.m. until 4 p.m. Monday through Sunday, but I figured one hour would probably be enough time for our purposes, so I turned off the engine and put the brake on.

We walked back south along the broad sidewalk, tipping our hats politely at the ladies and nodding to the gentlemen we happened to meet. We entered the Water Street entrance, a uniformed doorman ushering us in with a tip of his hat. Even on a Sunday afternoon the bar off to the right was crowded, men and women standing at the bar or seated at the many tables, enjoying a cold beer or a whiskey on an autumn day, the air thick with cigarette and cigar smoke.

We walked over to the front desk, a long, dark wooden rectangle against the far wall, framed by two marble columns. At one end, a young woman with a small child stood talking to one of the clerks on duty, so we approached the other clerk nearest the bar. He was a thin, older man with thick glasses, shuffling papers about and looking bored.

He glanced up at Riker and me as we approached and gave us a polite, practiced smile. His name badge read *Mr. Billings, Senior Clerk.*

"Good afternoon, gentlemen," he said, his voice pleasant but monotonous. "Welcome to the Blatz. How may I help you? We do have rooms available this evening, a double or two singles, if desired. Four dollars a night, or if you want a room with a private bath, four fifty."

"No, thanks, we don't need any rooms." I showed him my badge. "I'm Detective Barrington of the Milwaukee Police. This is Detective Riker. We're investigating the murder of Almanzo Firestone and would like to speak with Mrs. Firestone and the others in their party."

The man adjusted his glasses and looked thoughtful, his voice dropping several octaves as he glanced about. "Oh dear, dear, dear, yes. I heard about Mr. Firestone. Simply awful, dreadful, really. Probably a robbery. Nothing to do with the hotel, though, I can assure you. There's never been a murder here to my knowledge."

"That's reassuring to know," I said. "Now, if you'd be kind enough to tell us what room Mrs. Firestone is in. We have the full cooperation of your general manager, Mr. Suskind."

"Mr. Suskind, yes, yes, yes, of course. He told us to expect you. It's the Blatz policy to always cooperate with the police, not that we have reason to do so regularly. The Blatz is a very safe property, in an excellent neighborhood. Very safe."

"But things happen, even murder, in the best of neighborhoods," I said. The woman with the small child had stopped talking to the other clerk and was trying to hear what I was saying. I removed my hat and nodded politely at her. She gave me a curt smile, thanked the clerk who had been attending her, and walked away, the small child in tow.

"What room is Mrs. Firestone in?" I said again.

"Oh, yes, yes, yes, of course, forgive me. Yes, one moment, please." He scanned the register briefly, his finger moving steadily down the page. "Well, let me see. Mr. and Mrs. Firestone are in the Valentine Suite, named after Valentin Blatz, of course. It's made up of rooms 402, 404, and 406, with 404 being the sitting room. Mr. Ricci is in the adjoining room, 402, and Mr. Goodacre is down the hall in 415. Both of those gentlemen are traveling with the Firestones."

"Thank you."

"You're quite welcome. We at the Blatz strive to give excellent service."

"I'll be sure and let Mr. Suskind know how helpful you've been."

"Oh, I do appreciate that, Detective, thank you," He smiled more sincerely then and looked most pleased. "The name's Billings, Roger K. Billings, Senior Clerk. The *K* is for Kenneth."

I made a notation in my notebook. "A good, solid name. By the way, were you on duty last night, Mr. Billings?"

He adjusted his thick glasses once more, pushing them up the bridge of his nose. "Yes, yes, yes indeed. Yes. It was a fairly quiet evening for a Saturday night, rather unusual, but I will tell you this."

"What?"

He leaned across the counter and lowered his voice, glancing about to make sure no one else was within earshot. "One of the bellboys, Ralph, told me he heard arguing from Mr. Firestone's suite just before he went to the theater for his evening performance."

"Arguing? What did he hear?" I said.

Mr. Billings leaned across the counter a little farther. "The boy was making a room service delivery across the hall, and he distinctly heard at least two, possibly three, men arguing and shouting quite loudly in the sitting room of Mr. Firestone's suite."

"What were they arguing about?" Riker said.

"Ralph said he didn't stop to listen as he had another room service call to make, but he heard one of the men say, 'Why don't you get a divorce? You don't even like women,' and the other one shouted, if you'll excuse the language, 'To hell with you.' Then one of them said, 'if I find out you've been stealing from me, so help me I'll kill you, summon you from the beyond, and torture the death out of you,' or something to that effect."

"Interesting. Quite a turn of a phrase. Is this bellboy working today?" I said.

"No, no, no. No, he won't be back until day after tomorrow, but really I don't think he could tell you any more than I just have. His name's Ralph Ardmore, though, if you do want to question him."

I made another note. "Thanks, we might. For now, I think we'll start with Mrs. Firestone."

Billings leaned back and straightened up, adjusting his glasses again. "Oh, Mrs. Firestone has just gone out to lunch, I'm afraid. I should have mentioned that earlier. She stopped at the desk and asked if I had any messages for her, and then she asked for a restaurant recommendation. I suggested our fine dining room here at the hotel, but she said she wanted a change of scenery. Can't say I blame her, given the circumstances and all. Lovely woman, I've always admired redheads, but she did not look well at all, poor dear lady, all in black. Mourning, you know."

"Of course," Riker said. "To be honest, I'm surprised she even wanted to leave her room."

"A little fresh air will do her good, I imagine, though I'm afraid it's a gloomy, overcast day today. Seems fitting, in a way. Still so dismaying. About Mr. Firestone, I mean."

"Yes, it is. What about the other gentlemen? Where might we find them?" Riker said.

"Mr. Ricci and Mr. Goodacre? As far as I know, they're in their rooms, but of course it would be impossible to keep track of the comings and goings of all our guests. This is a large hotel."

"Of course. Well, we'll just go and see, if you don't mind," I said.

"I don't mind at all. Like I said, we here at the Blatz always cooperate with the authorities."

"Not that you have much reason to," I said.

"No, no, no. Not much reason to at all. The Blatz is a very safe property in an excellent location."

"So you've said," Riker said.

"Well yes, yes, but it's true. Quite true, yes. Oh, we have an occasional theft or something, but it's usually due to guest carelessness. Never anything serious, I assure you."

"People can be careless," I said, "and quick to blame someone else. Well, I'm sure you must have business to attend to, Mr. Billings, so we should let you go."

"Oh, yes, yes, indeed. Mr. Ricci and Mr. Goodacre are on the fourth floor, gentlemen. The elevators are just past the desk, across from the ladies' and gentlemen's lounges."

"Right, good day then," I said.

"Good day."

Riker and I left the desk and walked the length of it to the passenger elevators, our hats in our hands.

"Interesting fellow," Riker said as we waited for the elevator to arrive.

"Billings? Yes. Quite the company man, but he clearly enjoys his gossip. I can just picture his ears perking up when that bellboy told him about the argument last night."

Riker nodded. "I'm sure. What do you think it was all about? And who do you think was involved?"

The etched brass doors slid open and we stepped inside. "Four, please," I said to the operator.

"Yes, sir," he replied, closing the doors with a whoosh and a click.

"The argument? I don't know, but hopefully we'll find out."

Soon enough, the operator stopped the cab and opened the doors once more. "Fourth floor, gentlemen," he said.

"Thanks," Riker said as we stepped into the hall. "Which way is 402?"

"To your right, sir. Good day."

"Thanks, good day," I said as the elevator doors closed. We walked down the plush carpeted hall and knocked on the door of 402. It was opened by an attractive man with dark hair and olive skin, probably in his mid-thirties. He wore a white shirt with a green tie, dark, cuffed trousers, and black socks, no shoes.

"Oh, I thought you were someone else," he said, staring out at us. "Can I help you with something?" His voice was deep and resonant, and his breath smelled of alcohol and tobacco.

"You're Lorenzo Ricci?" I said.

"That's right. Who are you?"

"I'm Detective Barrington and this is Detective Riker, of the Milwaukee Police Department."

"Oh. And you've come to ask me some questions about Almanzo, or more accurately, Almanzo's murder, naturally."

"That's right. May we come in?"

"Sure, sure. Why not?" He stepped aside and motioned us into the room, closing the door behind us. "I'm just finishing up a telephone call, if you'll excuse me," he said, walking back to the desk where the telephone receiver was on its side. He picked it up, turning away from us. "Listen, dollface, I gotta go, but come see me tonight, room 402. Yeah, nine's fine. Bye." He hung up the phone and turned back to us. "Sorry about that, just ordering room service for later."

"This is indeed a full-service hotel," I said.

"Yeah, a real classy joint. I'd offer you a drink, but I don't have any clean glasses, and I'm almost out of bourbon anyway." The bed was unmade, and dirty clothes were scattered about, along with newspapers and magazines. The ashtray on the desk was full of cigarette butts.

"That's quite all right, Mr. Ricci. We're on duty anyway," Riker said.

"Stinks for you," he said. "I figured the police would come asking questions sooner or later. Pretty horrible what happened. I heard they found his body in an alley not too far from here. Muriel had to go identify him this morning."

"Muriel being Mrs. Firestone?" Riker said.

"Yeah. Crazy. They made her go look at his dead body. Kind of creepy."

"It's actually standard procedure, Mr. Ricci," I said. "Even though he had his wallet on him, mistakes have been known to happen. Always more cut and dried if someone who knew the victim can make a positive ID."

"I suppose. Glad I didn't have to do it, though. Morgues give me the creeps. Have you caught the lowlife who killed him yet?"

"No, sir. Not yet," Riker said.

"So, what gives, then? What do you want from me?"

"Just to ask you some questions," Riker said.

"Ask away, but I don't know nothing. Not about his murder, I mean." He sat down at the writing desk and picked up a glass tumbler less than half full of what I assumed was bourbon. The nearly empty liquor bottle stood on top of the desk, its top off. Another empty bottle was in the trash can next to the bed.

"Sometimes people know more than they think. We'll also be talking to Mr. Goodacre and Mrs. Firestone. Your full name is Lorenzo Ricci?" I said, taking out my notebook once more.

He finished his drink and put the tumbler down. "Actually, that's my stage name. My real name is Lawrence. Lawrence Adrian Ricci. Almanzo's the one who suggested Lorenzo. When we first met, he had plans for us to be a team. The All-Seeing Almanzo and the Amazing Lorenzo."

"Has a nice ring to it," Riker said.

"Yeah, but it hasn't exactly worked out that way. I'm Almanzo's associate and understudy, or at least I *was*."

"I wasn't aware spiritualists had understudies," Riker said.

"I wasn't an understudy so much as an apprentice or protégé. He was teaching me the tricks of the trade, but I was a quick learner. More so than he expected, I think."

"But I thought it was a divine gift, not something that could be taught," I said.

Lorenzo snorted. "Divine gift? There's a laugh. If Almanzo could really predict the future, he wouldn't be dead now, would he? Al put on a good show, but that's all it was. A show, theatrics, stuff anyone could learn, like magic."

"Some people believe otherwise," Riker said.

"Some people believe in the Easter Bunny and the Tooth Fairy."

"But not usually adults," I said.

"The goon says some people will believe anything if they want to bad enough, despite any evidence to the contrary, and on that I think he's right."

"The goon?" Riker said.

"Goodacre, Al's manager. Cynical little bastard, which is one of his few redeeming qualities."

"I take it you don't care for him," I said.

"I'd say the feeling's mutual," Ricci said.

"And neither one of you believes in spiritualism?" Riker said.

"I believe it can make me a buck or two. As for Firestone, he really thought he had some kind of crazy ability, or at least he wanted people to believe he did. Even his wife Muriel thought he had divine powers. In fact, she thinks she has the gift, too. Or pretends she does."

"Maybe she does have powers," Riker said.

Ricci laughed again. "She may have powers all right, but they ain't supernatural, they're 38-24-36, red hair, and gams that go all the way up. She has the kind of gifts I can appreciate."

"And it sounds like you do," I said. "I understand Mr. Firestone's matinee performance this afternoon was canceled in light of what happened."

Ricci nodded. "Yup, and right now the goon's trying to cancel the whole damn tour, and they're going to give everyone their money back. Stupid. I should have gone on in his place this afternoon. Hell, I could have completed the tour. That's the way it shoulda been, but they felt it would be better not to proceed."

"They?"

"Goodacre and Muriel."

"Understandable, I suppose," Riker said.

"If I may be frank, I don't see what difference canceling the performance or the tour made. Almanzo is just as dead."

"But he is dead, Mr. Ricci," I said.

"Yes, his hubris was his downfall. Like I said before, I think he truly believed he was the all-seeing Almanzo, and that nothing terrible would ever happen to him. But clearly he was dead wrong, and, as the saying goes, the show must go on."

"That's true, but it's not like he just came down with laryngitis and you stepped in for the sake of the audience. Don't you think proceeding as planned would have been a bit callous under these circumstances?" Riker said.

"Because I'm supposed to be grieving?"

"Something like that, yes."

He shrugged his massive shoulders, rolled up his shirt sleeves, and loosened his tie. "I've got bills to pay, you know? Grieving doesn't pick up my bar tab or pay my restaurant and hotel bills. The goon doesn't seem to be worried about money, but I need the dough. So I'm thinking since they want the tour canceled, I might start a tribute tour on my own. In Al's memory, of course."

I raised my eyebrows. "A tribute tour?"

"That's right. Maybe the fact that he's dead will even help draw the crowds. I could summon his spirit onstage."

"That would certainly be novel," I said.

"You have to have some kind of a gimmick these days, mister. The believers are waning, and audiences have been dwindling. Times are tough in this business. I won't do the full shows, of course, but I'll do the card readings and the audience participation, and the finale will be summoning Almanzo's spirit right there onstage in front of everyone, all done with special effects. It will be an amazing performance."

"A show like that will take some money to put on," I said. "Do you have any backing?"

"I will." He picked up the bourbon bottle and drained its contents into his glass, taking a swig. "I've been working on it. I've been thinking about going off on my own for a while now."

"I wish you much luck," I said. "But getting back to the events at hand. Do you know why Mr. Firestone may have been in that alley last night?"

He swirled the bourbon about in his mouth before swallowing. "I have a pretty good idea."

"And what would that be?" I said.

"Eh, the whole evening was crazy. Al wanted to host a cocktail hour before dinner in his suite for him, Muriel, me, the goon, and some pretty young thing who's the president of his fan club. The goon arranged for her, Al, and himself to have dinner after the show last night, and Al thought it would be a good idea to have her up for cocktails beforehand. He liked to show off, you know, while at the same time saving money by having drinks up here using a bottle he had the goon pick up at the liquor store."

"Thrifty," I said. "I imagine ordering drinks in the bar downstairs would have been considerably more."

"You got that right, and Al's never been one to spend money unnecessarily."

"Yet he got a suite when a standard room would have sufficed."

"He writes it off as a business expense. He and Muriel often hold private séances, tarot card and crystal ball readings in the sitting room of the suite. Plus, like I said, he likes to impress. He spends a small fortune on his fancy clothes, and then there's that stupid monocle. It's just clear glass, you know. All for looks."

"A true showman," I said. "So, what exactly was it about the night that made it crazy, as you say?"

"Things got a little heated, for one. Al and Muriel didn't get back from the evening performance until almost eight thirty, and I'd already had a few cocktails by the time he showed up. We had a few words."

"What about?"

"Me not being included in the dinner plans, for one. The cheap son of a bitch didn't want to pay for Muriel or me. It irked me, you know? I'd had a few drinks 'cause I was pissed. And then Muriel started in on me for drinking, so to hell with all of 'em."

"Was the president of his fan club there at that time?" Riker said. "I'm sorry, I didn't catch her name."

"You didn't catch it 'cause I didn't throw it. I honestly don't remember her name. Started with an *L*, I think, but I'm not sure. But yeah, she got there around a quarter after eight. Pretty little thing, but kinda nuts. Real fan of Almanzo's, all gaga for him. If she only knew."

"Knew what?" I said.

"What he's really like. What he really likes. *Who* he really likes. If she knew the truth she'd feel a whole lot differently about him. She's a kook, and klutzy, too. She spilled a perfectly good drink all over the rug right after Al and Muriel got in. That didn't sit well with Al at all. He was plenty steamed, but he couldn't say anything to her. The three of them went downstairs shortly after that."

"And what happened after dinner?" I said.

"From what the goon tells me, Almanzo wanted to get some air after they finished eating, so he went for a walk."

"Down a dark alley, alone, apparently," Riker said.

"Almanzo wasn't always the brightest. His brains were in his pants, if you know what I mean."

"Not really," I said. "You mentioned before you had an idea of what he may have been doing in that alley."

"Yeah. In every city we went, he found a way to get some extracurricular activity of a certain illicit nature. It was only a matter of time until it caught up to him. I have a feeling whoever he met for his little fling shot him dead."

I glanced at Riker, who looked rather embarrassed. "So you're saying he had extramarital affairs?"

"I wouldn't call them affairs so much as one-night stands, a new one in every town. As his understudy, I usually arranged them at his request, and he paid me a little extra to do it. That way he kept his nose clean as far as appearances go in case anyone talked. The way I see it, most likely he hooked up with the wrong fling last night in that alley."

"That's certainly possible," Riker said. "And how did you go about arranging these flings, Mr. Ricci?"

"I asked around the hotel. Every city we go to, there's always someone in the know—a bellboy, desk clerk, waiter, concierge, or someone at the theater who, for the right price, will direct me toward the kind of entertainment Al wanted."

"And what exactly was that kind of entertainment?" Riker said.

"Not the kind Mrs. Firestone, or any dame, could provide, if you get my drift. The kind that fan club girl would find sinful and evil."

"And who directed you as to where to find last night's sinful and evil entertainment for Mr. Firestone?" I said.

"I ain't no stool pigeon, and I honestly don't remember, anyway. It was just a guy in the know, for a price."

"Are you trying to tell us you honestly don't remember who you paid to give you information on where Mr. Firestone could find a sexual partner for the evening? A male partner, if I'm understanding you correctly."

"Yeah, you're understanding correctly, all right. But I can barely remember what day it is or what city we're in half the time. It was just some guy."

"I see. Do you at least know who it was Mr. Firestone met up with last night? Or what the arrangement was as to how or where they were to meet?" I said.

"Nope. Not the slightest idea, sorry. I got the scoop, and I gave it to him before the show last night, while he was getting dressed. Al put on his gray suit with the baby blue tie that matched his eyes. He liked doing that. I will say his eyes were an amazing shade of blue. They really stood out against his dark skin and dark hair. People often mistook us for brothers, except my eyes are deep brown."

"And bloodshot," I said.

"Funny guy," Ricci said, taking another hefty drink.

"I can see the resemblance, Mr. Ricci," Riker said.

"Thanks, I guess. We did look a bit alike, but in every other way, we were very different. Not to mention I'm younger, taller, smarter, and better looking overall."

"And not conceited in the least," I said. "Was Mrs. Firestone aware of his dalliances?"

"Dalliances. Now *there's* a word," Ricci said, laughing. "You'll have to ask her. We never talked about it."

"All right, we will. By the way, did you and Mr. Firestone have words before the show last night?"

"Words? Of course we had words. We didn't just sit and stare at each other. I had to give him the lowdown for the night."

"Yes, I understand, but did the two of you argue at some point? I'm told voices were raised."

"Oh, that. It was nothin'. I mean nothing unusual. Al and I bickered sometimes."

"Yes, but I believe during this particular argument one of you said something about getting a divorce and not even liking women, and then the other one said to hell with you, or something like that," I said.

Ricci laughed again. "You dicks got ears all over the place, don't you? Honestly, I don't even remember what it was all about or what was said. Like I said, my memory ain't what it used to be, especially after a couple of drinks, or three or four. But I'm sure it was nothing unusual, just us bickering."

"It couldn't have had anything to do with his wife, could it?" Riker said.

He shrugged. "It could have, I suppose. To be honest, I was getting tired of arranging his little trysts, and I told him so. It was embarrassing, no matter how much he paid me. One guy in Jersey honestly thought I was asking for myself. I nearly belted him."

"But you couldn't say who it really was for," I said.

"No, I couldn't. That was part of the deal, and people thinking I was a pansy irked me, you know? So, last night I told Al he should just get a divorce and be done with it, but he thought that would hurt his reputation and his fans wouldn't like it. He accused me of flirting with Muriel, too. He was jealous. I told him he didn't even like women, so what did he care?"

"Did he have a reason to be jealous, Mr. Ricci?" I said.

"Well, like I said, Muriel has gifts a man like me can appreciate, and she seems to appreciate a man who's a man, if you know what I mean."

"So, he *did* have a reason," Riker said.

"Some might think so. But Al was also jealous of me onstage. He kept trying to hold me back, keep me in the shadows and out of the limelight. He even cut me out of the evening performances, limiting me to the matinee. He said I wasn't ready, but I was ready, I *am* ready, to be a star. I would have outshone him, given the chance."

"And now you'll have your chance," Riker said, "with the tribute tour you mentioned. Once you get your financial backing."

"Yes. Too bad it happened this way, but that's life, I guess. And death. So, it will be a tribute to the amazing All-Seeing Almanzo and all that he was. Well, maybe not *all* that he was." Ricci chuckled loudly and finished his drink, setting the glass back down with a clunk. "Can't go offending the ladies."

"I imagine elements of Firestone's life would be rather offensive to some people if they were known," I said. "There was also something said last night about an accusation of stealing, and a threat to kill someone and then summon their spirit back from the dead to torture it."

"That part was Al and the goon, who dropped in to see what me and Al were arguing about. I don't know the whole of it, but I got the impression Al was steamed at Goodacre about some of the financial stuff. He didn't think he was being on the up-and-up. They argued about it for a few minutes, then Al and me had to leave for the theater."

"I thought you weren't in the evening performances anymore," Riker said.

"I'm not, but I went to watch part of the show just for laughs. And because there's a cute little usherette there named Loretta. I sat in the audience for the first half, which didn't go so hot, then came back here when Loretta gave me the brush-off at intermission. Turns out she's dating the manager."

"That's too bad," Riker said.

"Her loss. The manager looks like a real chucklehead."

"And the cocktail party started at eight?" I said.

"Eight fifteen. Me and the goon got things started at eight, though, and the fan club girl got there at quarter after. Al and Muriel showed up at almost half past, which was late, 'cause the dinner reservation was for nine."

"Did you see Almanzo at all after he, Mr. Goodacre, and the fan club girl left to go down to dinner?" I said.

"Just briefly. I went downstairs to get something to eat on my own, since I wasn't included in the fancy dinner. I saw the three of them at a table, so I meandered over to say hello. They had just sat down and were looking over the menu. Al looked annoyed I was there, and so did the girl and the goon, so I left. I grabbed a hot dog at a diner down the street, then came back here. That was the last time I ever saw him. I really still can't believe it. I guess ya never know when you're gonna draw your last breath or take your last drink."

"Life is made up of firsts and lasts, Mr. Ricci."

"I'm sure you're not the first to say that, and you won't be the last."

"Indeed. May I ask where were you between nine and midnight last night?" I said.

"Nine and midnight? Once I got my hot dog, I came back up here. I listened to the radio for a while and had a couple of drinks. Eventually I fell asleep."

"You didn't go out on the town? On a Saturday night?" I said.

"I was tired and I felt lousy."

"I hope you're feeling better today. By the way, you said the first half of the evening show last night didn't go very well. What happened?"

"Lots of little things, and from what I hear the second half wasn't much better. Muriel forgot the name she was supposed to use, for one thing."

"She forgot her name?"

"Yeah. Stupid. For each show we give her a different name and change her appearance a little bit just in case, you know? Some folks go to more than one performance, so it has to look fresh."

"I'm not sure I understand," Riker said.

"Geez, she's a plant, okay? At one point in the show, Al says, 'And now, if I may, a volunteer from the audience, please.' Then Muriel raises her hand, and Al chooses her to come up onstage. Then he says, 'Your name, Madam?', and she gives him the prearranged name. Last night it was supposed to be Mrs. Robert Tattinger. Ethel Tattinger."

"Ah. And she forgot the name," I said.

"That's right. When Al asked her name, she just stared at him and finally blurted out 'Muriel Firestone'. It was pretty awkward. She blamed me for it because I'm the one that comes up with the names for each show. She said the name was too complicated. Should have been Smith or Jones or something, according to her. Dumb broad. Anyway, like I said, the show didn't go so well, Loretta wasn't interested, and I was tired, so I just went to bed. Alone."

"A first time for everything, I'm sure," I said. "Well, we won't keep you any longer, but don't leave town just yet."

"I've got nowhere to go at the moment. Our next stop was supposed to be Cedar Rapids, Iowa, I think, but if the goon cancels the tour, I'm out in the cold until I can get my tribute tour on its feet."

"Right. One other thing. Are you aware of anyone who would want to harm or kill Mr. Firestone?" I said.

He laughed harshly. "If I had a dime for everyone who did, I wouldn't need to do all this crap. But yeah. The goon comes to mind, for starters."

"You mean Mr. Goodacre?" Riker said.

Ricci stared at him through his bloodshot eyes. "Yeah. Funny how *he's* not worried about canceling the tour. *He's* not worried about being out of a job. He handled all of Al's finances, you see, if you catch my drift. And like I said before, he and Al had words last night before the show. Al seemed to think the goon was doing something underhanded, maybe even illegal, and I think he probably was, but that's all I know about it, and that's all I'm sayin'."

"That's a serious accusation," I said.

"I ain't accusing, just suggesting, and you're the one who brought up that argument first, not me. But my money's still on the fairy he met in that alley last night. Find him, and you'll find your killer. By the way, since you're demanding we stay here at the hotel for the time being, who's gonna be paying our hotel and meal bills? I don't have unlimited funds at the moment."

"Unfortunately your hotel and meal expenses are not admittable for reimbursement, Mr. Ricci," I said.

"I don't like the sound of that. And just how long will I be forced to stay here?"

"Until we conclude our initial investigation into the murder of Almanzo Firestone."

"And what does that mean? How long will it take?"

"It depends, but probably just another day or so until we've interviewed everyone involved. Once their statements have been recorded, you'll be free to leave, but if an arrest is made, you may be required to return to give testimony at a trial, if there is one."

"What if a conclusion is never reached? What if you don't find the murderer?"

"If, after a certain period of time, the culprit can't be located, the case will be considered unsolved and the investigation will be stopped. But first, as I said, we have to complete our initial investigation, which means talking to you, Mr. Goodacre, and Mrs. Firestone, among possible others."

"Well, make your initial investigation quick, Mr. Barrington, or I'll have to start washing dishes in the kitchen to pay my way."

"Right, we'll do our best to keep you out of hot water, Mr. Ricci, good day," I said, putting away my pencil and notebook. I motioned for Riker, and the two of us turned toward the door. Before we could open it, however, a knock came from the other side.

I turned back to Ricci. "Expecting someone?"

"Probably the goon." He got awkwardly to his feet, stepped around us somewhat unsteadily and opened it. A bellboy in a crisp, short red jacket, matching cap, white gloves, and black trousers was holding a small silver tray with a white envelope upon it.

"Message for Mr. Ricci," the boy said.

"I'm Ricci. Who's it from?"

"She didn't say, sir. She gave me a dime and told me to deliver this to you."

I couldn't see Ricci's expression, as he had his back to us, but I watched as he took the envelope off the tray, gave the kid a nickel, and shut the door. Without turning around, he opened it, read the enclosed note, and shoved it and the envelope into one of his pockets before turning slowly around to us once more. He was scowling, and his face looked pale.

"Bad news?" I said. "You don't look so well."

"Hmm? What?"

"Was the note bad news?" I said again.

"No, it's nothing. Excuse me, gents. I need to talk to Mrs. Firestone."

"The desk clerk said she'd gone out," Riker said.

"Oh. Well, when she returns. I need a drink." He crossed to the dresser and picked up the empty bottle. "Damn."

"We'll see ourselves out," I said, but he didn't appear to have heard. He was still staring into the void of the bottle, looking anxious.

Riker and I stepped out in the hall and closed the door behind us. "Jeepers, I wonder what that was all about?"

"If I had to guess, I'd say he has a drinking problem," I said as we walked down the hall to the elevators.

"Oh that, yeah, and how. But I meant the note. It seemed to upset him."

"I noticed that, too. A note from a female, probably not Mrs. Firestone, but possibly."

"Why not?"

"Because she knows what room he's in. In fact, there's a connecting door between the suite's sitting room and his room. If she wanted to send him a note, she could just deliver it herself rather than go to the trouble of having a bellboy do it, or she could simply slip it under the door."

"That makes sense. So, now what do we do? Talk to Mr. Goodacre?"

"Yes. I got the impression Mr. Ricci thinks Mr. Goodacre has been embezzling, or he wants us to think so, anyway."

"Yeah, I got that impression, too. Not accusing, just suggesting."

"Exactly. Though I do wonder if what that bellboy heard was really directed at Goodacre, or if it was actually Ricci and he's just trying to throw us off. Perhaps Ricci's financial backing was coming out of Firestone's pocket without him knowing it, and Firestone found out."

"Wouldn't surprise me," Riker said. "He doesn't seem exactly ethical."

"I agree."

"It will be interesting to see what Mr. Goodacre has to say."

"Yes, but before we talk to him, I want to go down to the lobby and have a word with the bellboy who delivered that note to Mr. Ricci," I said, pressing the elevator call button.

"To get a description of the woman who gave it to him."

"Yes. And while I'm doing that, see if you can find out the name of the girl Firestone and Goodacre had dinner with. Ricci said she was the president of his local fan club."

"I'll get right on it," Riker said as the elevator arrived and the doors slid open.

We rode down to the lobby in silence, not wanting to say anything more in front of the elevator operator. When we reached the lobby, I went off to the front desk to find Mr. Billings, who I figured could help me locate the bellboy who had delivered Ricci's note, while Riker used one of the telephone booths just past the bank of elevators.

I finished my chat with the bellboy, whose name was Carl, just as Riker was wrapping up his telephone call. "Find anything out?" I said.

"Yes, a girl named Florence Lufkin is the president of Firestone's fan club here in town. I got her home address and phone number."

"Good work."

"Thanks, but it wasn't too difficult. I finally called my wife, too, and let her know I'm on a new case and wouldn't be home until supper at six."

"How did that go over?"

"Like a lead balloon. I'm not even sure she believed me about being on a case, but it's okay. She'll get over it. Did you get a description of the female who wrote that note to Mr. Ricci?" Riker said.

"The bellboy didn't remember until I gave him a fifty cent piece. Amazing how that improves the memory."

"Yes, it usually does."

"Yeah, well, according to him she was young, early to mid-twenties, shoulder-length auburn hair, blue eyes, and a beauty mark above her lip. She was nice enough looking, in his opinion, wearing a gray dress with a blue jacket and a small blue hat," I said.

"Definitely doesn't sound like Mrs. Firestone. I get the impression she's older, more mature."

"Me too. In fact, I'd say Mrs. Firestone looks something like that." I pointed my chin at an attractive woman, probably in her mid-thirties, who had just entered the hotel. She was wearing a black dress and hat with a small black veil attached, black gloves, and a black leather handbag on her arm. "Unless I miss my guess, I'm willing to bet that's our Mrs. Firestone."

"And a killer figure, as Mr. Ricci said."

"Yes, he was rather descriptive."

She walked toward us and stopped at the elevators, pressing the call button as we stepped forward. She did have a nice figure, and her fiery red hair was swept up away from her face. Her red lips stood out against her pale complexion.

"Mrs. Firestone?" I said.

A faint look of surprise crossed her face. "Yes? Who are you?"

"Milwaukee police detectives. I'm Detective Barrington, and this is Detective Riker."

"Oh, I see. How did you know who I am?"

"Your red hair, for one thing, and your black mourning attire."

"I wear a lot of black in my profession, so this is nothing new, though the red hair is. Last season I was a blonde."

"Well, it was really just a lucky guess. The man at the desk described you as an attractive redhead, and so did Mr. Ricci."

"Really? Mr. Ricci said that?"

"In a manner of speaking, yes," I said.

"Well, Mr. Ricci seems to find anything in a skirt desirable, so that's not much. But you're too kind, and so is the man at the desk. I'm afraid I'm not looking my best at the moment, though. You're here about Alfred's death, of course."

"Alfred?"

"My husband, Almanzo. His real name was Alfred. Alfred Ernest Firestone. Almanzo was his stage name."

"Oh, yes, of course. Please accept our condolences."

"Thank you. This has all been just terrible." She touched her right temple with her hand, massaging it lightly.

"I can imagine it was quite a shock," I said. "Is there someplace we can talk in private, Mrs. Firestone? We have a few questions we'd like to ask you."

"I've nothing to hide and not much to say, I'm afraid, but if you want to talk we can sit on that bench there, if you like." She pointed with her other gloved hand to an upholstered bench across from the elevators between the doors to the men's and ladies' lounges. "I'm not in the habit of having strange men up to my room."

"As you wish," I said. "We've already spoken to Mr. Ricci, and we intend to talk to Mr. Goodacre next."

"Oh, you spoke with Lorenzo already?"

"That's right, not long ago."

"How did he seem?"

"He'd been imbibing a fair amount of bourbon, it would appear, and he was on the phone with what sounded like a young lady when we arrived," Riker said. "He asked her to come to his room this evening at nine."

"Oh, he did, did he? Typical. Did he happen to say whom?"

"No, I didn't hear a name."

"I can't say I'm surprised. He even went out carousing Friday night, to a variety of nightclubs and taverns. He got back quite late, even after promising he'd behave himself."

"Why would a single gentlemen need to behave himself?" I said.

"Because a young woman in a previous city got her father after him with a shotgun, and she wasn't the first."

"I see. That would be rather problematic, I imagine."

"Yes, it's not good for the show. It's bad publicity, and I'm beginning to think he'll never change. Anyway, ask me what you will. The police were here quite early this morning with the news of Al's death. It's been a long day already, and it's only early afternoon."

She moved slowly to the bench and sat down, crossing her legs at the ankles and smoothing out her dress as she set her handbag down beside her. Riker and I stood in front of her, blocking the view from the elevators and affording her at least a semblance of privacy.

"I promise we won't keep you long. Do you have any idea what your husband was doing in that alley last night?" I said.

She shook her head slowly, her little black hat and veil moving back and forth. "No, not really, and I'm not sure I want to know. I imagine he had an encounter with some ruffian who tried to rob him, and Alfred ended up dead. I was afraid this would happen sooner or later, but he wouldn't listen."

"What do you mean?" I said.

"Just that Alfred had a habit of going out alone late at night in strange cities, that's all. It was only a matter of time until he encountered a mugger or delinquent of some sort."

"Actually, Mrs. Firestone, Detective Riker and I are acting under the assumption your husband *wasn't* killed by a robber or mugger."

A look of surprise crossed her face. "Oh? Why is that?"

"The circumstances of his death were unusual."

"I see. I wasn't aware of that. But then who? We don't really know anyone here in Milwaukee."

"I understand. We're not ruling out a robber or mugger altogether, just exploring alternatives at the moment. Can you tell us what exactly happened last night?"

"Alfred had arranged for us to have drinks in our suite after the performance with some foolish girl who's the president of his local fan club. Mr. Goodacre was there, too, along with Mr. Ricci, of course. Mr. Ricci had been drinking heavily, and everyone was tense. Larry asked for a cigarette, and I told him to get one out of the desk drawer, completely forgetting my gun was in there. Larry took it out and started waving it around, causing this clumsy girl to spill her drink all over the rug. I thought she was going to burst into tears. She seemed rather unstable, if you ask me."

"Funny Mr. Ricci didn't mention that," I said. "About the gun, I mean."

"He probably doesn't even remember. He was stinking drunk, something else I'm beginning to think will never change. Anyway, I told him to put it back in the drawer, and he did, and Mr. Goodacre cleaned up the spill as best he could."

"Why do you keep a gun in your room, Mrs. Firestone?" Riker said.

"Al got it for me for protection a couple years ago. I don't like guns as a rule, though, so I usually keep it in a drawer. Strangely, I noticed this morning that it's missing."

I looked at Riker, who looked at me.

"Missing?" I said.

"That's right. I went to get more cigarettes from the desk drawer after I returned from the morgue. That's when I noticed it wasn't there."

"Did you report it?"

"I called the front desk and spoke with one of the assistant managers. He said he would inquire of the housekeeping staff. It wasn't particularly valuable, but still…"

"Who would have taken it?" Riker said.

"I have no idea. One of the hotel maids, perhaps. And really anyone who was at the cocktail party could have easily slipped it out of the drawer. As I said, Lorenzo put it back in there after I told him it wasn't funny him waving it about. That's the last I remember seeing it."

"Guns, even unloaded ones, should always be kept locked up, Mrs. Firestone," Riker said.

"Yes, I know. I suppose I should have put it in the hotel safe, but I just never gave it any thought. Is the fact that it's missing of some importance?"

"I really couldn't say at this point. What happened after the cocktail party?" I said.

"Al, this girl, and Mr. Goodacre all went down to dinner."

"It seems odd that you weren't invited to dine with them, Mrs. Firestone," Riker said.

"It may seem odd, but it wasn't, I assure you. Al and Clive—Clive Goodacre, that is—know I hate those kinds of things. Al actually doesn't like them much either, but he has no choice. It was bad enough I had to endure the cocktail party and that stupid reception Friday night."

"And what about Mr. Ricci? He also wasn't included in the dinner," I said.

"No, and that irritated Larry quite a bit. As I said, I was happy not to attend, but he felt left out. I told him not to take it personally. He and Al frequently had words, and so did Larry and Clive, but I explained that not being invited to dinner was more a budget concern than anything else. Still, Larry got drunk. I was quite annoyed at his behavior."

"Yes, he mentioned you were irritated with him when we spoke with him earlier. He seems pretty upset that the tour will be canceled rather than continuing it with him in the starring role."

"Well, it *is* called 'The All-Seeing Almanzo,' not 'The drunken, Womanizing Lorenzo.' If Larry took over the starring role, I think we'd lose money hand over fist. Clive's working on canceling the tour now, I believe."

"Mr. Ricci said he's thinking of starting a tribute tour on his own," Riker said.

"Did he? That should be amusing."

"And what about you, Mrs. Firestone? What will you do?" I said.

"Me? I haven't had the time to even consider it yet. But I'll get by. Al had an insurance policy, of course, and I also do tarot card readings and séances and such on my own. I'm known as Muriel the Mystic."

"Clever name."

"Thank you. I've been in show business my whole life. I started out in vaudeville as a kid. My parents were entertainers and I was part of the act, the DeLario Trio. DeLario was my maiden name. The three of us did impressions, voices, sang a bit, and even danced. It was only after I met Alfred that I realized I had the gift of spiritualism, and I focused my efforts on that."

"Better late than never, I suppose. Do you know what your husband did after dinner, Mrs. Firestone?"

She shook her head slowly, her little black hat and veil moving back and forth. "Not exactly, no. Clive said Al told him he was going to go for a walk after they'd finished, to get some fresh air. As to how or why he ended up in that alley, I really couldn't say. At least I would prefer not to, as I said before."

"If you have a theory or an idea, we would prefer you *did* say," Riker said.

She sighed. "Fine. As I said earlier, my husband tended to meet certain unseemly people late at night for activities society would frown upon. And an alley would be a good place for those activities, I would imagine, especially late at night. My husband was a good spiritualist, but he tended to lack common sense."

"I'm sure he put on a good show," I said.

"He did, as a matter of fact. He was very entertaining, but he wasn't a fraud. It wasn't *just* a show."

"In spite of the fact he used you as a plant in the audience?"

She looked surprised. "Who told you that? Larry?"

"Does it matter?"

"I suppose not. But that's just showmanship, you see. Theatrics. Al sometimes used tricks to entertain and convince people to study spiritualism. But true spiritualism is based on the belief that spirts of the dead have the ability to communicate with those in the living world, and he had that gift. The spirits of the departed can guide us when we have questions and concerns and help us to understand God and the afterlife. That's not easily demonstrated or explained onstage in front of a live audience."

"Fascinating," Riker said.

"I think so."

"And have you yourself spoken with the dearly departed?" I said.

"I don't possess the gift Alfred had, but yes, I have had some success as a medium."

"A medium?"

"Someone who mediates communication between the departed and the living, usually through a séance."

"Oh yes, of course. Muriel the Mystic," I said.

"That's right, though I have much still to discover. Now with my husband gone, I may not get the chance to learn more."

"It seems to me he could give you lessons from the great beyond."

"You mock me, you mock spiritualism, as many nonbelievers do. It's all right, we're used to it. You don't fully understand. You have closed minds."

"Our apologies, Mrs. Firestone. We don't mean to mock, but I confess I am a nonbeliever. A friend of mine, however, is very much a believer," I said. "He came with me to your husband's reception Friday night, as a matter of fact."

"Your friend, then, is very wise, Mr. Barrington."

"That's true, he is."

She closed her eyes halfway. "And I sense he's quite close to you, closer than anyone else, I think."

"Uh, well, yes. He's a good friend, a policeman."

"Yes, yes, I can sense that." She got to her feet and touched my temples with her gloved fingertips as she closed her eyes. "There's something else, too, but I don't quite know what it means. A lock. No, a key. A key without a lock. Does that mean anything to you?"

"A key without a lock wouldn't do much good, Mrs. Firestone."

"Nor a lock without a key. Or is it keys? I'm getting images of keys now, and a good-looking young man."

"Sorry, I don't know what that could mean," I said, though I had to admit I was impressed.

She dropped her hands to her sides and opened her eyes. "Don't you? Hmm. As I said, I have more to learn about my gift and how to use it. I'm actually better at tarot card readings, but I've left my deck upstairs."

"Pity," I said. "I'm pretty good at cards."

"I'm sure you are. Are you familiar with cartomancy?"

"Um, no. I'm not."

"It's basically like tarot cards, only using a regular deck of cards to tell fortunes and divination. It's been around since the fourteenth century."

"I see. And you do that, too?"

"I do. However, I specialize in tarot card readings, and I also conduct séances. In fact, I'll be holding a séance Tuesday night at seven in the sitting room of our suite, in an attempt to contact my late husband. Perhaps you'd both like to attend."

"Doesn't a séance seem, I don't know, a little sudden?" I said.

"Shortly after death is the best time, Detective. The spirit is still partly in this world. I'd actually like to do it sooner, but there are things to attend to and arrangements to be made. Death is different for those who believe in spiritualism. Sudden death is a shock, of course, but we don't see death in general as a tragic end. Rather, it's a transition to a different plane. I know I'll see Alfred in the great beyond."

"When did you last see your husband in this world?" Riker said. "You know, alive."

"He came back upstairs to our suite to change his tie during the dinner. That idiot girl spilled some kind of soup on it."

"How did he seem?" Riker said.

"Annoyed. In fact, very annoyed. Not just about the tie but about the whole dinner, and he was still steamed about her spilling her drink on the rug, and Ricci waving that gun about and being drunk. I got the impression Al didn't like this girl very much, yet he had to be polite and cordial to her."

"Because she was the president of his fan club."

"That's right."

"And where were you between nine and midnight last night?" I said.

"Is that when he was supposedly killed?"

"According to the autopsy the coroner completed," Riker said.

"I had dinner alone in my room a little after nine, after the cocktail party ended. Then I listened to the radio for a bit and studied my tarot cards. I got into bed around ten, I believe, read a few magazines, and eventually fell asleep. I didn't wake up until the police came early this morning."

"Weren't you concerned your husband never returned to the hotel last evening?" Riker said.

"I really wasn't aware he hadn't returned until this morning. Our room has two twin beds. I read for a bit and then fell asleep a little after ten. I expected Al would stumble in sooner or later, because it's nothing unusual for him to keep late hours. He was always a creature of the night, the shadows, and the darkness. I didn't realize he'd not come back at all until this morning when the telephone rang at seven. It was the front desk saying the police were in the lobby and wanted to speak with me. I looked over and saw his bed hadn't been slept in. I thought perhaps he'd passed out on the sofa in the sitting room, but he wasn't there, either."

"Are you aware of anyone who might want to harm your husband?" Riker said.

"Being a public figure, he got his share of fanatics, both good and bad. It happens. And he was known for going out alone and meeting unsavory characters late at night."

"Yes, but is there anyone close to him who had a grudge against him that you know of?"

"Since we're in a strange town, not many people here knew him at all. He and Mr. Ricci argued frequently. Alfred was considering dropping him from the show altogether because he's just too unreliable. And then there was an incident with Clive the other day."

"Clive Goodacre?"

"Yes, my husband's manager. Al was reviewing past receipts from the last few shows, going over some of the expenses. He told me things didn't quite add up the way they should, and he was going to talk to Clive about it."

"And did he?" Riker said.

"I honestly don't know. Probably, but if there had been any wrongdoing, Al would have fired him on the spot once he could prove it. He would have taken legal action against him."

"Interesting," I said.

"It still seems the most logical to me, however, that my husband simply met up with the wrong person last night in that dark alley. Honestly it was just a matter of time, and his time was up."

"Maybe you can ask him at the séance," Riker said.

"That's actually a good idea," she said. "Maybe I will. I hope you'll both attend. You could find it enlightening."

"Yes, well, we'll give it some thought," I said. "Our condolences again, Mrs. Firestone. We'll ride up with you if you're going to your room. As I said, we want to speak with Mr. Goodacre next."

"He's in room 415, down the hall from the suite, but please don't mention what I said."

"We promise to be discreet," I said.

"Very well." She picked up her handbag and pressed the elevator call button. When we reached the fourth floor, we walked with her to the suite, said our goodbyes, and continued to room 415 at the end of the hall. I knocked three times on the door.

It was opened by a small man in his mid- to late forties, with thinning silver blond hair and a matching mustache. His bluish green eyes sparkled, but he was otherwise average looking in every sense of the word.

"Mr. Goodacre?" I said. "Clive Goodacre?"

"That's right. I assume you're Barrington and Riker, is it? The police detectives? Though I'm not sure which is which."

"You assume correctly. I'm Detective Barrington."

"I thought you were the one in charge. I spoke with Mr. Ricci a short time ago to let him know I finally managed to cancel the rest of the tour, and he told me to expect you."

"May we come in?" Riker said.

"Of course, please do." He stepped aside as we entered, and I noticed his room was neat and tidy, with everything in its place and put away, the bed freshly made.

"I understand you were Mr. Firestone's agent and manager," I said.

"Yes, for the past year now, almost two. I arranged his bookings, took care of his publicity, handled his mail, that sort of thing."

"An important job," Riker said.

"I think so, though not everyone did. Still, Almanzo appreciated me and the work I did for him."

"I'm sure he did. You handled his finances, too? Paid the bills?" I said.

"Yes, of course I handled the books. That's part of my job." He looked at me suspiciously. "Why?"

"Just making sure I have the facts correct."

"Almanzo was very particular about the finances. He didn't trust Muriel with a dime, and he had all the money put into an account under his name only. He counted every penny."

"Interesting. You were with him last night?" I said.

"Earlier in the evening, yes. There was a cocktail party in his suite for him and Mrs. Firestone, Mr. Ricci, myself, and some silly young girl, president of his local fan club. The cocktail party was Al's idea."

"The silly young girl last night being Florence Lufkin, yes?" Riker said.

Goodacre raised his thin eyebrows in surprise. "My, my, you gentlemen are thorough. That's correct."

"How did that go?" I said.

"Not well, to be honest. The evening show was at six and ended about a quarter of eight, a little earlier than usual. Apparently, that didn't go well, either. Al and Muriel got back to the hotel close to eight thirty. Myself, Ricci, and this girl were all waiting for them. Ricci had already had several drinks."

"Was he intoxicated?" Riker said.

"He certainly seemed to be well on his way, but that's nothing new for him. Ricci went to get a cigarette from the desk and found Muriel's gun, which he proceeded to wave about, causing this clumsy Miss Lufkin to get hysterical and spill her drink all over the rug. She seems a bit emotionally unstable, if you ask me. Anyway, Mrs. Firestone told Ricci to put the gun away, which he reluctantly did."

"Guns should never be handled recklessly."

"Of course not. Miss Lufkin was quite upset. I'm sure she thought Almanzo would be furious with her about the stain on the rug, and even though he clearly was, he somehow managed to comfort her. One minute she's frightened by the gun, spilling her drink and on the verge of tears, the next she's staring moony eyed at Almanzo when he gives her his handkerchief and puts his arm on her shoulder to comfort her."

"Ah, she appealed to the male ego."

"Yes, and Al had a big one. Here she was, the president of his Milwaukee admirers, fawning over him. Even though he didn't like her, he loved the attention. Al had lots of crazy fans, you know, all types. One young girl even burst into his dressing room in Minneapolis last winter. Most upsetting. Fortunately, Mr. Ricci took care of her. As I say, he has a way with women."

"So we've heard," Riker said.

"Yes, but Miss Lufkin was different. She seemed to only have eyes for Almanzo."

"How did she get invited for drinks and dinner in the first place?" I said.

"She wrote Almanzo a letter a month or so ago, all excited that he was going to be performing here in her home town of Milwaukee. As his manager, I answered the letter immediately and invited her for cocktails and dinner here at the hotel last night after the evening performance. Since she's the president of his local fan club, I thought it would make good press. I also sent her an autographed picture of Almanzo along with two complimentary tickets to the Sunday matinee."

"Smart thinking. Something like that would indeed be good publicity," I said.

"Just doing my job. There have been similar dinners in other towns, though Almanzo never liked doing them. Last night was no exception. The girls always blather on about what a fan they are and how much they admire him, and ask silly questions, like, 'When did you first know you had the gift?' and 'Can you read my palm?' Things like that. It's no wonder he hated it, as does Muriel, but she knows they're necessary, and so did he."

"Because of publicity," Riker said.

"Yes, exactly. There aren't as many believers as there once were, so it's important to seize any and every opportunity. I even arranged for a reception Friday night here at the hotel for members of the press and local dignitaries, though not many of them showed up." He looked at me closely. "If I'm not mistaken, I think I saw you there."

"You did. I was there for a brief time, doing a preliminary investigation on spiritualism and on Mr. Firestone. Are you a spiritualism believer, Mr. Goodacre?" I said.

"Me? Well, let's just say there are things we don't understand, at least not yet. But do I think Almanzo was truly the All-Seeing? Not hardly, I'm afraid. As much as he tried to convince me and everyone else otherwise."

"I admit I'm also a bit of a skeptic. What time was dinner last night?" I said.

"Nine o'clock, just after cocktails in the suite. I made the reservations myself, of course. I requested a table in the middle of the dining room. Important to see and be seen, you know."

"Nine o'clock is rather late for dinner, isn't it?" Riker said.

"Maybe for small-town folks like yourselves."

"Milwaukee isn't exactly a small town, Mr. Goodacre," I said.

He waved his hand at me dismissively. "No offense meant, but you must admit this isn't New York or Chicago."

"That's true, it isn't. Some would say that's a good thing. And what time did dinner end, exactly?"

"Oh, around ten, I think, just a few minutes before, actually. We didn't have dessert, which surprised me because Almanzo almost never skips dessert, but he was understandably tired and irritable. Besides dumping an entire drink on the carpet in the suite, Miss Lufkin spilled soup on his tie during dinner, so he had to go up to change, leaving me alone with her. They're only interested in the All-Seeing Almanzo, not me, and I never know what to talk about with these fans. I was glad when Almanzo finally returned and I could stop trying to make small talk with her. We finished up, said our goodbyes, and I offered to see her home. Fortunately, she declined. She left us at the table."

"And then what did you and Mr. Firestone do?" Riker said.

"Al said he wanted to go for a walk and get some fresh air. He kept looking at his watch all through the meal, like he couldn't wait for it to be over. I offered to accompany him on his walk, but he said he wanted to be alone, so I went to the hotel bar and had a drink."

"And he left the hotel," Riker said.

"That's right. The last I ever saw of him, he was striding quickly across the lobby toward the Wells Street doors."

"How long did you stay in the bar?" I said.

"Forty-five minutes or so."

"Would anyone remember you being there? The bartender, perhaps?" Riker said.

"I doubt it. The bar was quite crowded and noisy, and they seemed short-staffed. After that I went up to my room. I remember it was almost eleven by that time. I got ready for bed and read for a while, then went to sleep. I got up once during the night to use the bathroom, but otherwise I didn't wake up until about seven when Muriel knocked on my door. She said the police were downstairs and wanted to talk to her. She feared something had happened to Almanzo because he apparently never came back to the suite. She told me she thought he'd been arrested."

"Had anything like that happened before?"

"Almanzo's had his share of run-ins with the local authorities in various towns, so it wouldn't have been inconceivable. I got dressed quickly and accompanied her downstairs to the lobby."

"What about Mr. Ricci?" Riker said.

"I don't know, honestly. She probably assumed he was sleeping one off, and he probably was. He's rather fond of alcohol. And women."

"So, you and Mrs. Firestone went down to the lobby," I said.

"That's right. Of course we soon learned that it was far worse than Almanzo being arrested. They told us a man's body was found in an alley earlier that morning and the body had Almanzo's wallet on it. They wanted Muriel to go to the morgue and identify him. When she returned a short while later, I could tell from the look on her face he was dead. Muriel and I don't always see eye to eye, but still I felt terribly for her. She looked just dreadful. They say it was murder."

"It *was* murder, Mr. Goodacre. Are you aware of anyone who would wish to harm Mr. Firestone?" I said.

He looked rather thoughtful. "Certainly someone of questionable morals who took advantage of the situation."

"What situation would that be?" Riker said.

"A well-dressed man alone, walking the streets late at night.

Someone probably tried to rob him, and perhaps Almanzo resisted, though that seems out of character for him. He's not exactly fierce."

"Robbery is one theory we're working on, but is there anyone else you're aware of personally?"

"Personally? Almanzo wasn't always well liked, of course. He could be blusterous and full of himself, but certainly that's no cause for anyone to want to harm him, much less kill him. But, of course..."

"Yes?"

"Well, Mr. Firestone and Mr. Ricci have had several heated arguments lately. Just yesterday before the show, I was walking down the hall when I heard them yelling at each other in the suite's sitting room."

"What were they arguing about?" Riker said.

"I went in to find out, but it was just the usual stuff. Mr. Ricci fancies himself ready to take over the show, or at least to have equal billing, and Almanzo doesn't see it that way. They quarreled fairly often about it. And rumor has it Mr. Firestone was thinking of dropping Ricci from the show altogether."

"That hardly seems reason to murder someone," Riker said.

"People have murdered for less," I said.

"True, and Ricci was familiar with a gun. I once saw him shoot a rat backstage at a theater in Ohio from ten feet away with a gun the stage manager had. Got it in the first shot," Mr. Goodacre said. "And the rat was moving fast."

"Impressive," Riker said.

"Yes, and he didn't seem too heartbroken when we broke the news to him this morning after Mrs. Firestone returned from the morgue. And then there's Mrs. Firestone herself. Her marriage to Almanzo was not exactly typical or happy."

"How do you mean?" Riker said.

"Mr. and Mrs. Firestone had more of a business relationship than a romantic one. They each got something out of it. Muriel got to travel, got to dabble in spiritualism as Muriel the Mystic, and got her bills paid by a man who wouldn't bother her in ways most men would."

"And what did Mr. Firestone get out of it?" Riker said.

"Respectability with his fans, and the ability to be more or less above suspicion in certain situations he was prone to put himself in."

"Mr. Ricci did mention that Mr. Firestone was a bit of a philanderer," Riker said.

"It's true, I admit, though I always looked the other way. Not my business, you know."

"Do you think Mrs. Firestone was aware of his philandering?" I said.

"Muriel? Oh, yes. She played dumb, but she knew. She found them distasteful, but she put up with it. Of course, she wasn't above having an affair or two of her own. It happens."

"That's quite a statement, Mr. Goodacre," I said.

"As I said, their marriage was more of a mutual arrangement, no love lost. I've no proof, but she's not as pure as she pretends to be, I can assure you. And it certainly appears she and Mr. Ricci had gotten friendly over the last several months or more. Al didn't like it one bit. He was afraid it would hurt the show. That was part of the argument between Ricci and Almanzo yesterday, too. Al was rather jealous of Ricci on many levels."

"I got the impression in speaking with Mrs. Firestone that she doesn't care for Mr. Ricci much," I said.

"Well, things seem to have recently cooled between them, if there really was anything there to begin with. Perhaps it was just my imagination, based on Mr. Ricci's rather crude comments about her. Either way, I wasn't all that surprised when Muriel agreed with me that we should cancel the rest of the tour."

"Do you think it's possible Mr. Ricci or Mrs. Firestone could have had something to do with Firestone's death?" Riker said.

"Anything is possible. Muriel has that gun, of course."

"Yes. Mrs. Firestone told us it's missing," I said. "She noticed this morning that it's gone."

He raised his eyebrows in surprise. "Really? That's peculiar."

"It's certainly interesting. But what motive would Mrs. Firestone have for wanting her husband dead?" Riker said.

"Personally, I think she was getting tired of him, the show, the touring, his little secret, distasteful, sexual encounters, everything, and frankly, so was I. Almanzo Firestone was a hard man to work for, and an even harder man to be married to, I would imagine."

"Then why wouldn't she just divorce him?" I said.

"Because Almanzo was almost broke, so there'd be no alimony to speak of. It's no secret he wasn't as hot as he once was. He used to have sold-out theaters, but lately he's been lucky to get half to three-quarters. Muriel could see the writing on the proverbial wall. Pretty soon people will stop coming to see him altogether, or at least, there won't be enough of them to make touring worthwhile. Then what? When the people stop coming, so does the money, not that there's all that much now. I tried to convince Mr. Firestone to cut his losses and give up after this season, but he refused. He loved the adoration. Mrs. Firestone didn't."

"I think I understand," Riker said.

"You do look like a bright boy. About a year ago, Muriel took out a hefty life insurance policy on Almanzo. Now she stands to collect. But again, I'm not saying she or Ricci had anything to do with Al's death whatsoever. I'm just supposing, you understand."

"We do understand, Mr. Goodacre, I assure you. Mrs. Firestone mentioned that insurance policy to us."

"Did she? I'm surprised, but I suppose she's no reason to hide it, especially if she is innocent, and she may very well be. My money is still on a street thug. Al had a bad habit of walking alone at night, in every city we went."

"You may be right about the thug. By the way, Mr. Ricci mentioned he was considering doing a tribute tour to Almanzo, on his own," I said, "since you decided to cancel the rest of Almanzo's show."

Goodacre laughed. "Good luck to him. Ricci's a drunk with minimal talent and little stage presence who gets by on his good looks, but those good looks are fading fast. Almanzo had already cut him out of all the evening performances and was probably going to drop him from the act altogether after this tour. Say, there's another reason right there why Ricci could have bumped off Almanzo."

"You certainly do have your theories. By the way, did Mr. Firestone discuss the finances of the tour with you recently, Mr. Goodacre?"

"The finances? Yes, of course. We discussed them regularly. It's only natural."

"But I understand he seemed to think things weren't exactly adding up right. That there wasn't as much cash flow as there should have been, is that right?" I said. "We were told you were brought into that argument in the suite yesterday. Something about things not being on the up-and-up."

"Who told you that? Never mind. I can guess with amazing accuracy, I'm sure. Almanzo never did understand business. He never could figure out positive and negative columns, or plusses and minuses. Attendance has been consistently down, but expenses continue to rise. It's simple math, really, but he seemed to think I might be doing something underhanded because there just wasn't much available cash. We discussed it and cleared the air. It was just a misunderstanding, certainly not an argument. Not between Almanzo and myself, anyway."

"I'm glad to hear it. Well, we won't take up any more of your time right now, Mr. Goodacre, but as we advised the others, please don't leave town just yet," I said.

"Don't worry, I won't. The only place left to go is home, such as it is, until I find a new client. It certainly won't be Mr. Ricci."

"Not surprising, I'd say, from what you've told us."

We gathered up our hats and left the room as Goodacre closed the door. While we waited for the elevator, Riker looked over at me.

"Interesting threesome," he said.

I looked back at him. "Yes, most definitely. And they were all supposedly alone in their respective rooms last night during the time of the murder, except for Goodacre claiming he was in a bar with no witnesses for part of the evening."

"Yes. Shaky alibis at best," Riker said. "And each of them pointing the finger at the others."

"Yes, I noticed that."

"And then there's the missing gun. If it really is missing. You think she lied about that?" Riker said.

"It's possible. But if she was telling the truth, I do wonder who took it."

"Ricci, Goodacre, or Miss Lufkin, perhaps," Riker said.

"Or maybe even Mr. Firestone himself."

"I suppose that's possible. They all had access to it during the cocktail party. Say, on a different subject, how do you think Mrs. Firestone knew about Alan? That whole thing with her getting a vision of keys, and a handsome young man…"

"Lucky guess," I said, as the elevator arrived and we stepped in.

"Or maybe she saw Alan and me at Friday's reception and asked her husband about us. He probably said something about meeting a Mr. Barrington and a Mr. Keyes, and she put two and two together."

"Yeah, I guess that makes sense," Riker said. "Certainly the logical explanation, anyway."

The elevator attendant was the same one who had taken us up earlier. "Lobby, please," I said to him.

"Yes, sir," he said, stifling a yawn.

We rode down in silence, stepping out as we reached the ground floor. I looked at Riker as the elevator doors closed behind us. "I want you to check with the restaurant here in the hotel. See if you can talk to the waiter who served the Firestone party last night. I want to confirm the time the meal began and ended. If they finished shortly before ten, like Goodacre said, that puts Firestone's time of death closer to sometime between ten thirty and midnight, I'd say. Also, check with the bartender on duty last night and see if he or anyone else remembers Goodacre being there sometime after ten."

"I'll ask about that right now."

"While you're doing that, I'll give the station a call, if you've got a nickel I can borrow."

"Sure, here," he said, handing me a nickel from his pocket. "How come you want to call the station?"

"Mr. Goodacre mentioned a *Journal* photographer taking pictures at Almanzo's dinner last night. I want to see copies of those. I'll have someone at the precinct request them and get the newspaper to send them over to my attention via courier. Meet me back here when you're done."

I finished my phone call and waited on Riker, taking the time to use the men's room. I mulled over the events, facts, and circumstances. Unfortunately, no fresh ideas were forthcoming, but there was much to discover yet, I felt. I returned to the elevators, and presently Riker appeared, looking eager and pleased with himself.

"Looks like you might have some good news."

"Yes and no. The bartender and one of the waitresses in the bar from last night didn't recall Goodacre at all, but they both confirmed it was quite busy and crowded, and that they were indeed understaffed. And I have to admit, Mr. Goodacre isn't very memorable."

"I agree. I thought that might be the case. What about the waiter from the restaurant?"

"I had better luck there. He was just finishing his lunch shift, and I caught him out back having a smoke. He remembered Firestone, Goodacre, and the girl quite well."

"Someone like Firestone would be hard to forget," I said.

"Yeah, that's the truth. Not too many men wear a monocle."

"He's the only one I've ever known. So, what did the waiter say about the time?"

"He said he remembers bringing them the check a little before ten or thereabouts. Jibes with what Goodacre said."

"Okay, then, so that narrows down the time of death considerably."

"It does, but there's something else, too."

"What's that?"

"He told me they all ordered the lobster thermidor with spinach and green peas, plus tomato soup. Firestone and Goodacre had brandies, and Miss Lufkin had a crème de menthe. The bill came to $15.90 plus tax."

"Not cheap, but not outrageous."

"No, not for a place like this. The waiter remembers Mr. Firestone looking in his wallet and saying to Mr. Goodacre that he only had twelve dollars on him, so he asked Mr. Goodacre to pay the bill and the tip."

"Firestone sounds like he was a cheapskate," I said. "It goes with having drinks from the liquor store in his suite rather than in the bar. Not to mention the watered-down champagne at his reception Friday night."

"Yes, last of the big spenders," Riker said. "But remember what the police report said? Firestone had seven dollars in his wallet when his body was found. A five and two singles."

"Say, you're right, good memory," I said. "That means that somewhere between ten p.m. and the time he was murdered, he spent five dollars."

"And a green carnation at Birdwell's flower shop costs five dollars," Riker said.

"Interesting. I think a visit to Birdy's flower shop and a little conversation with Mr. Birdwell is in order."

Riker's eyes flickered briefly. "Oh. I suppose that would be a good idea, given what we've found out."

"Unless you have any other ideas."

He shook his head. "No. Not really. Do you think he's open Sundays?"

"A florist? Possibly. A florist with a side business in sex? Most likely." I pointed over my shoulder to the phone booth. "I'm sure he's in the telephone directory. If you have another nickel, give him a call, discreetly, of course. Find out his hours and see if he will actually be there himself this afternoon."

Riker looked unsure, but finally he nodded. "All right." He walked over to the booth, entered, and closed the door behind him. I watched him fish another nickel out of his pants pocket and drop it into the slot as he lifted the receiver and dialed the number.

"Well?" I said when he had hung up the receiver and stepped back out of the booth.

"They're open until eight, and Birdwell's there all day."

"Excellent. You didn't tip our hand, did you?"

Riker frowned. "I may be new to all this, but I'm not an idiot. I told him I needed a pretty arrangement for my mother's birthday, and I inquired as to whether he was the proprietor, because I wanted him to do the work personally."

I smiled. "Nice job."

"Thanks. I do have some experience in stretching the truth and making up stories, for better or worse."

"Right, well, let's go. After we're finished there, we can stop and grab a late lunch at Art's Diner. I'm buying."

"That's the second best piece of news I've heard today. But be warned, I have a voracious appetite."

"Duly warned. Come on." I didn't wait for a reply but turned and headed toward the lobby. Riker followed quickly behind.

Chapter Eleven

Midafternoon, Sunday, September 14, 1947

Birdy's flower shop was a little over a block east from the hotel, near the corner of Broadway and Wells, wedged in between Frank's Hardware Store and Babcock's Curiosity Shop. It would have been an easy walk, but since I had parked in a one hour zone and we had already exceeded an hour, I thought I'd better move my car. Fortunately, there was no ticket under the wiper. Sure, I could get a parking ticket fixed, but sometimes it's just easier to obey the rules. Riker climbed in next to me, and we drove the short distance to Birdwell's, this time parking where there was no time limit.

"Ready?" I said.

His hands were on his knees, and he sat bolt upright, staring straight ahead out of the windshield. "If you don't mind, Heath, I'll wait out here."

"Why?"

"I don't want him to recognize me."

"I understand, but I don't think you need to worry about that. I'm sure a lot of young men and women have come and gone over the years, and I doubt he ever paid much attention to them. Besides, you've grown up, matured."

He didn't say anything for a minute, apparently mulling it over. "All right. I'll go in if you need me there, Heath. I mean, I'm a detective now. This is my job."

I looked at him, noting the agony in his face. "No, it's all right," I said after a moment. "Might be better with just one of us anyway. Don't want to make him too nervous. I'll go in alone."

"Thanks. I'll keep an eye on the car." His eyes were still transfixed straight ahead, but he now moved his hands up and down his thighs nervously.

I reached over and touched his shoulder briefly, giving it a squeeze. "It shouldn't take long." I exited the car and put my hat back on as I strode purposefully up the street toward the little shop with the dingy green awning, the words *Birdy's Floral* written in white script upon it.

I pushed open the single glass door and looked around, taking in the aroma of fresh flowers and feeling the refrigerated air on my face. A small counter was to the left and a display area was to the right, with floral arrangements on white metal stands and fabric-draped pedestals. A bank of built-in coolers with thick glass doors and shiny aluminum handles stood against the back wall. A little man was behind the small counter, wearing a dark green apron over a white shirt and black bow tie. If I had to guess, I'd say he was in his mid- to late sixties. What little hair he had left was as white as freshly fallen snow, and he had merry blue eyes that sparkled. He reminded me of someone's grandpa, not exactly the type of man I expected to be running a sex operation.

"Good afternoon, sir. How may I be of service?" he said, a soft smile on his pink lips. His voice was kind, gentle, and resonant, his cheeks rosy.

"Mr. Birdwell?" I said.

"That's right. What can I do for you?" He sported a gold and diamond ring on his right hand and a simple gold wedding band on his left.

"I'm Detective Barrington of the Milwaukee Police Department," I said, showing him my identification and badge.

"How do you do?"

I watched for a reaction, but I didn't notice one. "Are you the owner of this place?"

"That's right, twenty-five years in this same location. If you're looking for flowers for a sweetheart, I've got some fresh yellow roses sure to put a smile on any lady's face."

"No doubt, but I'm not looking for flowers today."

"Oh?"

"I'm looking for information."

"Hmm, well, information on flowers I can give you. Plants, too. Anything else, I'm afraid my mind's not what it used to be."

"How about information on Almanzo Firestone?"

His expression never changed. "Who?" he said, cocking his head.

"Almanzo Firestone, the famous spiritualist. He was staying at the Blatz and visited your flower shop here last night."

He scratched his chin. "You don't say."

"I do say."

"It's possible, I suppose. I get many customers in throughout the day, you know. Most don't give their names unless they're putting their purchase on account. I've heard of Almanzo Firestone, now that you mention it, but if he was in here, I didn't recognize him. Why would I?"

"No reason, I guess. But he was rather distinctive in appearance. Middle aged, dark hair, dark features, sporting a monocle."

"A monocle? Why didn't you say so in the first place? Not many of my customers use a monocle."

"So, you *do* remember him now."

He nodded agreeably. "Yes, yes, of course. He didn't say much, didn't stay long. A simple purchase and he was on his way. He paid cash, of course, being that he's from out of town. It was a bit late in the day, I believe."

"How late in the day?"

"Oh, let me think. Close to closing. On Saturday nights, I close at ten."

"That's rather late for a flower shop, isn't it?"

"Yes, well, I've nothing else much to do. My wife is deceased, and my children are grown and gone. You'd be surprised at who buys flowers late at night."

"I'm sure. What did he purchase, Mr. Birdwell?"

"Hmm, I don't recall exactly. A flower, perhaps."

"You don't recall or you'd rather not say?"

He looked puzzled now, but cautious. "I'm not sure what you mean by that, Detective."

"Almanzo Firestone purchased a carnation from you last night. A green carnation. Does that help your memory?"

He swallowed a couple of times, suddenly nervous. "A green carnation? Why yes, he did buy a green carnation, come to think of it. For his lapel. Why are you asking, anyway? What's this all about?"

"Almanzo Firestone was murdered last night in an alley not too far from here not long after leaving your shop."

His complexion turned a chalky white, and a bead of perspiration appeared on his forehead. "Murdered? Really? That's terrible. It's getting so a man's not safe on the streets anymore."

"One should never take his safety for granted, Mr. Birdwell, nor depend on others for it."

"Yes, yes, I suppose that's true. I hope you find whoever did it. I'm afraid I'm not much help."

"Not yet, but you might be. Do you know who killed Almanzo Firestone?"

"Me? Why should I know anything about it? Just because he bought a flower from me?"

"Not just any flower, but a green carnation after he gave you the password."

His right eye started twitching, and his forehead broke out in a full-blown sweat now. "I…I don't know what you mean." His voice went up an octave.

"I'm sure you do. You run a side operation out of this little shop, Birdy, supplying men with a little pleasure for a big price. You keep most of the money and pass on less than a third to the unfortunate person who has to fulfill your customer's desires. I intend to shut you down, but how far that goes depends on you. If you tell me who you arranged to have Firestone meet last night, it will be easier on you."

"I want to talk to my lawyer. He's very good, you know. You'll find yourself walking a beat if you don't leave me alone, Detective," he said, his voice angry now.

"Go ahead. Call him." I slid his telephone over to him across the counter. "In the meantime, I'll call for a black-and-white to have you arrested on suspicion of running a prostitution ring and possibly being an accessory to murder. It will be in both the morning and evening papers, I assure you. I'm sure the local radio stations will pick it up too, maybe even the national ones."

"No! You can't do that!" He was almost shouting, his face red. "It would ruin me. My family. I have children, grandchildren…"

"On the other hand, you could give me the information I want. Then I could make a call to the vice squad and let them know to go easy on you, provided you promise to behave. I could let them know you cooperated with the investigation."

His eyes narrowed as his mind raced in thought. "You've no proof of anything. You're bluffing."

"Am I? The concierge at the Blatz says differently."

"Lamont Woodley? He'd never—"

"But he did," I said, "and he's willing to testify, as are two other employees from two other hotels." It was a lie, of course. I hadn't yet spoken to the concierge at the Blatz or anyplace else, but I thought Birdwell was going to faint.

"Please, I'm sure the young man never hurt Firestone." His voice was now soft and pleading.

"That remains to be seen. Who did you call last night to service the All-Seeing Almanzo?"

"After he bought the flower, I made a call and talked to a young fellow I've used a few times before. He...he goes by Scotty, I don't know his last name. He's worked for me a few months. I told him I had a delivery for him."

"Which was code for you had business for him. And he was to meet his trick in the alley, isn't that right? He was to look for someone wearing a green carnation."

"Please, I have children and grandchildren."

"So you mentioned. You should have thought of them before, Mr. Birdwell. This Scotty accepted the delivery order?"

"Yes, yes. It was late, but he said he could be in the alley in about fifteen minutes. I let the customer know, and then he left and I closed up shop for the night."

"Where can we find this Scotty fellow?"

Mr. Birdwell wiped sweat from his forehead and face with a white handkerchief he'd pulled from his apron pocket. "Webster's boardinghouse. Most of the boys stay at Mrs. Webster's. It's cheap and close by."

I jotted the name down in my notebook. "Got it, and thanks. I wouldn't go anywhere if I were you. The fellows from the vice squad will want a few words. They should be here shortly."

"But you'll talk to them, right? Tell them I cooperated?"

I looked him in the eye. "I'm a man of my word. But I don't know if it will do any good, to be honest. The vice squad doesn't like men like you much, and frankly, neither do I. I'd make that call to your lawyer now if I were you. Good day." I turned on my heel and left, leaving him shaking in disbelief and shock behind the counter, his white shirt now soaked in sweat.

I filled Riker in on what I'd found out, and then I made a call to the station on my car radio, informing them to send the vice squad over to the flower shop and arrest Leslie Birdwell. As promised, I mentioned that he had cooperated in my investigation, for what it was worth.

When I was finished, I looked over at Riker, who was still sitting upright, drumming his fingers on his knees. "So that's that, then. Birdwell's finished."

"Yes, I'd say so. Up to the judge to decide what happens to him now."

Riker nodded slowly. "I imagine so. Won't be good for him." He looked over at me then. "You didn't mention me at all, did you?"

"No, I didn't. I didn't have to. The mention of the concierge at the hotel was all it took to push him over the edge, a fact I wouldn't have known if it wasn't for you."

He looked relieved. "Good. That's good. I mean, it's good he gave you the information, and good that I could help. Now what?"

"What do you think our next move should be?"

"Well, I suppose we should go talk to this Scotty guy."

"That's what I think, too. I'll radio the station and see if they can get me an address on that boardinghouse. It's apparently not too far from here."

Riker looked over at me again. "It's not. It's over on the corner of Kilbourn and Cass, only about a five-minute drive from here. I stayed there a long time ago."

"All right, saves me a call. Let's go, and maybe you can fill me in on this Mrs. Webster."

"She's all right, Heath. She honestly doesn't know about Birdwell. She thinks all us boys do is make deliveries for him."

"Deliveries, indeed. That's one word for it, anyway."

"What about lunch, by the way? I seem to recall you saying something about buying."

"Right you are. Sometimes I get so preoccupied I forget to eat."

"No wonder you're so thin," Riker said.

"You sound like my mother. Come on, we can grab something at the diner before we go to Webster's." I headed my car toward Art's Diner, my mind whirling.

CHAPTER TWELVE

Late afternoon, Sunday, September 14, 1947

After two egg salad sandwiches, two orders of chips, and three malted milks, one for me and two for Riker, we climbed back into my car and drove to Webster's boardinghouse. It was a ramshackle three-story gothic-style building, with a wraparound porch, gingerbread trim, and attic dormers. The clapboard siding was covered in peeling gray paint. The trim was a slightly lighter shade of gray and had probably once been white.

"Are you coming in this time, or do you want to wait here in the car again?" I said as I shut off the engine and applied the brake.

"I'll come in. Like I said, Mrs. Webster doesn't know anything about Birdy's or that part of my past. It will be nice to see her again, actually."

"Right, let's go then."

We got out of my car and walked down the cracked sidewalk to the gate, where Riker paused to look up at the old, spooky-looking house. "It's been a long time," he said. "Brings back memories both good and bad."

"I can imagine. Shall we?" I said, opening the gate.

"Sure," he said, letting out a deep breath. We went through the gate and across the walk, and climbed the worn steps up to the porch, which seemed to sag beneath our weight. I rang the bell twice as Riker stood next to me, fiddling with his hat. After several minutes, a tall woman in a high-collared dress, partly covered by a starched white apron opened the door. Her long hair was streaked with shades of gray and silver and gathered at the back of her neck. Her nose was large and prominent, and her eyes dark. She appeared to be in her late sixties or early seventies, but she stood straight, her shoulders back, proud and statuesque.

"Yes?" she said in a deep, unusually pitched nasal voice.

"Mrs. Webster?" I said.

She slowly looked from me to Riker, taking us in.

"I am she. But I'm not interested in buying whatever it is you're selling—vacuums, encyclopedias, brushes, whatever it is, I don't need it, I already have it, or I can't afford it. I'm baking today, and I don't have time for salesmen."

"Actually, ma'am, we're not selling anything. I'm Detective Barrington, this is Detective Riker. We'd like to speak with a young fellow named Scotty. We've been told he lives here."

She gave us a suspicious look. "Scotty? Why do you want to speak with him?"

"We just want to ask him some questions, Mrs. Webster," Riker said.

"About what, may I ask?" She stared at Detective Riker, looking him up and down. "Did you say your name is Riker?"

"Yes ma'am, Grant Riker."

"I know you, don't I? I remember you. Little Grant Riker."

Riker nodded and gave her a gentle smile. "Yes, it's me. I'm glad you remember me. It's good to see you again, Mrs. Webster. It's been a few years."

"Before the war," she said.

"Yes, a long time."

She moved her head up and down slowly. "You're a police detective now?"

Riker looked embarrassed. "You may recall I enlisted in the Navy, and I joined the police force when I got out. I made detective just a short while ago."

She reached over and pinched his cheek hard. I noticed her hands were large, with long fingers. That had to hurt and was sure to leave a mark. "Little Grant, all grown up. Good for you."

"Yes, ma'am," he said, rubbing his cheek where she'd pinched him.

She nodded slowly. "And I'm still here. A little older..."

"You look the same."

She smiled. Her oversized teeth were dull and gray, but her dark eyes sparkled with joy. "Flatterer. You always were. I've gained a few pounds, my hair's gotten grayer, and the lines on my face are deeper, but you? You look good, Grant. You were always a handsome lad, but now you've grown into yourself. Married?"

"Yes, ma'am, and I have a little girl, Jane Marie."

Mrs. Webster beamed. "That makes me so happy, my dear. I always thought you'd turn out okay. I was so worried when you went off to war. You never kept in touch. I didn't know what became of you."

"I'm sorry about that. I meant to, honestly. I did write you once from overseas, but the war just consumed me, it consumed all of us."

"Yes, of course. I understand. Most of the boys who leave I never hear from again. But it's good to see you now. Good to know you've done well for yourself. You must bring your wife and little girl by for tea sometime. I'd like to meet them."

"Oh, uh, yes, sure. Mrs. Riker is pretty busy these days, what with the baby and all, you know."

"I suppose so. But surely you could find time to bring them over for a little while, couldn't you? Oh, I do love babies. I never had any of my own, of course."

"Well, I'll ask her. I'm afraid I can't promise."

She gave him a hurt look. "You're not ashamed for her to meet me, are you?"

"What? Gee, no, not really." I could tell Riker felt suddenly awkward. "She's just busy, that's all. But I'll be sure and ask her."

"Good, good. Don't forget." She looked back to me then. "Now then, why do you want to speak to Scotty? Is he in some kind of trouble? He's a good boy, you know."

"We just want to ask him some questions."

"So I understand. But you still haven't told me what you want to ask him questions about."

"His whereabouts last night, for starters."

She frowned ever so slightly. "I see. Well, if you're here inquiring about his whereabouts, you must think he's gotten into some kind of trouble. But I can assure you Scotty was playing pinochle with me last night. I lost nearly every game."

"I'm sorry to hear that, about you losing, I mean," Riker said. "I hope you weren't playing for money."

"We just played for fun," Mrs. Webster said.

"Of course," I said. "I was only joking."

"Witty, you are," she said dryly.

"Some people think so. Was Scotty with you the entire evening?"

"That's right. We played several games."

"I see. Well, we'd still like to talk to him. We're investigating a murder, and Scotty may have some vital information."

Her ample bosom heaved up and down. "I don't see how. I'm sure he doesn't know anything about a murder. He's a nice boy."

"Yes, I'm sure he is. But we still want to talk to him."

"Please, Mrs. Webster. I'd really appreciate it," Riker said.

Her expression softened once more. "Well, I'll ask him, but he's very private, you know. I think he's up in his room. He shares it with the Jenkins boy. Come on in and have a seat in the parlor, and I'll check. I don't allow visitors upstairs, so he'll have to come down if he's willing."

"Thank you, we do appreciate it," I said.

We removed our hats, and Riker and I stepped inside as she stood back, closing the door behind us. She motioned toward a cozy-looking room through a red-draped doorway to our left.

"Make yourselves comfortable, gentlemen," she said. "I'll be back shortly. Well, perhaps not shortly. My rheumatism doesn't allow me to move as quickly as I used to." She climbed slowly up the stairs toward the second floor.

When she had gone, I looked around at the room we were in. There was nothing special about it, really. The furniture and furnishings were clearly old and worn, but everything was clean and tidy. An upright piano was opposite the doorway, with an overstuffed sofa in front of one of the windows and a couple of mismatched chairs facing it in front of the fireplace. I paced about as Riker looked around, clearly reminiscing.

"You all right?" I said.

"Hmm? Oh, yeah, fine, fine."

"That Mrs. Webster is interesting."

"Yes. She has gotten a bit older, yet she's still the same. Just like this place. It looks exactly the same as it did all those years ago. If I didn't know better, I'd swear those were the same wilted flowers on the piano that were here back then, too."

"I get the feeling Mrs. Webster doesn't make a lot of money on this place."

"She doesn't. Never has, I don't think. Fellows were always behind on their rent, and she always let it slide. Sometimes for months. She has too big a heart."

"She certainly is unusual."

"What do you mean?" Riker said. He sounded defensive.

But before I could respond, a tall, gangly, rail-thin young man appeared in the draped doorway, dressed in an undershirt and baggy trousers, barefooted. He looked nervous as he glanced at us.

"Hullo," he said dully.

We both turned to look at him. "You're Scotty?" I said.

He nodded, his eyes bloodshot and so dilated they looked almost entirely black. "That's right. Mrs. Webster said you wanted to see me. Said you was cops."

"That's right. I'm Detective Barrington, and this is Detective Riker."

"What do you want?"

"What's your full name, Scotty?" I said.

"What's it to you?"

"We're investigating a crime, we're talking to you about it, and we need your full legal name for the record."

"Smith."

"Really? Is that the best you can do?"

"People do have the last name of Smith, you know."

"True, but somehow I doubt that's yours."

He sniffed and rubbed his eyes. "Aw, who cares? Scott Herbert Hale, if you must know. Quite a name, ain't it?"

"Yes, a good name," Riker said.

"It's okay. It's really Herbert Scott Hale, but I switched it around so it sounds better. Anyway, I didn't do nothin', and I didn't see nothin' either." His bloodshot eyes darted back and forth between us as he spoke, his speech now rapid.

"In regard to what?" Riker said.

"In regard to anything you think I might have done or seen in regard to that crime you said you were investigating." He was nervously wringing his hands.

"That covers a lot of territory," I said. "Won't you sit down?" I motioned to one of the chairs.

"I'm fine," he said, shifting his weight from foot to foot. "I'd prefer to stand."

"Suit yourself. Where were you last night, say between ten and midnight?" Riker said.

He swallowed a couple of times and blinked his eyes rapidly. "I was here. Ma said this is about that fella's murder. I don't know nothin'. And I didn't know him."

"Ma?"

"Mrs. Webster. Most of us call her Ma. She said to say I was here playing pinochle."

"Were you?" I said.

He sniffed and wiped his nose with a dirty handkerchief he'd pulled from his back pocket. "Aww, no use in lying, I guess. I don't even know how to play pinochle. Do you?"

I shook my head. "No, I never learned. Cribbage is my game of choice."

"I don't know that one either."

"It's an entertaining diversion. So, if you weren't here playing cards with Mrs. Webster, where were you?"

He put his handkerchief away and shoved his hands in his front pockets, causing his trousers to slide down precariously low before he pulled them back out and yanked up his pants. "I never met a detective before, but I've known my share of cops. Can't say as I care for them."

"There are good ones and bad ones, trust me," I said.

"Maybe."

"Mrs. Webster seems to think highly of you," Riker said. "In my opinion, that means a lot."

"Ma's kind. She looks out for me, for all of us, tries to protect us."

"Quite admirable," I said.

"I don't trust cops, but I find it doesn't do much good to lie to them. They always find out."

"Sometimes. It's generally better to come clean, unless you have something to hide. By the way, how did you know it was a man that was murdered?" I said.

"Huh?"

"You mentioned you don't know anything about the fellow that was murdered, and that you didn't know him. How did you know it was a man?"

He shrugged his bony shoulders. "It's always a man, ain't it? Who goes around murdering women?"

"Tell that to Jack the Ripper."

"Who's that?"

"Never mind, it's not important. Mr. Birdwell told us he called you last night about a delivery job."

I watched his face, expecting a reaction, but there was none.

"Oh." He wiped his nose with the back of his hand. "Guess I'm not surprised. You wouldn't be here if you didn't already know what I might have to hide, and you wouldn't know how to find me unless you already talked to Mr. Birdwell."

"You're very perceptive, Scotty. How old are you?"

"Nineteen. I'll be twenty next May."

"Where are you from?"

"Sparta. I came to Milwaukee when I was seventeen. Someday I'll get out of here. Not just this place, but *this* place, if you know what I mean. I'll make something of myself. When I turned sixteen, I tried to enlist. I lied about my age, but they wouldn't take me. Then the war ended, so here I am. But it's only temporary." He sniffed, blew his nose with the dirty handkerchief again, and then shoved it once more into his back pocket.

"Of course. I wish you well. But about last night…" I said.

"Yeah. All right, so I was there."

"Where?" Riker said.

"Don't play dumb." Scotty sneered at us. "You know where. The alley. Near the Blatz Hotel. It's not far from here."

"Why were you there?" I said.

He snorted again, this time wiping his nose on his bare arm, not bothering with the handkerchief. "A flower delivery, like you said before. I was supposed to meet a fellow. Again, I'm sure you know all this. I was there for the delivery job Birdwell called me about."

"You were there to meet a fellow wearing a green carnation," I said.

"That's right. That's how it works. I figured you already knew that. I didn't know who he was, and I didn't care. I met him like I was supposed to. He seemed okay. Kind of fancy, had one of those round eyepieces over one eye. Saw that in a movie once, but I never saw one in person before."

"A monocle."

"Yeah, that's what they's called. Different. I asked him if he wanted to go somewhere, but he said he was from out of town and had nowhere to go, so we just did it there in the alley. We'd just barely got started when shots rang out. First one, followed by another. I thought it was a truck backfiring at first cause it sounded like it came from the street, but then the guy fell over. He was bleeding and gasping, and I knew he'd been shot. I got up and ran, and I didn't look back."

"You got up?"

Scotty gave a half laugh. "I was on my knees. If I hadn't a been, I might have gotten shot too."

"It's possible. Did you see where the shots came from?" Riker said.

"No sir, I didn't see nothin'. I heard the shots, saw him fall over, and I got up and took off down the alley. I ain't no sap. I came straight back here."

"And you didn't call the police?" I said.

"No. That would have been stupid, now, wouldn't it? I kept my yap shut."

"Why would that have been stupid?" Riker said.

"Because they would have wanted to know what I was doing there. But I didn't do nothin' wrong."

"That's debatable," I said.

"I ain't what they call musical, if that's what you're thinking. I ain't like that."

"Musical?" Riker said.

"Sure, you know. Guys say 'I heard he was musical' when they're talking about somebody, only they ain't talking about playin' no instruments. They're talking about fairies and pansies."

"I see," I said.

"Yeah, I ain't that way, see? I only do it for the money. I have a girl back home. Rose. Rose Fielding. Sweet and pretty."

"In Sparta."

"Yeah. When I get out of here, I'll send for her. We want a big family someday."

"I wish you well, Scotty, but I must caution you about this way of earning a living. No good will come of it," I said.

"Yeah, I know, but it's not so easy to quit. Ma suspects something, I think. She's told me a hundred times to clean up my act, get all my ducks in a row."

"She's a wise woman," Riker said.

"Yeah. You gonna arrest me now? Take me away and lock me up?"

I studied Scotty for a brief moment, pondering what to say, what to do. "We certainly could. Prostitution is illegal in all forty-eight states. But I have to ask myself, would it do you any good?"

He snorted again. "Do me any good?"

"I mean, if we arrest you, you will go to jail. Then someone, possibly Mrs. Webster, will post bail and get you out, though it sounds like it would be a financial hardship for her. The case would go before a judge, and most likely he'd find you guilty."

"Depends on the judge. I had one as a client once, you know," Scotty said with a smirk. "He was a regular. Big tipper, too."

"Be that as it may, if the judge finds you guilty, you may serve time in prison. I don't like to think what would happen to a boy like you in prison," I said.

"Aw, I can take care of myself."

"Sure you can. You'd be real popular, no doubt. And when you eventually got out of prison, you'd have a police record. Then what? Would prison have reformed you? Even if it did, would you then be able to get a real job? Hard to do with a police record."

"Hard enough to do without one," he said. "I've tried a few times."

"You do have options, Scotty," Riker said.

"Geez, what do you care?"

"Because I stayed here once when I was about your age. I lived here at the boardinghouse," Riker said. "Like you."

Scotty looked at Riker suspiciously. "Oh yeah? For real?"

"Yes, for real. You probably don't believe me, but it's true."

"Aw, so what?"

"Believe it or not, Scotty, the police are not your enemy. We're here to enforce the law and to protect the citizens. Even though you're breaking the law, I don't think you're a threat to society. At least not yet. But if you continue, we'll have no choice but to arrest you. Birdwell's will be shut down either way," I said.

He looked thoughtful then. Finally, he nodded slightly. "If you shut Birdy's down, I won't have any money coming in."

"How much do you typically make in a week?" I said.

"Depends. Sometimes fifteen to twenty bucks, sometimes less, sometimes more."

"That's a lot of flower deliveries," I said.

"Some of it is tips or referrals, you know. If I do a good job."

"You'll have to find a new job now," Riker said. "A more upstanding source of income."

"Yeah, sure, that's easy for you to say. What can I do? Jobs are hard to come by these days for a bum like me."

"Now that you're of age, you could still enlist in the service. Once you're out, you may find it easier to get employment," Riker said. "That's what I did. I was a Navy man."

"But you'll need to get help with your nose problem first," I said. "Which is where I suspect most of your money is going." I took out my pencil and notebook and jotted down a name and phone number, then handed the paper to him.

He looked suspicious as he took it. "What nose problem?"

"That's the number for Dr. Wilchinsky. Give him a call. He's treated others like you, and he's discreet."

"I can't afford no doctors, especially if you're really going to shut down Birdy's."

"Just make an appointment for him to treat you. I'll take care of the payments," I said.

Scotty looked at us suspiciously. "Why would you do that? Why do you fellas care? Did you used to live here, too?" he said to me.

"No, I didn't. But Riker's telling you the truth when he says he did. He went through a rough time also, but he turned himself around, and I believe you can, too."

"But the Army won't take you until you're clean," Riker said.

"The Army, huh? I bet I'd look good in a uniform. Rose would like me like that."

I looked at Riker and then back at Scotty. "No doubt she would."

"I'll think about it, I suppose."

"Make the call, Scotty. Today, not tomorrow. Or we will be back."

He stared down at the paper I handed him. "Sure. I suppose I should thank you. Both of you."

"For what?" I said.

"For not arresting me, I guess. So, thanks." He stuffed the paper in one of his front pants pocket, wiped his nose with his arm once more, and then turned and went out into the hall.

Riker looked over at me as I watched Scotty take the stairs two at a time to the second floor.

"Ready to go, Heath?"

"Yes. I think we're through here for now. We can see ourselves out. No doubt Mrs. Webster is busy in the kitchen. I believe she said she was baking today."

"And she's an amazing cook. If we stick around, we might get to sample some of her cookies or pies."

"Don't tell me you're still hungry after an egg salad sandwich, chips, and two malteds."

Riker grinned. "Maybe a little."

"Honestly, I don't know where you put it. But we don't have time to waste. Come on."

We stepped out on the sagging front porch of the boardinghouse and put our hats back on, pulling them low to shade our eyes from the afternoon sun as we went down the broad wooden steps.

"That was all quite fascinating," I said.

"What was?"

"Mrs. Webster, for starters."

"What about her?"

"She was tall for a woman, and such big hands and feet. It looked like she was wearing a size ten or eleven shoe."

"She's always been bigger than life."

"I'm sure. And that voice. It's rather affected, wouldn't you say?"

Riker bristled. "Maybe. Who cares? What are you getting at, Barrington?"

"Only that Mrs. Webster has an Adam's apple."

"So?"

"So, that, sir, was no lady."

Riker stopped short on the sidewalk and looked at me. "I beg to differ. Mrs. Webster is more a lady than any lady I know."

"But she's a he," I said. "Or at least she was. I've never met anyone like that before."

"I bet you have."

I shook my head. "No, I would have been able to tell. I can always tell."

"I seem to remember you were fooled on the first case we worked on together."

"That person was just dressing up for a role, but Mrs. Webster is different."

"To me she's just Mrs. Webster. Always has been."

"But how does she live her life? Does she date?"

"I've never known her to date, but she might if she was given the chance. It's not about sex, though, it's about her being true to her heart. Does that make sense?"

I scratched the back of my head and adjusted my hat. "I think it does. In a way it's just like you and me, I suppose. But it can't be easy."

Riker shook his head. "I never said it was easy, and neither did she. In fact, I'm sure it's quite hard, harder than it is for us. She keeps to herself, though she does have a few friends. She doesn't go out much and has no family to speak of. She gets the groceries delivered, and she makes her own clothes. But she's happy enough, which is more than a lot of people can say. And she has her boys to keep her company, at least. We all know. Most of us never cared. The ones that did care didn't stick around long. And the rest of us just didn't talk about it. She took care of us and watched out for us when no one else would. She was like a mother to us, which is why most fellows call her Ma. Does it bother you?"

I paused and looked at him. "No, I guess it doesn't, not really. It's just different, that's all."

"We're all different. It's what makes life interesting. Normal is just a word in the dictionary, Heath."

"You know something, Grant? You're absolutely right. She seems like she's a nice lady."

"Yeah, that's who she is. A nice lady."

"But I got the impression you didn't feel comfortable with the idea of your wife meeting her," I said.

"Oh, well, that. Mary Jane wouldn't understand someone like Mrs. Webster."

"But you're not embarrassed by Mrs. Webster?"

"No." Riker shook his head slowly. "But Mary Jane is really naïve and innocent."

"And Mrs. Webster is, well, different?"

"Touché, Heath. You're right. You know, I think maybe I will bring her and the baby around when this case is finished. Maybe it's time to open up her eyes a little bit."

"That's up to you, Grant. Just be aware if you do, it might raise questions about yourself that you'd rather not answer, questions about your past, and even your present."

"Yeah, but I think Mrs. Webster would be hurt if she thought I was embarrassed and didn't want Mary Jane to meet her."

"No doubt, but she'd get over it. I'm not sure Mary Jane will, if you decide to go ahead with it."

"I think perhaps that's a chance I'm willing to take. I owe it to Mrs. Webster. And to myself."

"I'm glad to hear it. Speaking of Mrs. Webster, though, I hate to say this, but I think we must consider her a suspect."

"What? Why? What motive would she have for killing Firestone?"

"To protect Scotty. Perhaps she thought if she shot Firestone, it would scare Scotty straight, so to speak. Get him to change his ways once and for all. And think about it. She said Scotty was in all night playing pinochle with her."

"To give him an alibi," Riker said.

"Yes, but it also gave her an alibi. When she went upstairs she told him to say he was playing cards with her all night. I'm sure she didn't expect him to tell us the truth, so the pinochle story protected her and Scotty both."

Riker scratched his head. "Gee, that makes sense."

"It does. She probably took the call from Birdwell, let Scotty know he was wanted on the telephone, and then perhaps listened in to what was said from another extension. She heard Birdwell say he had a delivery for Scotty to make. At ten o'clock at night, that made her suspicious, so she followed Scotty. She fired two shots into the dark alley when she saw Scotty drop to his knees. Perhaps she didn't intend to kill Firestone, but merely scare him and Scotty both, but Firestone got in the way. And someone like Mrs. Webster would be likely to have a gun, and to carry it on her person whenever she went out."

"Why do you say that?"

"For protection against prejudiced, ignorant people who could be cruel and threatening. You said yourself she rarely goes out anymore, and that's probably why. It makes sense she'd have a gun for protection, just in case."

"I suppose so. That's pretty sad."

"Yes, it is. But I'm only supposing right now. She must be considered a suspect, and further investigation is warranted, but right now I'm just guessing."

"You're usually a pretty good guesser," Riker said.

"Sometimes. Sometimes guesses lead me to other guesses. It's a process, hard to explain."

"Okay. I really hope it doesn't turn out that Mrs. Webster killed him, though."

"I do too, but we have to consider the possibility. There's also a chance Scotty is our killer."

"How do you figure?"

"Perhaps he thought Firestone looked like he had money. When Firestone dropped his pants, Scotty stepped away, maybe on the premise of making sure the coast was clear. Then he turned and shot him. Before he could grab the watch and wallet, he got scared off by something, or someone."

"Yeah, I suppose that's possible, but my gut tells me he's innocent. Of murder, at least, and the same with Mrs. Webster."

"Time will tell, hopefully. My instincts agree with your gut, but that only goes so far. By the way, it was nice what you did for him back there."

Riker shrugged. "I've been there. Never the drug thing, thankfully, but I knew kids like him. Let's hope he turns himself around, if he's not a murderer. It was nice what you did, too, offering to pay for the doctor and all."

"I hope he'll make that call."

"He will. I'll telephone Mrs. Webster later and make sure he calls, or she'll box his ears but good."

"I'm sure she would, and that would hurt something awful," I said. "She looks pretty strong."

"She is," he said, rubbing his cheek once more where she'd pinched him. It was still rather red. "Where to next?"

I pulled out my pocket watch. "It's half past five. I think we've covered quite a bit for one day. Let's head back to the station and wrap things up, start fresh again tomorrow morning."

"Sounds good to me. It's getting dark, and I promised Mary Jane I'd be home by six."

"You'll never make it. By the time we get back to the station, sign out, and you drive home, it will be half past six at least—and she was already irritated with you."

"Yeah, I know. But this is my first real case, I can't just get up and leave in the middle of questioning a suspect because I told my wife I'd be home for dinner."

"I'll drop you off at your place directly from here. Then I'll go back to the station and type up the preliminary notes on the case. When I'm done, I'll sign us both out."

"But taking me home is out of your way, and my car is at the station."

"You can take the streetcar in tomorrow and get your car. Besides, I've got nothing to do but go home to an empty apartment."

"Not seeing Alan tonight?"

"No, I'll give him a call, though, just to say good night, and maybe ask him if he wants to go to the movies tomorrow night. *The Ghost and Mrs. Muir* is playing at the Downer."

"Doing more research on ghosts and spirits?"

"No, just a coincidence. It's supposed to be a good film."

"Yes, I've heard that. Tell Alan hello for me."

"Will do. Now let's get you home."

"Thanks, Heath. Mary Jane will appreciate that, I'm sure."

"I'm happy to do it, but meet me at the station tomorrow morning at nine o'clock sharp. I want to pay a visit to the president of Firestone's fan club."

"Florence Lufkin? Think she'll be home on a Monday morning?"

"I had Sergeant Stilke do some checking for me. Miss Lufkin was working as a secretary for the First National Bank but was discharged a couple of weeks ago and apparently has not found gainful employment as of yet, so she should be home."

CHAPTER THIRTEEN

Early morning, Monday, September 15, 1947

Ever eager, Riker was waiting for me as I climbed the stairs to the detectives' room, his hat in his hand. He looked more rested than he had the day before, his eyes clear and alert. The time, I noted, was half past eight.

"Morning, Heath."

"Good morning. I figured you'd be the first one in again," I said.

He gave me a smile, and I swear he was practically blushing. "I almost wasn't. Mary Jane was feeling romantic this morning, happy I was home for dinner last night, thanks to you, and the baby was sleeping soundly for once. I just made it to the streetcar stop on time."

"So, all is forgiven for not picking her up after church and not getting home until dinner?"

"More or less. But I had to promise I'd be home for dinner tonight. Six o'clock on the dot."

"I see. Well, while you were being romantic I've been thinking on the case."

"Oh yeah? What are you thinking?"

"Lots of things, but too soon to hypothesize anything yet."

"Big words for so early in the morning. Well, I'm ready, willing, and able, so let's go see what Miss Lufkin has to say." He was almost bouncing up and down as he spoke.

"Slow down, Trigger," I said, laughing. "Let me put my liverwurst sandwich in the icebox, check my desk, make a couple phone calls, and have a cup of coffee first. Give me twenty minutes and I'll be set, deal?"

"Okay, deal. I'll just go over my notes again or something while I wait."

I had my cup of coffee and finished up what I needed to do in just over fifteen minutes, aware Riker was chomping at the proverbial bit to get going.

"All right, Trigger, saddle up and let's ride," I said, coming up to him as he paced the floor in front of the file cabinets.

"Yes, sir!" He took the steps down two at a time ahead of me, and we signed out on the board at ten minutes to nine. It was a brighter day than yesterday, the clouds having lifted as sunshine and light surrounded us. We chatted back and forth about the previous day and our thoughts, suspicions, and ideas as we drove. When we reached Oakland Avenue, I slowed down and Riker checked the addresses. A few blocks later he said, "This is it, Heath. 1410 Oakland Avenue. She must live above that pawnshop."

"Right, let's go then." We left the car at the curb and entered a side door to the left of the pawnshop's plate glass window. The door was unlocked, so we climbed the rickety wooden stairs to the second floor and knocked on the first door to our right.

The door to 2A was opened by a fairly attractive-looking girl, probably in her early twenties. Her shoulder-length hair was auburn, with a wave, and she had a beauty mark above her lip. She was wearing a gray skirt with a pink cashmere sweater over a white blouse, low sensible black shoes on her small feet, and a simple gold chain about her neck from which hung a capital letter *F*. I couldn't help but notice she fit the description of the person who wrote that mysterious note to Ricci.

"Miss Lufkin? Florence Lufkin?" I said.

"Yes, that's right. Who are you? What do you want?"

"I'm Detective Barrington, and this is Detective Riker of the Milwaukee Police," I said, showing her our badges. "We'd like to ask you a few questions."

"What about?" She fidgeted with the chain around her neck, the *F* attached to it bouncing back and forth.

"About the murder of Almanzo Firestone. I understand from his agent you had drinks and dinner with him the night he was killed."

"Oh, that. It's just awful what happened to him. I heard about it on the radio, and of course it was in the papers. I just couldn't believe it, so unexpected. Have you caught the person who did it?"

"That's what we're trying to determine, miss," Riker said, "exactly who is responsible."

"Yes, of course. You might as well come in." She stepped aside and Riker and I entered. It was a small place, but clean and tidy enough. The smell of rose water hung in the air.

"May I take your hats?"

"Thank you," Riker said. She placed them on a small side console, then ushered us to the chintz sofa as she seated herself in the armchair by the window. A large crucifix hung on the wall over the sofa, and on the coffee table was a well-worn Bible, along with multiple books on the occult, the spirit world, and fortune telling.

"Nice place you have here," Riker said.

"Thank you. It's small but affordable. The man who owns the pawnshop downstairs is my uncle, Hugo Petersen. Sometimes I help him out cleaning in the store or running the register in exchange for a deal on the rent."

"Seems like an equitable solution," I said.

"It's okay, but it's not free. He reminds me frequently he could get more for this place renting it to someone else, and he gets livid if I'm late on paying. I still owe him for this month's rent."

"Doing business with relatives can always be tricky," I said. "So you live alone?"

"I do. I should probably get a roommate to help with the bills, but I like my privacy too much and it's only a one-bedroom, and a small one at that. Oh, did you want something to drink? I don't have a lot, but I could brew a pot of tea."

"No thank you, Miss Lufkin. We won't keep you long, but we do have a few questions," I said.

"About dinner and drinks Saturday night, yes. Strange thing, that. I mean how it all came to pass. Like it was ordained to happen."

"How so?"

"Well, I'd never met Mr. Firestone before, not in person anyway, though I'd seen his performances a few times. I'm the president of the local chapter of his admirers. So, when I heard he was coming to Milwaukee, I wrote him a letter welcoming him. Just a few days later,

I received a letter back from Mr. Goodacre, his agent, asking me if I'd like to have cocktails and dinner with the All-Seeing Almanzo, and he also included an autographed picture of Mr. Firestone, which I put in my scrapbook, and two free tickets to the Sunday matinee. Can you imagine? Of course I replied immediately in the affirmative. I planned on taking my friend Shirley to the Sunday show."

"I'm sure that must have been thrilling for you," Riker said.

"Oh, yes. It certainly was. I even splurged on a new dress and a visit to the beauty parlor, and so did Shirley. My hair is generally flat, so I had them add this wave," she said, touching her hair ever so gently.

"It's quite attractive," Riker said.

"Thank you, I wanted to look my best, though it looked better on Saturday. I wash my hair on Mondays, so it will be completely gone after today. I was just thinking of doing that when the two of you arrived unannounced."

"Please forgive the intrusion," I said.

"It's all right. I can do it after you leave if you don't stay too long."

"This shouldn't take more than a few minutes, Miss Lufkin. Now then, about Saturday night?" Riker said.

"Yes, well, the agent arranged it all. I was to meet him, Mr. and Mrs. Firestone, and Mr. Firestone's protégé, Mr. Ricci, in Mr. and Mrs. Firestone's suite at the Blatz at a quarter past eight o'clock. The Valentine Suite. Isn't that something? Such a romantic name."

"Actually the suite is named after Valentin Blatz. He was the founder of the Blatz brewery," Riker said.

"Oh, I didn't know that. Still, I'd never been in a hotel suite before, much less for cocktails. It all sounded so glamorous. I had to take the streetcar and a bus to get there from here, but I was a little early. I got there at just a few minutes after eight, which gave me a chance to use the ladies' room and freshen up. Then I went upstairs to the fourth floor and knocked on the door of the suite. I expected Mr. Firestone to answer it, but it was a little fellow who turned out to be Mr. Goodacre. He invited me in and got me a rum and ginger ale. Mr. Ricci was there already, fairly drunk, I must say. Mr. and Mrs. Firestone arrived closer to half past eight. They came right from the theater. They were both dressed so beautifully."

"And how did you find the All-Seeing One?" Riker said.

"It's funny. He was shorter than I thought he'd be. Onstage he seems larger than life, but he was still quite attractive, and taller than Mr. Goodacre. Mr. Firestone and Mr. Ricci look a lot alike, actually."

"We met Mr. Ricci earlier. I noticed the resemblance," I said.

"Yes, he's handsome, but I can't say I cared for him. He drinks too much, in my opinion, and he's a bit of a letch."

"So I've heard," Riker said.

"You heard correctly. At one point in the evening, after Mr. and Mrs. Firestone got there, Mr. Ricci got a handgun out of a desk drawer and started waving it about. It startled me so much I spilled my drink on the rug. I'm a little clumsy, but it really wasn't my fault. Mr. Ricci was clearly intoxicated, and I was afraid the gun might go off. It made me terribly uncomfortable. I could tell Mr. Firestone was angry with me. I was so upset I nearly cried."

"I'm sure he understood, Miss Lufkin," I said.

"Oh, I could tell he was upset the way he was glaring at me. But then, I looked at him and he just handed me his handkerchief and put his arm around my shoulder and I felt okay, I felt safe. A short while later, Mr. Goodacre said the three of us should go down to dinner. Believe me, I was more than happy to get out of there at that point."

"Understandably. So, the three of you dined? Mr. Firestone, Mr. Goodacre, and you?" Riker said.

"Yes, right there in the hotel, though after what happened in the suite, I'd lost my appetite."

"Still, you managed to finish your lobster," I said.

She looked surprised. "My heavens, how did you know that? How did you know what I ordered?"

"Just doing my job, miss."

"I see. Well, I'd never been in a fancy restaurant like that before. It was the kind of place someone like Mr. Firestone would dine, all right. And I'd never had lobster before, either. It was the special, so all three of us had it. I must say it was delicious."

"And how did the rest of the evening progress?" Riker said. "Did it get any better after the cocktail party upstairs?"

"Not much, I'm afraid. I could tell Mr. Firestone was still upset about the stain on the rug, and I knew he wasn't too keen on having dinner with me. I'm sure it was his agent's idea, you know, publicity. Speaking of publicity, just as we were finishing, a man from the newspaper showed up. He took our pictures and asked some questions."

"Famous spiritualist has dinner with president of local fan club," I said.

"Yes, it was supposed to run in the Sunday issue of the *Journal*. But naturally…"

"Of course. To be honest, I wasn't aware spiritualists had fan clubs," I said.

"Admirers, Detective, not fans. I'm the president of the local chapter of his admirers. Sixteen members total, including me and my friend Shirley."

"I stand corrected, Miss Lufkin," I said. "But I wasn't aware they had admirers, either."

"Almanzo was so much more than a spiritualist, don't you see? He was so talented, so gifted, a real showman. People listened to what he had to say."

"A showman he was. So, the two of you got to know each other?"

"Sort of. Almanzo was polite and cordial, but I could tell he wasn't really enjoying himself. He's not a very good actor or conversationalist. Or wasn't, I guess I should say. Still, it was a night I'll never forget. He was a sight to see, resplendent in a navy suit with a red tie, a carnation in his lapel, and a monocle. I've never seen anyone wear a monocle before. I kept wanting to ask him how he kept it from falling down. It seems like it would be so uncomfortable, you know?"

"They are unusual, but Mr. Firestone was a bit flamboyant," Riker said.

"Definitely. I'm afraid I'm terribly clumsy, though. Just as I think he was forgetting about my spilling my drink in the suite, I dropped my soup spoon and the soup splattered all over Mr. Firestone's tie. Isn't that always the way? I could tell he was quite annoyed, though he was too much of a gentleman to scold me. Most men would have left it, but Mr. Firestone went up and put on a fresh tie, leaving me alone with Mr. Goodacre for quite some time. It was rather awkward."

"How so?"

"I don't know, it just was. He kept asking me silly questions, treating me like a bobby-soxer. I'm twenty-two, you know. I'm not a kid anymore. Anyway, I was glad when Almanzo finally came back, even though he still looked perturbed. He'd put on a pretty blue tie this time. We finished dinner but skipped dessert, which is fine by me. I have to watch my figure."

"You parted ways at that point?" Riker said.

"Yes. We all stood, and he shook my hand. I was surprised at how soft his skin was. His fingernails even had clear polish on them, can you imagine? I couldn't help but stare. My father's hands are all calloused and rough, but Almanzo's were as smooth as a baby's bottom."

"I imagine summoning the dead and foretelling the future doesn't require much heavy lifting, Miss Lufkin," I said.

"That's true, I suppose. It's more mental."

"It certainly is that," Riker said. "So, he shook your hand?"

"That's right. I thanked them both kindly and Mr. Goodacre told me he would see me home if I liked. Mr. Firestone, however, said he wanted to go for a walk. He seemed most anxious, checking his watch several times all through dinner like he had another appointment, but he said he just wanted to get some air. Anyway, I told Mr. Goodacre not to bother. The bus stop the next block over takes me to the streetcar stop, which practically takes me all the way back here to my place. Mr. Goodacre shook my hand and said he was pleased to have met me, and then I left, never to see either one of them again." She sighed, her eyes half closed. "It's a night I'll never forget, in spite of everything that happened, or maybe partly because of it."

"Certainly a tragedy," I said. "Mr. Firestone's death, I mean."

"Hmm? Oh, yes, of course. I've seen lots of his performances. I even went to Minneapolis last winter to see him at the State Theater. Do you know how cold and miserable Minneapolis is in the winter?"

"I've never been, but I've heard tell," I said.

"Well, you heard correctly. Much worse than here. Except for that awful blizzard we had last January."

"That was one for the history books indeed."

"Yes. I'm not too keen on the cold, but still I went to Minnesota. My cousin Frida lives there in the Twin Cities, and she goes steady with a boy named Wally who works at the theater there in the box office. So, I got a ticket and even a backstage pass, can you imagine? How could I not go?"

"Indeed, that does sound too good to pass up," Riker said.

"Yes. I took the mid-morning train and got there in time for the show. I spent the night at Frida's, and then took the early afternoon train back."

"You mentioned you had a backstage pass, but you didn't get to meet Almanzo?" I said.

She shook her head. "No, unfortunately. I went to his dressing room, but there was some hullaballoo over something, so I didn't get to go in. Not sure what it was all about."

"That's too bad," Riker said.

"Yes, but still, he was magnificent in the performance, well worth the trip. He had such a way of speaking. Absolutely mesmerizing. But now his voice and his talent have been forever silenced. A tragedy, as you said. But God's will, of course."

"God's will? How so?" Riker said.

She shrugged. "It just is. I believe everything is God's will. That blizzard in January, for example. God brought that down on us sinners for something we had done. Humans are just instruments in his hands. We do his bidding, you see, and he punishes us as he sees fit."

"Frankly, Miss Lufkin, I don't see," I said. "That sounds to me like removing personal responsibility from your actions."

She pouted. "You sound like my neighbor, Mr. Levitz. He lives in the back apartment, 2B. He doesn't see the truth either, or refuses to see it. He thinks God is benevolent and forgiving."

"Actually, Miss Lufkin, it does state in the Bible, 'For God so loved the world, that he gave his only son,'" Riker said. "That sounds pretty benevolent to me."

"Yes, well, in Mr. Firestone's case, God gave him his talent, and God took it away," she said.

"Someone with a revolver took it away," I said.

"But only as God directed them."

"And what reason would God have for doing that?" Riker said.

"The Lord works in mysterious ways, Detective," she said, fiddling with the gold letter about her neck again. "We may never know for sure, but most likely Mr. Firestone did something to anger God, and he was thus struck down."

"Convenient," Riker said.

"Not really, it's just how it is. I believe his was a death foretold in the stars."

"Oh? You mean you somehow knew beforehand?" Riker said.

"No, of course not. But it was foretold, nonetheless. Nothing could be done to stop it."

"Isn't it unusual for a fan—excuse me—an admirer of a fortune-teller and spiritualist to also be religious?" I said.

"I don't think so. I think it's all intertwined. Almanzo was a man of God. God gave Almanzo the talent to see the future, to speak to the dead, and he used it well."

"To turn a profit by being a prophet," I said.

She scowled at me. "I can tell you're a nonbeliever. But beware, Detective. Both of you. He is watching."

"If he's watching me, I'm sure he's getting quite a show. By the way, Miss Lufkin, what was in the note you sent Mr. Ricci earlier?" I said. It was a gamble, but it paid off.

Her face turned pale. "Note?"

"Yes, we happened to be in his room when the bellboy delivered it. We spoke with the bellboy afterward, and his description of the girl who gave it to him fits you to a T."

"Oh, that note. Well, uh, yes, of course. I wrote Mr. Ricci a condolence note, that's all."

"How kind of you. But what about Mrs. Firestone?" Riker said. "It seems she would have been the one to send a condolence note to."

"Yes, I suppose so, but I only met her briefly at the cocktail party in their suite, so I thought Mr. Ricci would be a better choice."

"But you said you never met Mr. Ricci, either, except briefly during the cocktail party. In fact, you said he was obnoxious and rather annoying and you didn't care for him," Riker said.

"Yes, but I, uh, wanted to show there were no hard feelings. Because of the incident with the gun and all."

"Did you send a condolence note to Mr. Goodacre?" I said.

"No, I didn't. I guess I should have sent one to him and Mrs. Firestone, too. Maybe I still will." More fiddling with the necklace.

"Yes, I guess you should have sent them both notes. Or perhaps not." Riker said.

"By the way, why were you discharged from your position at the First National Bank?" I said.

She looked surprised. "Not that it's any of your business, but my supervisor, Mr. Mungston, claimed I was tardy seven times in sixty days."

"Were you?"

"No, it was only six times and all with good reason, but it's for the better anyway."

"How so?" Riker said.

"It's God's will, of course. He wanted me to leave the First National Bank because he has something else destined for me to do, I'm sure."

"And what would that be?"

"I really couldn't say. It hasn't been disclosed to me yet, but I'm sure it will all come to light."

"Fascinating. By the way, your necklace is quite interesting. Is that *F* for Firestone?" I said.

"What? Oh, no, I'm not that big an admirer. It's for Florence, my first name. Most people call me Flo."

"A charming name," Riker said.

"Thanks. I was named after my aunt. I wear this necklace every day. It reminds me of her, especially as she gave it to me just a month before she died."

"She must have been a lovely lady."

"She was."

"Well, we won't keep you any longer, Miss Lufkin, but we'll be in touch," I said as the three of us got to our feet.

"Why will you be in touch? I've already told you everything I know."

"As things come up, we may have more questions, things we didn't think of before."

"I see. Well, right now I need to wash my hair, so if you'll excuse me…"

"Yes, thank you for your time," I said. "Good day."

"Good day, gentlemen."

We gathered up our hats, left her apartment, and returned to the street, where we walked the short distance to my car.

"What do you make of her?" I said.

"She's something. That bit about the note she sent to Ricci didn't ring true to me."

"Not at all. If that was a condolence note she sent, I'm the Queen of England. I'm willing to bet it was something else entirely, and not signed," I said.

"Not signed?" Riker said.

"Correct. If I had to guess, I'd say it said something like, *Meet me in Lake Park by the old lighthouse*, or something, *on Monday, at four p.m.*, or something like that. *I'll be in a green dress*, or blue, or whatever."

"But why? What could she want to meet Ricci for? And why wouldn't she sign the note?"

"That remains to be seen. It's also possible, I suppose, that the note *was* signed. That she was lying about never having met Mr. Ricci, and that they are comrades, of a sort, in a dirty business."

"You mean they were in on Firestone's murder?"

"It's possible. That whole scene in the suite with the gun, Ricci making advances on Miss Lufkin, it could have all been an act," I said.

"So, she's a suspect along with Mrs. Webster, and maybe even Scotty."

"Yes."

"But what's her motive? In love with Mr. Ricci? Even if that's true, it wouldn't be a motive to kill Firestone."

"No, it wouldn't appear so. Perhaps she acted alone, thinking she was performing God's will. Or maybe she's totally innocent. There are other suspects, of course. Mr. Goodacre, Mrs. Firestone, and Mr. Ricci, and possibly some combination of them all. Detective work is really about considering each of the possibilities, and then slowly eliminating them until you're left with one."

"You make it sound easy."

"It's actually not difficult if you pay attention to the details and all the little things. Like how you noticed the carnation on Firestone's lapel. If it wasn't for you, I probably wouldn't have paid any attention to that."

"Huh. I think I understand. It's like solving a crossword puzzle. You look at the clue, then come up with possible solutions, paying attention to the letters, if any, that are already there, to help you."

"Yes, that's a pretty good analogy. Come on, let's head back to the station," I said, as we reached my car. "Those photos from the *Milwaukee Journal* are supposed to be delivered this morning, and they may be more letters to our crossword puzzle."

CHAPTER FOURTEEN

Morning, Monday, September 15, 1947

We entered the police station and checked in on the blackboard by the sergeant's desk. "Morning, Sparrow," I said.

"Barrington, Riker," Sergeant Sparrow said, looking up at us. "You two were out and about early this morning. I came on duty at ten and saw you'd already come and gone."

"Hot on the trail, as they say. Any messages?"

He glanced at a few notes on his desk. "Nope, nothing for you two. A courier from the *Milwaukee Journal* dropped off an envelope for you, though, Barrington. I had Porter take it up to your desk. I had to tip the courier a quarter, you know."

"Great, thanks. I owe you one."

"Sure, still waiting on those ballgame tickets you promised me, too, by the way."

"Baseball season's over," I said.

"I have a feeling I'll be waiting next year, too."

"Okay, I'll see what I can do. How's the wife and kids?" I said.

"All doing well. Baby number five is due soon. Still hoping for a boy this time."

"Name him after me," I said, "and I'll buy you a cigar *and* get you those ballgame tickets."

"Sure you will," Sparrow said. "But it will probably be another girl."

"As long as she's healthy," I said.

"Yeah, yeah, I know. But a boy would still be nice." The phone on his desk started to ring. "Gotta go," he said, picking up the receiver.

"See you in the funny papers, Sparrow," Riker said. We turned and climbed the stairs to the detectives' room, running into Spelling on his way down.

"Morning, Barrington," Spelling said, glancing at Riker and then back at me. "I see you took my little student here under your wing. The chief said you actually requested him."

"I did. Riker has got a sharp mind and a photographic memory, and he's already been a big help to me. Your loss, my gain. How's your vandalism case?"

"I think I've got it covered, and I did it all on my own."

"Good to hear. I guess I'm not as swift as you. I'll take all the help I can get," I said.

"You'll need it," he said, smirking. "I heard about that All-Seeing spiritualist fellow. Shot dead in an alley in the middle of the night, no witnesses, no motive. Good luck trying to solve that one."

"No witnesses we know of at present," Riker said.

"Somebody told me he was shot taking a leak against the wall. They found him with his pants down."

"Don't believe everything you hear, Spelling," I said. "Now if you'll excuse us…"

"Sure, sure. Be my guest." He bowed and waved us up the stairs as he continued down. "Say, I just had a thought," he said, calling after us. We stopped at the top and looked down at him.

"What?" Riker said.

"My cousin Bertha's got a Ouija board. Maybe she'll let you use it to solve your case. You know, ask the dead guy who shot him." Spelling snorted and laughed like a braying donkey as he turned and disappeared down the hall.

"Jackass," I muttered.

"Hee-haw," Riker said. "Don't let him get to you. Come on, let's take a look at those photographs the courier dropped off."

I shook Spelling out of my head and walked with Riker to my desk, where the large manila envelope had been placed in my inbox. "These are the ones the photographer from the *Milwaukee Journal* took the night Firestone was murdered. Let's go into the briefing room and take a look at them."

I spread out all six of the black-and-white 8x10s on the table and studied them. They were mostly closeups of Mr. Firestone and Miss Lufkin at the restaurant table, but there was also one of the two of them with Mr. Goodacre. I wondered which one the paper would have used if Firestone hadn't been murdered. Instead they ran a stock photo of him in his theatrical garb along with the attention getting headline: *The All-Seeing Almanzo Shot Dead in Dark Alley, Alley Cat Killer On the Loose.*

I picked up one or two of the pictures and studied them closely, then set them back down. "Not much to see here, I don't think. Just standard photos of Firestone, Lufkin, and Goodacre in the restaurant at the Blatz. Oh well, it was worth a shot."

"What's our next step, Heath? It seems we're no closer to figuring this thing out."

"I know. I feel like we're still missing a piece or two of the puzzle."

"Do you think there's a chance we're over thinking this? Do you think it could have been a random mugger or burglar?"

"I'm not ready to rule that out, but I don't think it's likely. We have six good suspects, all with moms," I said.

"Moms?"

"Motive, opportunity, and means. Mrs. Firestone, Mr. Ricci, Mr. Goodacre, Miss Lufkin, Mrs. Webster, and Scotty." I walked over to the blackboard and picked up the chalk, writing each suspect's name across the top. Down the side I wrote *Motive*, *Opportunity*, and *Means*.

"Mrs. Firestone had the insurance money among other things as a motive. Ricci's motive was wanting a chance at the spotlight. Goodacre's motive would be to prevent Firestone finding out about him embezzling, if in fact he was. Miss Lufkin may have felt she was doing God's work. They all could have easily followed Firestone, and they all had access to the gun. And we've already gone over Mrs. Webster and Scotty. So they all had moms." I walked back to the table once more and looked at the pictures from the newspaper photographer. Miss Lufkin was grinning like an idiot in every picture, Goodacre wore a very practiced smile, and Firestone just looked grumpy. "I wish these pictures were more helpful. I'm not sure what I was hoping for."

Riker picked one of them up again and studied it. "Hmm, maybe they are," he said.

"Helpful? In what way?"

Riker handed the photograph he'd been holding to me. "Take a closer look."

I studied it but saw nothing out of the ordinary. "Just a picture of three people."

"You mean you don't see it?" Riker said.

"See what?"

"Actually, it's more what you don't see. In every one of these photos, Firestone isn't wearing the carnation in his lapel."

"Right, he went to the flower shop *after* dinner, remember?"

"I do. And do you remember what Miss Lufkin said when she described Firestone? She mentioned he was wearing a navy suit with a red tie, a carnation in his lapel, and a monocle."

"Say, you're right! And she said when they parted after dinner, she never saw him again."

"But she definitely said Firestone had a carnation in his lapel. There's no way she would have known about that unless she saw him after dinner."

"Good thinking, Riker. I would have missed that."

"I think we may know who the killer is, Heath. She followed him after dinner, saw him buy the carnation, saw him go into the alley, saw what he was doing, and shot him dead, being the good Christian woman she is. If so, it wasn't premeditated."

"But why would she be carrying a gun if it wasn't premeditated?" I said.

"Maybe for protection, like you said about Mrs. Webster. And Miss Lufkin is a fairly attractive young woman out walking the streets at night. It makes sense."

"Yes. Yes, it does. And perhaps she had an accomplice. Remember the note she sent to Ricci."

"Jeepers, that's certainly possible. Now what?"

"I think we need to have another talk with Miss Lufkin and Mr. Ricci."

"Because you think Ricci and Miss Lufkin may have been in on Firestone's murder together?"

"Maybe. Your comment on the carnation and how Miss Lufkin described Mr. Firestone jarred something with me. Ricci described Firestone as wearing a baby blue tie that night. He also stated he never saw Firestone again after briefly stopping at the dinner table where

Firestone, Goodacre, and Miss Lufkin were looking over their menus, having just sat down."

"Ah, yes! But Miss Lufkin initially described Firestone as wearing a red tie with the carnation, until she spilled her soup and he went up to change it out for a blue one."

"Exactly. And according to the police report, Firestone was found wearing a baby blue tie. So Ricci apparently saw him later in the evening also, even though he says he didn't."

"So, they both lied," Riker said.

"It would seem so. But to what end we have yet to determine. Let's start with Miss Lufkin, then we'll swing by and talk to Ricci again."

CHAPTER FIFTEEN

Early afternoon, Monday, September 15, 1947

Riker ate the hot potato salad and frankfurters his wife had packed him for lunch while I had the liverwurst sandwich I had brought from home, and then we drove once more to the little pawnshop on Oakland, parking just out front in a two-hour zone.

"Hopefully she's still home," Riker said as he climbed out of the passenger side of my car.

"If not, we go to plan B and talk to Ricci first," I said, joining him on the sidewalk. "But only one way to find out." I walked the short distance to the door to the left of the pawnshop window and we climbed the rickety stairs to the second floor once more. We removed our hats, and I rapped several times on the door of 2A.

It opened a crack in answer to my knock, and I was greeted by a sliver of Florence Lufkin's face.

"Oh, you two again," she said, opening the door wider. "When you said you'd be in touch, I didn't think you meant this soon." She still wore the same clothes, only now her hair was up and freshly washed, her feet were bare, and she had put on a printed blouse instead of the white one.

"Forgive the intrusion, but we have just a few more questions for you, if you don't mind," I said.

"And if I do mind?"

"We'll have to insist," Riker said.

"That's what I figured. You might as well come in, then. It's been a busy day already," she said, stepping aside.

"How so?" I said as we entered her apartment for the second time that day and looked around. Nothing had changed. She didn't invite us to sit down this time, so we stood just inside the door.

"Mrs. Firestone came calling this morning shortly after the likes of you two left. I'd just washed my hair and wasn't looking my best. In fact, I still have to comb it out. No more wave, sadly."

"I'm sure it will still look very nice," Riker said.

"If I ever get enough time alone to attend to it properly," she said. "So much unexpected company on a Monday is unusual, to say the least."

"I wasn't aware you and Mrs. Firestone were well acquainted enough that she would come calling," I said.

"We aren't, or we weren't, anyway. She came by to thank me for being so kind to her husband on his last night alive. And she wanted to invite me to a séance she's holding to summon his spirit tomorrow evening at the hotel."

"We were invited to that, also. It should prove interesting," I said.

"Yes, I was surprised to be included, frankly, but pleased. Anyway, I brewed some tea, and we chatted for a bit. Of course, I spilled my tea all over my blouse, I'm so terribly clumsy, but she was very nice about it and waited while I changed. She seems like a kind woman. I feel so terrible for her having to endure this in a strange city with no one to comfort her."

"She has Mr. Ricci and Mr. Goodacre," Riker said.

"Ugh, yes. Mr. Goodacre is a bit of drip, though, isn't he? I got the impression that night at dinner he didn't really care for Mrs. Firestone, or Mr. Ricci. Mr. Goodacre and Mr. Firestone didn't seem too fond of each other, either. And I don't think Mr. Ricci is the comforting type."

"Possibly not," I said. "Speaking of dinner that night, Miss Lufkin, you mentioned when we were here this morning that Mr. Firestone was sporting a carnation in his lapel."

"That's right. His right lapel, which I thought kind of different. Most men wear carnations on the left."

"The photos the *Journal* photographer took don't show him sporting a carnation at all," I said.

"I saw the newspaper article. It just ran a stock photo of him in his theatrical garb. Of course he wouldn't be wearing a carnation."

"Yes, but I meant in the photos the photographer took that night at dinner, of you, Mr. Firestone and Mr. Goodacre. In none of those pictures did he have a carnation in his lapel, because he didn't purchase that carnation until after dinner, after you supposedly left him. Yet when we questioned you earlier this morning you described him as wearing it that night."

Her face flushed lightly and her hand went to her throat as if to fiddle once again with her chain and letter *F*, but she wasn't wearing it now, so she let her hand drop back down to her side. "Did I?"

"You did. Which means you saw him after he bought it, didn't you?" Riker said. "Sometime between ten and midnight, even though you said you never saw him again after you left him in the dining room of the Blatz."

"Okay, so what if I did see him? I was waiting at the bus stop on Wells to go home after dinner. He came down the street almost right past me, but he never noticed me. He seemed anxious, in a hurry. The bus wasn't due for another twenty minutes, so I figured I'd try and see what he was up to, where he was going. He was acting different, kinda queer. All during dinner, he kept checking his watch, like he had some place to go, so I was curious, you know? So, I tailed him. You know what that means, I suppose."

"You followed him," Riker said.

"That's right. I watched him go into a little flower shop, which also seemed strange being open that time of night. It was just a minute or so after ten. When he came out, he had that carnation on. He even stopped to smell it once or twice. He seemed nervous, always looking around. He paced back and forth in front of the shop for a good ten minutes or so, constantly looking at his watch. I thought for sure he'd see me, but he still didn't. I stuck around, even though I knew I'd miss my bus. The lights went out in the shop, and still Almanzo paced. He checked his watch one more time, crossed the street, and went down a ways and into an alley. As he moved off, another man appeared from out of the shadows, like he'd been waiting for Almanzo to do something, too. I don't think Almanzo noticed him."

"What did the other man do?"

"He just stood there for a short while. Then after a few minutes, he followed Almanzo toward the alley, and I followed him. I felt like I was in a spy film, it was all so cloak and dagger, if you know what I mean."

"Yes, of course," Riker said. "So what happened?"

"The second man stopped on the sidewalk at the entrance to the alley. He took out what looked like a gun, and then I heard a couple of pops, then the second man turned and ran, and I screamed."

"And then?" Riker said.

"The man looked back me cause I was screaming, then he took off again, into the night. I just stood there for a while, shaking and scared. I pulled myself together eventually and went back to the bus stop and came home."

"You didn't call the police? Or call for a doctor?" I said. "Or even check to see if Mr. Firestone was alive?"

"No. I didn't know for sure what had happened, and I really hadn't seen anything specifically. Plus I didn't know if that man was still lurking nearby. I also didn't want to get involved."

"But you were involved. You *are* involved, Miss Lufkin. What did this man with the gun look like? Can you describe him?" Riker said.

"I don't know. Average. Dark suit and hat, clean shaven, I think."

"Would you be able to pick him out of a lineup?" I said.

"A lineup? Gee, wouldn't that be something? Just like in the movies. How exciting! Isn't that exciting?"

"Not how I'd describe it, Miss," Riker said.

"Well, it would be exciting for me. Anyway, I might be able to pick him out of a lineup given the chance. It's hard to say, though there was something different about him."

"Oh? What's that?" I said.

"I can't think of it right now, but it may come to me. If it does, I'll let you know."

"I see. Why didn't you tell us any of this before?"

"I told you, I didn't want to get involved."

"Miss Lufkin, you're a witness to a murder," I said.

She shook her head. "I don't think so. I really didn't see anything, just heard a couple pops, and then I saw a man running, that's all. I couldn't even swear what he was holding was a gun. Maybe it was a pipe or something. Besides, whoever the man was, *if* he shot Almanzo, he was just doing the Lord's work. It's all preordained, you see, like I said before."

"So you think God wanted this man to kill Mr. Firestone? Wouldn't it be easier just to strike him down with a bolt of lightning?" Riker said.

She rolled her eyes and sighed. "People always say things like that, but God doesn't work in that way. He uses people as his instruments."

"A true multi-instrumentalist," I said.

"A what?"

"Someone who can play multiple instruments."

"Don't make fun, Detective. He may strike you down."

"I'll take my chances, but personally I don't think God works that way. He's not vindictive. By the way, if you think of whatever was different about that other man, or anything else, let us know immediately. Here's my card. If I'm not in, you can leave a message at the desk, or ask to speak to Detective Riker."

"I suppose." She took my card, glanced at it, and then set it on the table by the door.

I looked at her hard. "Lying to a police detective is serious, Miss Lufkin, as is omitting evidence. You could get yourself into a lot of trouble. More than you already are."

"I didn't lie, did I? I just didn't mention that I had tailed Firestone."

"You lied about not seeing him again after dinner, and you lied by omission. And you didn't notify the police about seeing a man firing a gun into a dark alley where apparently Mr. Firestone had gone just moments earlier."

"Okay, so arrest me."

"Don't think I wouldn't," I said.

"But you won't. It would never hold up in court, and you know it. I don't even know for sure that man had a gun, and the noises I heard may have been a truck backfiring. Now, if you'll excuse me, I have to get ready for a date, and I still have to comb out my hair."

"A date? On a Monday afternoon?" Riker said.

"It's later this afternoon, and what's wrong with that?"

"Not a thing, not a thing. By the way, I see you're not wearing your gold letter *F* anymore," I said.

Her hand went once more to her throat. "No, I took it off when I washed my hair, and I've misplaced it somewhere. I'm always doing that. I'm clumsy and I lose things."

Well, hopefully it will turn up. Thank you for your time. Good day," I said.

"Good day, gentlemen. Hopefully this will be the last time I see you both today."

"We'll see what we can do, Miss Lufkin," I said, and then we turned and exited, going slowly down the stairs and out on the sidewalk as we put our hats back on.

"You were pretty easy on her, Heath. I mean, she lied to us and omitted evidence," Riker said as we walked to my car.

"I know, but I have a feeling we'll find out more from her by going easy on her, at least for now."

"Why is that? Do you think Miss Lufkin was telling the truth this time? About the second mystery man?"

"I don't know exactly. But I got the feeling she was still keeping something from us."

"Like what?"

"I'm not sure. She seemed like she was being coy about the mystery man she saw."

"Oh?"

"It may be just my imagination. She said something was different about him, but then she couldn't think of what it was. I find that curious."

"Why would she be coy about that?"

"Perhaps Miss Lufkin is lying about there being a second man," I said.

"Hmm. That's possible, I suppose. Maybe she made the mystery man up to take suspicion off of herself."

"It's been done before. We confront her with evidence she was lying about the last time she saw Firestone, so she makes up another lie to cover herself."

"Good theory," Riker said.

"Thanks, but I have another theory, too."

"Do tell."

"That there really was a mystery man that night, but Miss Lufkin wants to keep her options open. She doesn't want to tell us flat out she would never recognize the guy, but she doesn't want to say she would definitely recognize him, either."

"How come?" Riker said.

"Miss Lufkin might be engaged in, or planning to engage in, a little thing called blackmail, possibly with someone we all know, which is why she was being coy. If the person she plans to blackmail doesn't cooperate, she suddenly remembers what he looks like, you see?"

"Ah, yes. And if he *does* cooperate with her, then Miss Lufkin doesn't recall."

"Very probably."

"But if she really did see a man shoot Firestone, that removes Mrs. Firestone and Mrs. Webster from the list of suspects," Riker said.

"Yes, I suppose you're right. Let's get in the car and wait for a bit. If Miss Lufkin's date shows up, I want to see who it is, and if she goes anywhere I want to know where. I want to see what she's up to."

"You mean you want to tail her."

I smiled. "Right you are, Detective."

Chapter Sixteen

Afternoon, Monday, September 15, 1947

I moved my car to the side street and turned it to face the pawnshop just across Oakland. I parked beneath a giant elm, which cast the car in shade, making it difficult to see us should Miss Lufkin leave the building and glance our way. Then we waited, keeping our eyes on the door to the left of the plate glass window. We passed the time talking about Spelling, the chief, Alan, whether or not we thought Jackie Robinson was going to make Rookie of the Year, and how we believed President Truman was doing overall. We were just discussing the rumor that Truman was planning on creating a Central Intelligence Agency when Florence Lufkin made her appearance across the street. She still wore the gray skirt she had on earlier, but now sported a slim, black plaid coat, white gloves, and a black handbag over her right arm. Her freshly combed shoulder-length hair was now down, and on top of it was a black pillbox hat with a pink band.

"There she is, Heath. She must be going to meet her date."

"Yes, I see her. She's heading north, probably to the streetcar stop up the block. Do me a favor and open my glovebox. There's a streetcar map in there, underneath the one for the City of Milwaukee."

"Right," Riker said, opening the glovebox and rummaging around. "Gee, you keep it pretty neat in here."

"It's just the way I like it. Makes it easier to find things. I get rid of stuff that I have no use for."

"I wish you'd tell that to Mary Jane. She even saves old gift wrap. She unwraps every gift carefully, then irons it and puts it away. String, too, and boxes, and every old greeting card she's ever gotten. And don't get me started on her clothes."

I smiled. "A lot of people are like that after living through the Depression. They don't want to throw anything away. Find the Oakland and Locust stop on the map."

He scanned it briefly. "Got it."

"Okay. I'm going to move my car around the corner and up a couple blocks, just close enough so we can see which streetcar she takes."

I moved into position and parked again, sliding down just a bit in the seat so we wouldn't be spotted but could still see her. She waited on the platform for approximately ten minutes, until the southbound streetcar slowed to a stop and she got on.

"All right, what's the next stop for the south bound trolly?"

"Bradford Avenue. Then North Avenue."

"Good, I'll drive us down to the Bradford Avenue stop and see if she gets off there."

We beat the train by a few minutes and waited as it slowed to a stop, discharged a few passengers and took on a few more, but Miss Lufkin did not get off. "On to North Avenue," I said, putting my car in gear again.

We had better luck there, with Florence Lufkin exiting next to last. She adjusted her hat and checked her face in her compact, then started walking east at a steady pace.

"I think we best go by foot from here, Riker," I said, pulling over to the curb and shutting off the engine, "but we'll have to keep our distance."

"Right. Where do you think she's headed?"

"Only one way to find out," I said, climbing out while keeping Miss Lufkin in my line of vision. "Let's go."

We slowly walked two abreast, staying at least a block behind her. She stopped at the corner where North crosses Farwell, opened her handbag, and took out her compact to check her face powder once more. I wondered if she had spotted us in the mirror of her compact, but if so she didn't react. She put the compact back into her handbag and continued on her way, walking briskly until she turned into what looked like a tavern.

"Let's cross to the south side of North Avenue and watch the front door," I said.

"Louie's Bar and Grill," Riker said as we got closer. "Doesn't look like the type of establishment Miss Lufkin would patronize. Kind of seedy and run down."

"Which may be precisely why she chose it."

"Why's that?"

"Because it's unlikely anyone in there would know or recognize her," I said.

"Ah, that makes sense. A perfect place for a secret rendezvous. So now what?"

"Now we wait again. You'll find a large part of detective work is just sitting or standing around waiting. Waiting for something to happen, waiting for someone to appear, waiting for someone to leave, waiting for just about anything and everything."

"Good thing I'm a patient man."

"Yeah, same here. Goes with the job. Here's a dime, go buy a newspaper from that newsstand over there, will ya?" I said.

"Sure, what for?"

"To give us something to do and something to hide behind. We'll look suspicious if we just stand here, but two gents standing on the sidewalk reading a newspaper isn't so unusual."

"Clever. Be right back."

He bought the *Milwaukee Journal* and gave the first section to me, which I opened and pretended to read as I kept my eyes on the front door of Louie's across the street over the top of the page.

"Interesting," I said after a few minutes. "No one else has gone in there."

"What's interesting about that?"

"That means whoever she intended to meet was already there waiting for her, or they're late, or perhaps a no-show."

"Shouldn't one of us go in and see?" Riker said from behind the section of paper he was holding.

I shook my head slightly, the paper rustling in my hands. "As much as I'd love to find out what's going on in there, I don't think it's possible to do it discreetly. It looks like much too small a space, and she knows both of us. We'll just have to wait until she leaves."

"Then when she leaves, we go in and question the bartender about who she was with?"

"Yes. Though I think it might be best to split up at that point, one of us tailing her to see if she makes any other stops."

"Flip a coin?"

"Doesn't matter, you choose."

"Okay, I'll tail her, you go in."

"Fair enough. What time do you have?"

Riker glanced at his wristwatch. "A quarter after three. She's been in there fifteen minutes now."

At a quarter of four, both Riker and I were getting restless. At four, I was beginning to wonder.

"I know I said I was patient, Heath, but how long do we wait? My arms are aching from holding up this newspaper."

"I know. Take a walk up the block and back for a break. I'll do the same when you return."

"Sounds good, thanks." He folded up his paper, tucked it under his arm, and strode west on North Avenue. When he returned, I did the same. It felt good to relax my arms and my body. When I got back to Riker, I asked the time again.

"Four fifteen. She's been in there an hour and fifteen minutes."

I shook my head. "Something's not right. I think we should go in."

"But what if she sees us?"

"It's a chance we'll have to take. A woman like Miss Lufkin wouldn't meet someone at a place like this to begin with unless she had ill intent. And it's doubtful a meeting of ill intent would last over an hour. I'll pull my hat down, go in, and have a quick look around. If I spot her, I'll turn around and leave, like I ducked into the wrong door, hopefully before she recognizes me. I'll take my tie off and try to change my appearance a little, just in case."

"What should I do?"

"Just stay here and keep watching. I'll signal for you if I need you."

"Okay. What's the signal?"

"The signal? I'll open the front door and wave to you or something."

"Oh," he said, looking slightly disappointed. "I thought maybe there was some special thing you did, you know, smoke, or using a mirror to send Morse code or a secret whistle, or something like that."

"You watch too many movies and read too many detective novels, Riker. Just watch the front door."

"Right, will do. Be careful."

"Like I tell Alan and my mother, I always try to be." I crossed the busy street, pulled my hat low, and removed my tie, tucking it into my suit coat pocket before entering. The place was dark, and it took a few moments for my eyes to adjust, but I slowly looked around the interior. Near the door was a Panoram jukebox machine playing a short musical film, but no one was paying much attention to it. A couple of men at the bar were nursing some tap beers. In the far corner sat a man and a shady-looking woman who seemed like they were well acquainted, or about to be, but I saw no sign of Florence Lufkin. Maybe she was in the ladies' room or what passed for one in a joint like that, so I figured I should wait a while before signaling Riker. I stepped up to the bar and ordered a Coke, no ice, pushing my hat back on my head.

When the bartender served it, I gave him a dollar and told him to keep the change.

His eyebrows shot up in surprise. "Thanks, big spender. What brings you in?"

"I'm looking for a girl."

"Aren't we all?" He studied me briefly. "Clean cut, well dressed, big tipper, hmm. We get girls in here from time to time, but I doubt they're the kind you're looking for."

"Actually, I'm looking for one in particular. About five foot four, auburn hair, slender, wearing a gray skirt and black plaid coat, with a black hat that has a pink band around it. Oh, and she's wearing white gloves, or at least she was when she came in."

He laughed heartily. "When you say one in particular, you mean it."

"Yeah, I'm funny that way."

"You're funny all right."

"Have you seen her recently?"

"Yeah, sure. She was here, talking to some fella over at that table there," he said, pointing with a stubby finger, the end of which was missing.

"What did the man she was talking to look like?"

"Nice enough looking, but nothin' special. What's it to you?"

I ignored his question. "When did they leave?"

"I don't know, exactly. Twenty minutes, maybe half an hour at most."

"Where did they go? They didn't leave through the front."

"How do you know that?"

"I was watching, that's all. You have a back door to this place?"

"You ask a lot of questions, friend."

"And you don't provide a lot of answers." I slid off my stool, walked to the door, and stepped outside, motioning for Riker, who quickly discarded the newspaper and jaywalked across the street in a hurry, dodging the heavy traffic as cars honked at him. I turned and walked back to the bar. "I'm a police detective," I said, showing him my badge. "Now where did these two go?"

"I figured you were a cop or a private dick."

"Good deduction."

"She in some kind of trouble?"

"You're going to be in some kind of trouble if you don't tell me where they went, and when. Ever hear of obstruction of justice?"

"All right, all right, I don't want any problems with the cops. The man gave me a couple bucks to let them out the back way."

"I see. How about I give you a couple bucks in exchange for the two he gave you?" I said, hoping to get some fingerprints off them.

"I put 'em in the till. Probably in some other customer's pocket by now."

Riker entered, letting the door slam behind him, and came up next to me as I turned to look at him.

"Is she here?" he said.

"They left out the back, about twenty or thirty minutes ago," I said, and then turned back to the bartender. "Where's the back door?"

"Through the storeroom." He pointed with his thumb to a door just to the left of the bar. "It opens on to the alley. It's where I get my deliveries."

"Right, let's go," I said to Riker.

"Aren't you going to finish your Coke?" the bartender said.

I didn't bother to respond. With Riker following behind, I walked through the storeroom and out the back door into the alley. It was a narrow, dark, foul-smelling space that ran from Murray Street to Farwell Avenue, east to west. It was filled with trash cans, litter, empty bottles, and a few rats that went scurrying and squeaking when we approached.

I wondered what Firestone would have had to say about their actions according to myomancy. We both took out our guns as a precaution.

We stopped just outside the door, each of us looking left to right, and up and down. "No sign of them," Riker said. "But what's that awful smell?"

"Rotting garbage, urine, animal feces, and who knows what else in a place like this." I glanced down at my shoes, already dirty from the muck. "And I wore my good Allen Edmonds today, too. Damn," I said.

"They'll clean up, a little spit and polish. Now what? Back to her place? Or back to the station?"

I paused a moment. "I'm not sure just yet."

"Why would they sneak out the back like that?" Riker said.

"She may have spotted us and wanted to give us the slip. Looks like she did just that. I wish I knew who the man was that she met up with. Ricci? Goodacre? Someone else?"

"Could have been Ricci, based on that mysterious note she sent him," Riker said.

"Yes, possibly. And the fact that he lied about not seeing Firestone again after he stopped by their dinner table. It's possible they were in on Firestone's murder together, and she wanted to meet Ricci here, away from prying eyes and ears, to discuss what to do next, especially now that you and I have been nosing around. Perhaps she glanced out the front door, saw us across the street, and the two of them decided to sneak out the back way."

"Makes sense, Heath. It seems to me we have enough to arrest her and Ricci on suspicion of murder if it turns out he's the one that was here with her."

"Pretty weak case at this point. If only we knew for sure who the man was and what they were doing. The bartender described the man as nice enough looking but nothing special."

"That could be Ricci or Goodacre."

"Or any one of a thousand other guys," I said. "Let me think a moment." I paced up and down the alley, kicking an occasional empty tin can out of the way, and glancing here and there into deep, dark doorways that led to places unknown. I sidestepped a murky oily puddle, and that's when I saw it. One foot, encased in a black shoe, sticking out from behind a few battered trash cans. I stopped short in my tracks and let out a low whistle. "Riker! Come here, quick."

"What is it?"

I holstered my gun, moved a couple of the cans out of the way, and stooped down. "Lorenzo Ricci," I said.

Riker put his gun away and bent down beside me. "I'll be a monkey's uncle. Well, now we know who she met."

"Yes, it would seem so." Ricci's face was a grisly shade of white, drained of all color. I checked his vital signs just to be sure, though there was no question. "He's dead all right. Shot twice, just like Firestone by the looks of it, only Ricci was shot right in the chest."

"How did we not hear the shots?"

"North Avenue is busy, especially this time of day, and we were on the other side of the building across the street. Lots of traffic. Trucks backfire, horns honk, cars rumble by. We probably just missed it."

"Yeah, I suppose so. What's that in his hand?"

I looked closer, prying the fingers of his right hand open. "A gold *F*, on a broken chain. Like the one Flo Lufkin was wearing this morning," I said, careful not to touch the necklace itself.

"Looks like Lufkin's definitely our gal, then."

"But she wasn't wearing it when we spoke with her this afternoon. She said she misplaced it, remember?"

"Maybe she found it and put it on before she left her apartment," Riker said.

"I suppose. I'll have the necklace sent to the lab for fingerprinting."

"If they were in on killing Firestone together, maybe she decided to eliminate him. She felt he might spill the beans. How's the saying go? The only way to keep a secret between two people is if one of them is dead."

"Gruesome but true. Miss Lufkin may have asked him here to discuss the situation, and perhaps she could see he was panicked and nervous, so she decided to do away with him."

"It all adds up," Riker said. "She takes out a gun, they struggle, he pulls off her necklace, and she shoots him then flees."

"But she might have been blackmailing him, like we said before. She sent him a note asking him to meet her here with a payment of some kind or else."

"But if that's the case, why kill him, I wonder?" Riker said.

"Maybe he refused to cooperate. Or maybe he threatened her physically. Or maybe he tried to kill her in the alley, so she killed him first. Or he made the payment as promised, and she decided to kill him anyway to avenge the death of her idol, Almanzo Firestone."

"All good possibilities," Riker said. "I think now we have enough to arrest her."

"You think so?" I said.

"Sure. Don't you?"

"I don't know. Certainly it warrants questioning her more."

"She could have easily taken the gun from the Firestone suite that night, or she may even have her own gun. Maybe she got one from her uncle's pawnshop."

"Maybe. Better get the lab and the coroner out here. We'll need pictures and fingerprints before they take the body away for an autopsy. Take care of that for me, will you?"

"Sure, I can do that."

"Good. We need to question that bartender officially and get his statement, as well as statements from the rest of the patrons who were in there. Don't let anyone leave just yet. Maybe one of them saw or heard something." I took out my pocket watch and noted the time for the record. It was twenty minutes to five. "Better call your wife and tell her you'll be late for dinner tonight, Riker. So much for your promise to be home by six."

"That's a call I'm not looking forward to. What time do you think we'll be done?"

"Hard to say. When we finish here, we still have to go back to the station and write up our reports for the chief. If I had to guess, I'd say we won't get home until eight at least. I'll give Alan a call later and tell him I won't be able to make it to that movie at the Downer."

"I have a feeling Alan will be more understanding than Mary Jane, but that's the way it goes, I guess. Back in a bit," he said, going back into the storeroom.

I stayed in the alley with the body, which was lying in a puddle of murky blood, dirt, and oil. The flies were already swarming about. Nasty little things. I used my handkerchief periodically to mask the smell of the alley until Riker returned.

"All set?"

"Yeah, a black-and-white just got here. They're holding everyone inside until we can question them."

"Okay, we'll do that first."

"Good idea. Most of them were none too happy about not being able to leave. Oh, and the lab and coroner are on their way," Riker said. "I also requested a black-and-white to head over to Miss Lufkin's and have her picked up on suspicion of murder."

"Whoa, we didn't talk about that, Riker. I never okayed that."

"Sure, we talked about it. What do you mean?"

"We discussed it, and I said I wanted to question her further, that's all."

"Oh. But she has to be the murderer, Heath. And we can't let her skip town. If she saw us following her, she could be halfway to Canada by now."

"She may well be the murderer, and she may be on her way to Canada, but having her arrested is premature."

"Sorry. I was just trying to think for myself."

"Do me a favor and don't do that anymore. At least not right now."

He looked sheepish. "Okay, so now what?"

"We could call back and cancel the squad," I said. "Did you call them last?"

"No, I did that first. I called Mary Jane last. She was not happy."

"I imagine not. Well, you're efficient, if nothing else. They've probably already picked Miss Lufkin up at this point, then. Well, let's wait and see what happens. Maybe she'll crack under the strain of being arrested and confess. For now, we've got more work to do."

"At least it looks like Scotty and Mrs. Webster are in the clear," Riker said.

"On that I agree, if the two murders are connected. I can't see any reason why Scotty or Mrs. Webster would have to kill Ricci."

Chapter Seventeen

Morning, Tuesday, September 16, 1947

"Morning," Riker said, coming up to my desk with two cups of coffee in his hands.

"Good morning," I said, looking up at him. "You're actually in late today. It's five after nine. I've been here since eight thirty."

"That's early for you."

"Sometimes. There are days I'm here even earlier. Is one of those for me?" I said, nodding at the two cups in his hands.

"Yes, if you want."

"I definitely want."

"I thought you might. This one is black, just the way you like it," Riker said, holding out the cup in his left hand.

"Thanks," I said as I took it from him and inhaled the aroma. "How was your night?"

"Cold. Cold wife, cold meatloaf, cold green beans, and cold mashed potatoes, served with lukewarm coffee. Mary Jane was pretty annoyed I didn't make it home until almost nine. That's partly why I'm a little late this morning. We had words over breakfast, which consisted of lumpy oatmeal and burned toast."

"Sorry to hear it. I wish I could have let you go last night, but she's going to have to understand that sometimes detective work doesn't punch a clock."

"Yeah. I think she knows that, but that doesn't mean she likes it."

"Probably made worse because you promised her you'd be home by six. You shouldn't make promises you can't keep."

"Bad habit of mine, I guess. Anyway, how was your night?"

"I couldn't sleep, so I spent forty-five minutes trying to clean my Allen Edmonds shoes and get the smell of that alley out of them. I even threw the shoelaces away and put in new ones." I glanced around and saw Spelling standing nearby, looking through one of the filing cabinets. "I was supposed to go to that movie with Ellen last night, but I didn't get home until almost nine, either. Fortunately, she understands these things happen."

"Ellen? Oh, right, Ellen's a good girl. You're lucky to have her," Riker said.

"Yeah, I am."

"What brought you in early?"

"I telephoned the Blatz and spoke with the manager, Mr. Suskind. I told him I wanted Mr. Ricci's room left uncleaned and no one admitted."

"What for?"

"Just thinking about that note Miss Lufkin wrote to Ricci. I'm wondering if it was on his person when he was killed or if perhaps it's in his room. I'd like to know what it actually said."

"Smart thinking. Maybe there's other evidence there, too."

"Yes, that's what I was thinking. We won't know until we look. Mr. Suskind has given us permission to search. You know they always cooperate fully with the police," I said, a slight smile on my face.

"Even though they don't have much reason to. The Blatz is a very safe hotel," Riker said, smiling back.

"In an excellent location. I think we should head over there soon."

"Just say the word. Speaking of Florence Lufkin, anything come up about her arrest? Or shouldn't I ask?"

"They're holding her over at the women's prison. No weapon was found on her person. She's demanded to speak with her lawyer."

"Jeepers, sounds like I really messed that one up."

"Not necessarily, though maybe you were just a tad overeager. Right now I want to wait for the coroner and have a look at the forensics report to see if the bullets they took out of Ricci are from the same gun used to kill Firestone. And I want to search Ricci's hotel room, like I said, and also get a warrant to search Miss Lufkin's apartment. *If* she's the murderer, she might still have the gun in her apartment if she wasn't smart enough to dispose of it."

"I can get started on that warrant if you want."

"Sure, that would be helpful."

"Glad to do it," Riker said, looking at me as he sipped his coffee. "You know, I'm new to this detective thing, but I can tell you've got something else on your mind, too. What is it? In addition to looking tired and worried, you look puzzled."

"Hmm? Oh, yes, I guess I am all those things—tired, worried and puzzled. I'm just not certain Florence Lufkin is our murderer."

"Why?"

"I don't know, really. It's all just too convenient."

"You'll feel better if we find the murder weapon in her apartment," Riker said. "Or if she's confessed."

"Yeah, that would definitely make me feel better. Let me know when you have that warrant approved," I said, taking a large drink of my coffee as the phone on my desk rang. I picked it up quickly, setting my cup back down. "Yes?"

"It's Miss Blake, Mr. Barrington. The chief wants to see you and Mr. Riker pronto in his office."

I sighed. Somehow, I wasn't surprised. "Right, we'll be there five minutes ago." I hung up and looked at Riker. "The chief wants to see us."

"That can't be good. Think it's about Miss Lufkin's arrest?"

I stood up, grabbed my suit coat, and started walking, Riker following behind. "We'll soon find out."

Miss Blake was behind her small desk, outside the chief's office. "Go right in, he's expecting you," she said, never looking up from her typing.

"Right, thanks," I said.

"Uh-huh," she said, pulling out the full sheet of paper and adding a fresh one.

The chief was in his usual place, and I noticed three cigarette butts in his ashtray, the smoke still hanging in the air. He did not look pleased.

"Good morning," I said, trying to sound cheerful.

"Is it? This is my ninth day in a row in this office. I was hoping to go home early today, but now this," he said, pointing to the newspaper atop his cluttered desk. "See the morning *Sentinel*, gentlemen? The headline reads *Alley Cat Killer Strikes Again*."

I glanced at the article then back at the chief. "Sensationalism, that's all. Alley cat killer. Catchy, anyway."

"I don't like catchy, Barrington. I like criminals caught."

"But we did catch her, Chief," Riker said. "We had her picked up last night on suspicion of murder."

The chief scowled at Riker. "And by her, you mean Miss Florence Elizabeth Lufkin."

"That's right, sir."

"It may interest you two to know Miss Lufkin has retained the services of an attorney, a Mr. Hinkley. Apparently he does some work for her uncle, Hugo Petersen, who runs a pawnshop and loan." The chief lit up another cigarette and blew the smoke in our direction.

"Obtaining legal counsel is always a wise idea," I said, trying to discreetly wave the smoke away.

"Yes, Barrington, I know that, and so does she, obviously. I just got off the phone with this Mr. Hinkley. He wants to know why his client was arrested last night. He's threatening to sue the department for false arrest and demanding she be released immediately."

"She was arrested on suspicion of murder, Chief," I said.

"On what evidence and whose order?"

Riker looked most uncomfortable. "Well, I made the call, sir. As for evidence, she was with the victim right before he was shot, and she wrote a note to him beforehand. She admitted writing him the note when we asked her about it. We were with Mr. Ricci when he received it."

The chief's bushy caterpillar eyebrows shot up and came together. "What did the note say?"

"I, uh, don't know for sure, sir. We never actually saw it. Ricci crumpled it up and put it in his pocket," Riker said, clearly flustered. "She claimed it was a condolence note for Mr. Firestone's death, but it might have been a blackmail note asking him to meet her at this bar. It might still be in the pocket of the pants he was wearing when he was shot."

The chief looked like he had a migraine as he puffed on his cigarette. His shirt collar was undone, his tie pulled down, and his shirt sleeves rolled up to his elbows. He picked up a typed piece of paper from his desk. "According to the preliminary report from the morgue, Mr. Ricci's personal effects consisted of a wristwatch, a pencil, a ticket stub to a movie theater in Kansas City, a pair of brass cufflinks, a matching tie pin, a leather coin purse with one thin dime and a nickel inside, a pack of Camels with exactly three cigarettes remaining, a book of matches from some bar in St. Louis, and a worn leather wallet containing an identification card, a condom, a telephone number for some girl named Alma in Minneapolis, a pocket comb, and three one dollar bills. In the inside breast pocket of his suit coat they found a bloodstained letter from his sister in Albuquerque dated two weeks ago, forwarded to the Blatz Hotel by way of the Broadway Hotel in Gary, Indiana. We're attempting to reach his sister via the Albuquerque police department. There was no mysterious note found on Mr. Ricci's person from Miss Lufkin or anyone else. But do go on."

Riker shifted his weight from one foot to the other, then back again. "Well, Ricci probably destroyed it, or maybe it's in his hotel room."

"Riker and I plan on searching his hotel room this morning."

"Talk to Suskind?"

"Yes, sir. He's giving us his full cooperation," I said.

"Figured he would. He's a good man. You say Miss Lufkin was with Mr. Ricci right before he was shot, and that she wrote him some mysterious note. Please tell me you have other evidence you used to warrant having her arrested."

"Yes, sir," Riker said. "Miss Lufkin lied to us the first time we questioned her. She lied about having seen Firestone after dinner the night he was killed. She first told us they parted ways after eating and she never saw him again, but she later confessed she followed Firestone that night, and even saw the man who shot him."

His eyebrows went even higher. "She told you she saw the man who shot the All-Seeing Almanzo, yet you arrested her for his murder?"

Riker looked a little pale now. "Well, she neglected to tell us about this man when we first questioned her. She was obviously keeping something from us. She may have been lying about seeing a man, and if there was a man, she said she may or may not recognize him if she saw him again. And we arrested her on suspicion of killing Ricci, not necessarily Firestone, sir."

"I know you're a new detective, Riker, but you're not that green. You were a cop, for crying out loud. Not telling you the whole truth, even outright lying, doesn't warrant arresting her on suspicion of murder, nor does being with the victim shortly before he was killed, or writing him a mysterious note," the chief said, rubbing his eyes with his left hand, the cigarette burning down quickly in his right.

"But she met him yesterday afternoon at a seedy bar on North Avenue," I said, trying to help. "That's probably what the note was about, like Riker said."

"Can you prove she met him there?" the chief growled. "Did you see the two of them together? Did anyone?"

"Well, no, sir. We interviewed the bartender and patrons after we found his body, but no one could give a positive identification of Mr. Ricci," Riker said.

"I know. I read that in your report."

"But I'm sure it was him that she met," Riker said. "Why else would he be dead in the alley?"

"Any number of reasons, actually," the chief said. "He may have been waiting for her, jealous of whoever it was she met, and that person killed him. Ever think of that?"

"No, sir. I...I guess I didn't. I just figured that when she realized we were tailing her, she and Ricci slipped out the back way. They struggled, and she shot him. A short while later, we found Ricci dead in the alley."

"Yes. As I said, I read your report. And I also read Miss Lufkin's statement. She admits she was at the bar. She claims she met her date there, they had a drink, and then they left out the back. They said goodbye in the alley and she went home alone. She claims she never saw Mr. Ricci."

"Well, of course she'd say that," Riker said.

"And she *did* say that."

"But obviously she's lying. Did anyone ask her who this date was? Did anyone talk to him?"

"Mr. Riker, I shouldn't have to tell you that corroborating or contradicting her story is part of your and Mr. Barrington's job as the lead detectives on this case—not mine or anyone else's."

"Yes, sir. I'm sorry, sir," Riker said.

"We'll get right on that, sir."

"Do that, Barrington. In the meantime, do either of you have any other evidence to hold Miss Lufkin?"

"Oh, I almost forgot!" Riker looked excited suddenly. "Yes, I do.

I mean, we do. Ricci was clutching in his hand a gold letter *F* attached to a broken chain, just like the one Miss Lufkin was wearing when we spoke with her yesterday morning."

"That wasn't listed in the report from the morgue of his personal effects," the chief said.

"That's because when the coroner arrived, I had it put in an evidence bag and sent to the lab last night to be dusted for fingerprints. I did mention that in my report, sir," I said.

The chief scowled at me, shifted through some papers beneath the morning *Sentinel*, and then picked one up, scanning through it. "Right. I see that now. I must have missed it the first time. Well, that's something to go on, at least." He ground out what was left of the cigarette and picked up one of the phones on his desk. "Miss Blake, call the women's jail and have Florence Lufkin's prints sent over to our lab and compared against the gold chain found on Lorenzo Ricci's body. Might as well have her whole file sent over while you're at it. Send it special courier. I want it yesterday." He hung up the telephone without another word and stared at us. "I'll let you both know when it gets here."

"Right, thanks, Chief," I said.

"You're dismissed."

"Yes, sir," Riker and I both said.

Riker and I left his office, our tails between our legs. Miss Blake was on the phone requesting Miss Lufkin's file.

"Jeepers, he seemed pretty sore," Riker said.

"Rightly so. He takes the heat for everything we do."

"But I still say Florence Lufkin is our gal. Want me to get to work on that warrant to search her apartment?"

"Might as well, though I'm not sure if we'll use it. I have a couple other ideas."

"Like what?" Riker said. "Searching Ricci's hotel room to see if we can find that note?"

"Yes, and I want to talk to Miss Lufkin again once she's released to find out the name of this supposed date she was with."

"I'm willing to bet she won't be able to tell us anything. She'll say something like she only knew his first name and doesn't have any way to contact him."

"It's possible. It's also possible she's telling the truth."

"Maybe, but I just don't see it, Heath."

"Don't close your eyes to anything until you're sure, Grant. I'll let you know when the chief calls."

"Okay, see you in a bit. You know, I feel just like I did the night my daughter was born, pacing in the waiting room at the hospital, anxious, nervous, and slightly nauseous."

"I know the feeling," I said. I walked back to my desk and Riker went to his. And then we waited.

It was well over an hour before Miss Blake summoned us to the chief's office again. I closed the door behind us and we both stood in front of him, trying to read his expression.

"What did you find out, Chief?" I said.

"The file arrived a little over half an hour ago along with the prints, which went directly to the lab for analysis, which I asked them to rush."

"And?" Riker said, anxiously.

"The analysis just came back. Inconclusive."

Riker looked crestfallen. "Really?"

"Yes," the chief said. He picked up the file from his desk and flipped it open. "The chain and gold letter were too small to lift any complete prints from, and the partial prints they did manage to get were smudged. Inconclusive. There's just not enough evidence to hold her at the moment, and no reason we can do so legally."

"But even if they couldn't get any prints, that necklace has to belong to Miss Lufkin. She was wearing one just like it yesterday morning," Riker said. "I mean, it's too coincidental that there would be two people involved in this case that wore a chain with the letter *F* on it."

"That may well be, Riker, but without fingerprints we can't prove it belonged to her." The chief picked up the phone again. "Miss Blake, contact Miss Ryerdon at the women's jail and arrange for the release of Miss Lufkin. That's right, charges are dropped for now. I'll sign the paperwork. Right." He hung up the phone and stared from Riker to me.

"Sloppy, boys, sloppy."

"I'm sorry, sir. I take full responsibility," I said.

"Good, because I'm blaming you, Barrington. Solve this case, but make it tidy, understand?"

"Yes, sir," I said.

"You two are dismissed. Again." He lit up yet another cigarette as we left his office.

"Good day, Miss Blake," I said as we passed her desk.

"Uh-huh," she said, not looking up.

"Gee, Heath, the chief shouldn't have blamed you. It was my idea to have her picked up," Riker said when we got back to my desk.

"I know, believe me, I know. But I'm the senior dick, so I shoulder the responsibility."

"I'm sorry. I'll make it up to you."

"You will, don't worry."

"What are you thinking? You said before you were mulling over some new ideas."

"Beats the hell out of me anymore," I said. "Did you get that warrant?"

"I submitted the paperwork to the judge while we were waiting for the chief to call us back, but we probably won't hear for a few hours at best."

"All right. Let's head back to the Blatz, have a look around Ricci's room, and talk with Mrs. Firestone and Mr. Goodacre. They're probably wondering what's happened to Ricci, and I doubt anyone's notified them yet of his death."

CHAPTER EIGHTEEN

Late morning, Tuesday, September 16, 1947

We stopped briefly at the front desk of the Blatz Hotel to get the key Mr. Suskind had left for us to room 402. Mr. Billings wasn't on duty, but the clerk handed it over to us no questions asked once we showed him our badges. From there we went directly to the elevators and then to room 402, not bothering to knock. The door swung open quietly, and we stepped in, closing it behind us. The drapes were open, the bed made, and the lights off. Ricci's dirty clothes were piled on the desk chair and a pair of his soiled underwear hung from the table lamp. Stale cigarette smoke hung in the air.

"He certainly wasn't the clean and tidy type," Riker said, looking about.

"No, he wasn't. Smells in here, too, like a mix of vomit, bourbon, and cigarette smoke. I feel sorry for the hotel maid who has to clean this place up." I opened the closet, noting a green suit, a couple of neckties, a pair of brown leather shoes, a pair of brown trousers, and two dress shirts. On the floor next to the suit sat a battered leather suitcase. "Take a look through the dresser and the desk, and through the pockets of the clothes on that chair, while I look through the things in here."

"Right, will do."

I searched carefully but found nothing out of the ordinary—a button in one of the suit pants pockets, a piece of unchewed chewing gum, and a lone sock, balled up inside the suitcase. I put everything back where it was and closed the closet door, turning to Riker. "Find anything?"

"No, sir, not really. Just his socks and underwear in the dresser. In the pockets of the clothes on the chair, I got a brown shoelace, and two phone numbers on slips of paper, one for a girl named Agnes, and another for a Dolly Sinclair. Dolly's has two stars drawn next to it, along with an address here in Milwaukee."

"Ricci worked fast. They just got to town on Friday, and according to him, he didn't go out Saturday night."

"But remember Mrs. Firestone said he *did* go out Friday night. That's where he most likely met Dolly, and maybe Agnes, too."

"Two for a Friday night," I said. "What about the desk?"

"A fresh bottle of bourbon in the bottom drawer, an ashtray with four cigarette butts in it, all Camels, a box of matches, a fresh pack of cigarettes, and a theater program for the performance Saturday night. That's about it."

"Hmm. I'll search the bathroom. Take a look under the bed and through the nightstands," I said.

"Okay."

The bathroom didn't take long. Just the usual toiletries lined up on the sink, an open package of condoms, and a wad of used tissue in the wastebasket. The floor had what looked like a dried puddle of urine on it. I poked my head out when I'd finished. "Any luck?"

"I found a hotel envelope with two playing cards in one of the drawers. Kind of odd. A six of hearts torn in half, and the king of spades."

"That's it?" I said.

"That's all that was in the envelope. Must have been some kind of magic trick or something. But he certainly liked his girlie magazines. There must be four or five of them in the one nightstand drawer. I flipped through them all, thinking maybe the note had been tucked inside, but unfortunately not. Some of the pages were stuck together, but I managed to get them apart."

"I don't want to think about why they were stuck together."

"Ricci clearly liked the ladies."

"And they clearly liked him, including Agnes and Dolly. Good thinking to look between the pages of the magazines, but I doubt he would have gone to much trouble to hide that note. In fact, there wasn't even a reason for him to keep it. So, if it wasn't on his person, and it isn't lying about, it's probably not here."

"He must have thrown it away or destroyed it," Riker said.

"Seems likely. But it was worth a shot."

"What next?"

"I've an idea. Hand me that slip of paper with Dolly's phone number, will you?"

"Sure," Riker said, retrieving it from the pants pocket draped over the chair. "Here ya go."

"Thanks." I moved over to the desk, lifted the telephone receiver, asked the hotel operator for an outside line, and then dialed *O*.

"Operator," a soft female voice said.

"Klondike 5 4947, please," I said, reading from the scrap of paper with two stars on it.

"One moment, please."

She connected me, and it rang four times. Finally, on the fifth ring, another female voice, less soft, answered.

"Hello?"

"Dolly, it's Larry Ricci," I said, trying to mimic his voice as best I could. "Lorenzo."

"You've got a lot of nerve. You were supposed to take me to dinner last night. I canceled my bridge game and sat by the phone until almost ten o'clock."

"Sorry, doll, I got tied up."

"I bet, and I bet I know who tied you up. The one who walked in on us in your hotel room Sunday night. The one you said was just a friend, only you seemed a little too friendly. I should have known. Men. Lying, dirty, double-crossing men."

"I'll make it up to you. It was all a misunderstanding."

"And why should I believe you? You can drop dead for all I care."

"Now listen, dollface—"

"You listen. You're a typical love 'em and leave 'em type, I should have known better. You'll be leaving town, and I'll never see or hear from you again, and that will be too soon for me!" She slammed the phone down. I hung up and turned to Riker.

"What was that all about?" he said.

"Apparently, Ricci was supposed to go to dinner with Dolly last night, and she was pretty irked that he stood her up, so she's not aware yet that he's dead. Also, someone walked in on the two of them here in Ricci's room on Sunday night," I said, "someone he may have also been involved with."

"You think it could have been Mrs. Firestone?"

"Possibly. Or maybe Miss Lufkin, or even Agnes. Or all of the above, or someone else entirely. Obviously Ricci wasn't a one-woman kind of guy."

"But you said one of them walked in on Mr. Ricci and this Dolly, and I get the feeling they weren't playing canasta at the time," Riker said.

"I get the feeling you're right. If he was also involved with whoever walked in on him, that person must have been pretty angry, I'm guessing. Curiously, Dolly never said it was a woman specifically."

"You mean it may have been a man?"

"Possibly. Maybe Ricci played for both teams, like someone else I know," I said, looking at him.

"That's hard to believe, but I guess he could have. And don't look at me like that. By the way, you're pretty good with voice impressions. You sounded a lot like Ricci."

"Thanks, I guess I was believable."

"You were. Now what?"

"Now we break the news to Mrs. Firestone and Mr. Goodacre about Mr. Ricci's demise, assuming they haven't already heard."

I locked the door to 402 behind us, and we went next door to the Valentine Suite, knocking on the door to the sitting room. Getting no response there, we moved down the hall to the suite's bedroom door, but there was no answer there, either. Finally we tried Mr. Goodacre's room at the end of the hall. Better luck this time, as he answered the door, looking crisp and neat in a white shirt, blue tie, and black pleated trousers with freshly shined black cap toe shoes.

"Oh, you two again."

"We get that a lot, it seems. Good morning, Mr. Goodacre. Do you by chance know where Mrs. Firestone is?" I said.

"She's here with me, actually. We were just discussing plans and arrangements for the future."

"Plans and arrangements?" I said.

"That's right. How best to go about finalizing everything, now that the tour's been officially canceled. Some of the theaters are willing to give us our deposits back, but some aren't. Some have already sold tickets that will need to be refunded. It's complicated."

"I can imagine. I'm sorry to interrupt, but we'd like to speak with both of you if we may."

"If you must. You can put your hats on the dresser." He stood aside and motioned us in. Mrs. Firestone was by the window, still dressed in black but not wearing a hat, veil, or gloves. She looked tired.

"Mrs. Firestone," I said. "I hope we're not intruding."

She turned her head and stared at us. "Of course you're intruding. What a silly thing to say. What do you want?"

"It's about Mr. Ricci," Riker said.

"What about him?" she said.

"Yes, what about him? I knocked on his door earlier but there was no answer," Goodacre said, closing the door and moving into the room with us. "As much as I dislike the man, I figured he should be in on this conversation. Have you checked the bar?"

"Then I take it neither of you have heard," I said, ignoring his last comment. "I regret to inform you Mr. Ricci is dead."

"What?" Goodacre said.

"It happened late yesterday afternoon," I said, looking from Goodacre to Mrs. Firestone.

"Are you sure?" Mrs. Firestone said. She sat down on the bed by the window. "Maybe he's just in an alcohol-induced coma."

"No, ma'am, he's definitely dead. I know this must come as a shock to you both, so soon after Mr. Firestone's death," I said. "Please accept our condolences."

"But how? Why? Did he fall and hit his head or something?" Goodacre said.

"No, sir, it does not appear to be accidental or self-inflicted," Riker said. "He was murdered."

"Murdered? Him, too?" Mrs. Firestone said. "Oh my, I need a glass of water."

Riker went to the bathroom and returned with a tumbler full of water. He handed it to her on the bed. "I'm sorry it's not very cold, ma'am."

She took the glass and sipped the water delicately, leaving red lipstick prints on the rim. "It's fine. Thank you. You say it happened yesterday afternoon?"

"That's right."

"And you're just now informing us?" Mr. Goodacre said.

"My apologies for the delay, but I'm surprised you hadn't already heard. It was in this morning's newspaper," I said.

She looked at me. "We're from out of town, Detective. Why would we read the local news? I don't even listen to the radio news broadcasts. It's all too depressing, and most of it doesn't apply to us."

"Some people like to know what's happening in the world," I said. "But maybe in your line of work you rely more on crystal balls, tarot cards, and all that."

"Even at a time like this you like to make fun, to mock," she said.

"You're right, of course. My apologies," I said sincerely.

"I can't believe it. Why would someone kill Lorenzo?" Goodacre said. "One of his lady friends, perhaps, in a jealous fit?"

"That remains to be seen," I said. "It's also possible whoever killed him also killed Almanzo. They were both shot to death in alleys."

"Oh dear. But if that's the case, that means it probably wasn't a random mugger," Goodacre said.

"That would seem to be correct," I said. "By the way, where were the two of you yesterday afternoon between three and five?"

"Here—where else would we be?" Mrs. Firestone said.

"Together?"

"No, of course not. I was in the lobby most of the afternoon catching up on my correspondence. I had to write friends and family and let them know about Alfred. It was a difficult task, but it had to be done. I also chatted with that nice Mr. Billings at the front desk. Mr. Goodacre was here in his room, I presume."

"That's right, I was. I had a frightful headache and a terrible stomachache. I don't think the fish I had for lunch agreed with me."

"Neither of you were near that alley where Mr. Ricci was shot?" Riker said.

"No, sir, I certainly was not. Dark alleys frighten me," Mr. Goodacre said, and then looked at Mrs. Firestone, who glared at us.

"I certainly was not, either. Unlike my husband, I stay away from dark alleys, Mr. Barrington."

"Of course, but I had to ask."

"Because that's the type of person you are," she said, finishing the water and setting down the glass.

"Also because that's the type of person I am, I have to ask if anyone can prove you were where you say you were yesterday."

"Mr. Billings would vouch for me," Mrs. Firestone said, "if you feel it's necessary to check. I went to the lobby around two in the afternoon, and stayed until nearly five."

"You were in the lobby the entire time?"

"I went upstairs to powder my nose once or twice, but otherwise yes, I never left."

"And you, Mr. Goodacre?" Riker said.

"I was in my room, so no witnesses, really."

"I see."

"I did call for room service, though. About a quarter of three, I called down and asked them to bring me up some saltines and an Alka-Seltzer. When they got there I asked them to come in and set it on the desk. I got up, ate the saltines and took the Alka Seltzer, and went back to bed. About an hour later, I called for them to come pick up the tray."

"So, the switchboard and room service can confirm you were in your room from at least three to four."

"Yes, I'm sure they could."

"Well, I'm glad you're feeling better, Mr. Goodacre," I said.

"Thank you. So am I, though this is all most upsetting."

"Most definitely. So, now what?" Mrs. Firestone said.

"Ma'am?" Riker said.

"I mean, my husband and his associate have both been murdered, just days apart. Am I to be next? Or Mr. Goodacre?"

"Me?" Goodacre exclaimed nervously.

"There's no reason to believe either of you are in danger," I said.

"Had he asked, I'm sure that's what you would have told Ricci yesterday morning, yet here he is dead," Mrs. Firestone said.

"I do suggest you both take precautions. I would advise against going out of the hotel alone at any time," I said.

"How long do you intend to force us to stay in this dangerous city?" Goodacre said.

"I don't think it will be long. What do the cards tell you, Mrs. Firestone?" I said.

"I haven't consulted my tarot card deck, and it's not used for that, regardless. It doesn't answer random questions."

"I have a random question perhaps you could answer," I said. "I understand you visited Florence Lufkin early yesterday morning."

"Yes, that's right. How did you know that?"

"It's my business to know things, Mrs. Firestone. Why did you call on her?"

"I wanted to thank her for being so kind to Almanzo on his last night on earth. She was the president of his admirers here in town, you know."

"Yes, all sixteen of them."

"I also wanted to invite her to the séance this evening. She seemed delighted by the idea and assured me she'd come."

"Surely you're not still planning on going ahead with that?" Riker said.

"Of course I am, now more than ever. Two unexpected deaths of people who were close to me, so close together. It's an opportunity that doesn't present itself often. I hope you'll both be in attendance. It could even prove beneficial to you in solving your case."

"I would find that most unusual and surprising, Mrs. Firestone."

"You are a true disbeliever, Mr. Barrington, but the dead can sometimes have much to tell us. As a spiritualist, I don't see it as an end, but merely a continuation to a different plane, a different form of existence. I'm saddened and shocked by the loss of my husband, and by Mr. Ricci's death, but I take comfort in knowing I can contact them at any time, and that I will see them both again soon."

"How fascinating. And what about you, Mr. Goodacre? Is that how you see death?"

"Well, uh, I must admit this has all been very distressing to me. Most upsetting. And frightening, but I understand what Mrs. Firestone is saying and why she feels the way she does."

"If you insist on holding this séance, Mrs. Firestone, I think you can count on me and Mr. Riker here attending."

"I'm glad to hear it, but you won't get much out it if your mind is closed, Detective."

"Oh, I think I can pry it open for an evening, and I'm sure Mr. Riker can do the same. We'll see you at seven, in the sitting room of your suite."

"Where is Mr. Ricci now?" Mr. Goodacre said.

"His soul has moved to the afterlife," Mrs. Firestone said. "Or near it. I can feel it hovering between the two worlds."

"Yes, yes, I know," Goodacre said, suddenly irritable. "But I mean his body. Where is he? Where is it?"

"The city morgue," I said. "The same place as Mr. Firestone until someone makes arrangements for his internment or the transfer of his body, perhaps back to his hometown. The department is attempting to contact his family. We found a letter from a sister in Albuquerque on his person. Are you aware of any other relations?"

"No, not really, I'm afraid," Goodacre said. "Muriel?"

"He spoke of his sister, Margaret, in New Mexico a few times, but other than that no one. If there is anyone else, his sister will know," Mrs. Firestone said. "As for Almanzo, I've sent a wire to his cousin and his one remaining uncle. They both live in Dubuque. Once I hear from them, I'll proceed with funeral arrangements. And as I said, I notified everyone else I could think of via post yesterday afternoon."

"Okay. And do either of you know why anyone would wish to kill Mr. Ricci?" Riker said.

"Perhaps someone had a grudge against spiritualists. Thankfully I'm just a manager," Goodacre said.

"But you're still a part of his entourage, Clive, so I'd keep your door locked, if I were you," Mrs. Firestone said.

Goodacre shuddered at the thought. "Say, maybe it was that fan club girl. She didn't seem to care for Lorenzo much."

"She'd be one of the few females who didn't," Mrs. Firestone said. "Though come to think of it, while Clive was trying to clean up the rug where she'd spilled her drink, she did sit at the desk that had the gun in its drawer. She could have easily taken it."

"Did you notice that, Mr. Goodacre?"

"I did see her sit over there, mainly to get out of the way while I was busy on my hands and knees. The hotel would certainly charge us for a stain like that on the carpet. I wasn't paying much attention to what any of the others were doing at that point, but she could have stolen the gun and murdered Ricci. I'm not sure why she'd want to kill Almanzo, though, but she may have had her reasons. She is an unusual girl, and she did seem emotionally unstable."

"Yes, I noticed that, too," Mrs. Firestone said.

"Right, well, my condolences to each of you once again. We'll see you tonight," I said. We picked up our hats and left, Mr. Goodacre closing the door behind us. Riker and I took the elevator to the lobby, and then we walked out to Wells Street.

"I'm confused, to say the least," Riker said.

"In what way?"

"In every way. I'm not used to people like that."

"There's no one kind of person, for better or worse," I said as we headed for my car.

"That's the truth. Interesting they didn't give each other an alibi."

"I noticed that, too. They could have easily said they were together yesterday afternoon if they were guilty."

"Right. Curious."

"Unless only one of them is guilty, or neither of them, and they're both telling the truth. Or they're both more clever than they appear."

"It's all enough to give me a headache. Say, how about some lunch? I'm hungry."

"Sorry, but I can't today. I have a tea date with my aunt Verbina at the Pfister."

"Oh, yeah. I remember you saying you have tea with her once a month."

"More or less, yes, when I can. She's quite a gal. You'd like her."

"No doubt. I'll just eat my meatloaf sandwich, green beans, and chocolate cake in the break room back at the station then. By myself."

"Sounds tasty."

"Leftovers from last night. I'll hold down the fort in case anything comes up."

"Right. Do me a favor, though. Give Mr. Billings a call and follow up on Mrs. Firestone's statement that she was in the lobby all afternoon yesterday. Also, verify Goodacre's alibi with the hotel switchboard and room service."

"Sure, I can do that."

"Thanks. I'll drop you back, but we'll have to hurry. My aunt does not tolerate tardiness. If you need me, call the Pfister and have me paged. I should be back by one thirty."

CHAPTER NINETEEN

Afternoon, Tuesday, September 16, 1947

I got to the Pfister hotel at 12:35 and found my aunt Verbina waiting for me in the lobby. She wore a smart red hat with a veil that just covered her eyes. To complement that, she had put on a red jacket over a white blouse, which accented her red and white striped skirt. Her earrings matched her brooch, which went nicely with her pearls. She checked her watch as I approached, tapping it impatiently with a gloved finger. "Five minutes late, my dear," she said.

"Sorry, darling. Business. Waiting long?"

"Never too long for you, and you know it."

I smiled. "I do, and I love you for it. I truly am sorry. I'm also afraid I don't have a lot of time. I need to be back to the station by one thirty."

"Well, then, let's get to it, shall we?" she said, looking up at me, her eyes merry and gay.

We crossed to the dining room, her on my arm, where the maître d' ushered us to a small table by a window for our afternoon tea. He held Verbina's chair for her, unfolded our napkins, placed them in our laps, and then handed us our menus. "Gilbert will be attending you both today, and will be with you shortly," he said, and then stepped quietly back to his station at the door to the lobby.

I put my hat on one of the empty chairs at our table and unbuttoned my suit coat with a happy sigh as a busboy appeared with water and then disappeared just as quickly after filling our crystal glasses. "It's good to be here with you, Auntie, truly. A welcome respite from the cares of the world."

"Thank you, dear. I feel the same way. I look forward to our monthly afternoon tea dates. And Gilbert always takes such good care of us, though that's probably partly due to the fact you tend to overtip."

"Good service is worth it," I said. "He's quite capable." *And he has a nice behind*, I added silently to myself.

Verbina looked at me as if she could read my thoughts. "Quite capable indeed, and then some. Shall we have the usual?" she said, scanning the petite menu briefly.

I smiled. "Why mess with perfection?" I gestured for Gilbert and gave him the order, two Earl Greys, warm scones with raspberry jam, and a side of heavy cream. Gilbert took it down on his pad with a little silver pencil, retrieved our menus, and with a slight nod of his head, turned and headed off toward the kitchen. I watched him go, a slight smile on my lips.

"So, what's new with you and Mr. Keyes?" Verbina said, pulling off her white gloves and setting them on top of her pocketbook.

"Hmm?" I said, diverting my attention back to her. "Oh, we're getting along really well, I think. He's been spending quite a bit of time over at my place."

Verbina raised a painted-on brow ever so slightly. "I hope you're being careful regarding your reputation, Heath. You can't afford nasty rumors, especially after that incident with Larry Crow trying to blackmail you."

"We're both being cautious, don't worry. I asked Alan to move into a two-bedroom with me. That way it would appear we were just roommates, saving money."

Her plucked eyebrows went up just a touch higher. "Oh my, that seems sudden, doesn't it?"

"We've known each other seven months already. It seems to me you married one of your husbands in less time."

"Hmm, point taken. What did Mr. Keyes say?"

"He said he had to think about it."

"Sounds like a wise man indeed. Why rush into things? Look how that marriage of mine turned out, after all."

"I know, but—"

She raised a hand to stop me in mid-sentence. "But you feel like you've known him your whole life, he makes you happier than anyone else has, and you want to be with him now and forever, to grow old together."

"Well, uh, yes, something like that. He's my best friend. I trust him with my life, my heart, with my everything, because I know he'll always be there for me, and me for him."

Verbina sighed. "Did you tell him any of that when you asked him to move in?"

"What? No."

"What did you say, exactly?"

"I don't know. I said something about how it would make sense financially, and that he's over to my place all the time anyway, and with a two-bedroom it would seem like we were just roomies, like I said, so we wouldn't have to sneak around."

"Tsk, tsk. Have I taught you nothing about romance all these years?"

I laughed. "*You* teach *me* about romance? You're a self-confirmed realist, a pragmatist, and all business. You have often told me marriage is nothing more than a partnership, a sizing up of what each can bring to the table. I don't recall you *ever* talking about romance."

She looked annoyed. "Then I have failed you. It's quite true that romance, my dear nephew, is but a temporary feeling of excitement and mystery that will soon fade."

"Now, that sounds like something you would say!"

"Because it's true, but not everyone sees it that way, including your Mr. Keyes. He's a romantic, for better or worse, and if you want to succeed with those types, you have to approach things on their level. You won't sway him by quoting statistics and reasons. Take him out to dinner at some private, dark, romantic place. Tell him how you really feel about him, and then ask him again."

"But what if he says no? Or that he still has to think about it? I'll have made a fool of myself."

"If he says no, take it as a temporary rejection. From what I've seen and from what you've told me, Mr. Keyes is just as smitten with you as you are with him. But prepare yourself either way. Personally, I think you've already made a fool of yourself by asking him the way you did the first time."

"Gee, thanks."

"You know it's true. These things take proper planning and strategy. Happily ever after has to be created and bartered for. It doesn't just happen. If you don't make things right, you'll prove yourself a fool. You and Mr. Keyes have a great deal to offer each other, and you will form a strong partnership, but you have to get him to agree. And to do that, you have to appeal to him on his level."

Gilbert arrived with our tea, scones, and jam. After he poured and stepped discreetly away, Verbina said, "By the way, I believe you told me on the telephone that you're working on a new case, aren't you? That magician's murder?"

"Spiritualist."

"Magician, spiritualist, it's all hocus pocus."

"Don't say that in front of Alan. He's somewhat of a believer."

"Well, everyone has their faults. What was that man's name again? Fire something. Firewood? Fireplace?"

"Firestone."

"Oh, yes. It was in the morning and evening papers and on the radio. Grisly, simply grisly. I suppose you can't share any details."

"You suppose correctly, Auntie. Police business, on a need-to-know basis only."

She sighed. "Oh well, it will all come out eventually, when you find Mr. Flintstone's killer."

"Firestone."

"What? Yes, Firestone. That's what I said."

"Actually you said Flintstone."

"Don't correct me, Heath, it's rude. And Flintstone is a noble name. The name of the great Saxon gods."

"Yes, well, the man who was murdered was named Firestone."

"Of course he was, that's what I said. And now there's been a second murder, according to the paper this morning. They say it could be the work of a serial killer, aptly named the Alley Cat Killer."

"Yes, I'm well aware of what the papers said. The chief read it to me personally."

"He did? Oh my, that doesn't sound good at all. Can you at least tell me if you have any leads? If the investigation is going well?"

"I do, and it's not. I must confess I'm puzzled and confused, by everything and everyone, including Alan."

"You'll figure it out, dear. You always do. By the way, how's your dear cousin Liz?"

"She's fine. I need to call her soon."

"Tell her hello for me, and your Mr. Keyes, too." She glanced at the watch suspended from a chain about her neck. "Oh, look at the time. It's nearly one, and you said you have to leave by a quarter after. Don't worry about me. I'll have the hotel call me a taxi."

"I can drive you home."

"Don't be silly, I'll be fine. I got here by myself, didn't I? And I'll be sure and avoid any alleys and alley cats, just in case. Hurry up now and finish, but don't gobble or gulp. And stir your tea back and forth, not round and round, dear. Simply hold your spoon vertically and move it back and forth, like a paddle."

I smiled. "You never change, Auntie, and for that I am forever grateful."

CHAPTER TWENTY

Afternoon, Tuesday, September 16, 1947

I made it back to the station at one thirty on the dot, signed in, and got upstairs to my desk, where I found the coroner's and forensic reports on Ricci waiting for me.

I hung up my suit coat and hat, had a seat, and looked over the reports carefully, taking notes. I also took the time to study the books I'd gotten on spiritualism, séances, the occult, crystal balls, and tarot cards once more. When I had finished, I motioned for Riker to join me.

"How was the lunch date with your aunt?" he said, making himself comfortable in the chair next to my desk.

"Fine, if a little rushed. I didn't want to be gone too long."

"I understand. They released Miss Lufkin. I'm assuming she's back at her apartment by now."

"Good. I'm sure she's plenty steamed at us," I said.

"Yes, I'm sure she is, but you still want to question her about the man she said was her date, don't you?"

"I do," I said, "but first things first. The coroners and forensics reports were waiting for me when I got back. I just finished looking them over."

"Oh? What did they say?"

"According to the forensics report, the bullets from Firestone and Ricci came from the same gun all right."

"Wowzer, so the same person killed them both."

"It appears that way. If only we could find the gun. Any news on that warrant?"

"Still waiting on Judge Whitaker. It was delivered to him, so all he has to do is sign it."

"Can't rush a judge, unfortunately," I said.

"I imagine not. What did the coroner's report say?"

"Firestone was shot from about ten feet away, Ricci from about six feet. Ricci died almost instantly. Interestingly, he didn't have any scratches or marks on his face or body. No hair or skin under his fingernails, and none of his clothing appeared ripped or torn, just bloodstained and dirty from lying in the alley."

"So, there was no struggle," Riker said, sounding disappointed.

"Apparently not. If Ricci had grabbed Florence Lufkin's chain in an attempt to fight her off or while attacking her, there most likely would have been some marks on his face or neck, or he would have been shot at close range as they struggled, not head-on from six feet away."

"But then how did Ricci end up clutching Lufkin's necklace?" Riker said.

"We don't know for certain it *was* her necklace. Only that it was similar to the one she wore."

"But it had an *F* on it," Riker said.

"Lots of names start with *F*."

"True, but like I said before, it's too coincidental two people involved in this case wore a chain with the letter *F* on it."

"Yes, I know. But at this point, we can't prove it belongs to her, and we can't prove it doesn't."

"Well, I still think it's pretty cut and dried. Miss Lufkin and Ricci were having an affair. They perhaps met backstage in Minneapolis when she went there to see Firestone's show. He got her the gun and convinced her to kill Firestone after telling her about his sexual activities. What Firestone was doing was unnatural to her, unseemly, disgusting. She probably believed God wanted her to shoot him. That note Ricci received was most likely from her, asking him to meet her in that bar. Maybe she decided she wanted money for her part in the killing, or she just wanted to see him, to profess her love for him. He goes to meet her and breaks things off with her, but asks her for her necklace as a remembrance or something. She gives it to him, then shoots him when they go out to the alley, angry and heartbroken."

"Interesting and plausible."

Riker beamed. "Thanks. I think so, too."

"Were you able to reach Mr. Billings at the Blatz?"

"Yes, quite a chatty fellow. He confirmed Mrs. Firestone spent the afternoon in the lobby from about three until nearly five, writing notes and letters at one of the desks and visiting with him. Mondays are slow days in the hotel business."

"I can imagine. So her alibi checks out. Interesting."

"Yes, and so does Mr. Goodacre's. Room service records show he called down for saltine crackers and an Alka-Seltzer at two minutes past three, and then he called again to have the tray picked up at three minutes after four."

"Good thing for Mr. Goodacre the Blatz keeps good records," I said.

"Yeah, so now what?" Riker said.

"Now we wait to see if the judge approves that warrant. Just in case your theory isn't quite correct, I still want to question Miss Lufkin about that supposed date of hers, but we might as well wait until we have the warrant and go over to search her place. At this point, if she *is* the murderer, I'd rather her think she's off the hook for now, just in case she hasn't yet disposed of the gun."

"And if the judge doesn't get the warrant back to us today?"

"Tomorrow's another day. I'm sure the judge will have the warrant by morning."

"I guess it's true what you said before. Being a detective is all about waiting for something to happen, waiting for someone to appear, waiting for someone to leave, and waiting for just about anything and everything."

"True words, Riker. If we don't get that warrant by six tonight, we'll go have dinner and go to that séance afterward. Better call your wife again. It's going to be another late night."

Chapter Twenty-one

Evening, Tuesday, September 16, 1947

The warrant still hadn't been approved by six, so Riker and I signed out and grabbed some dinner downtown, getting to the Blatz just a few minutes to seven. Since we were running late, this time I used the valet to park my car. If the chief didn't like it, I'd pay for it myself. Riker and I hurried into the lobby toward the elevators, where we literally ran into Florence Lufkin as she exited the ladies' lounge, causing her to drop her handbag on the floor, its contents scattering across the tile.

"I do beg your pardon, Miss Lufkin," I said as I stooped down to help her retrieve her things.

"Watch where you're going, Mr. Barrington, and Mr. whatever your name is."

"Mr. Riker," he said, bending down also. "Grant Riker. Here's your lipstick."

She grabbed it angrily out of his hand, along with the compact I was holding, and stuffed them back into her bag along with her other items before standing up and dusting herself off.

"I hope you're not injured," I said.

"No worse than being arrested on suspicion of murdering Mr. Ricci and spending a night in jail, thanks to you two idiots. It was most humiliating."

"That was all just a terrible mistake, Miss Lufkin," I said. "I do apologize. By the way, how was your date yesterday afternoon?"

"My date?"

"The fellow you met at the bar on North Avenue," Riker said.

"Oh, him. Not that it's any of your business, but it was fine. I met him at the bar and grill, we had a drink, and we went our separate ways. I can't say I cared for him much." She walked over to the elevator and pushed the call button, glancing at her wristwatch.

"What was his name? How did you meet him?" Riker said.

Miss Lufkin glared at him. "His name is Bob, and I met him at the, uh, grocery store. I don't know his last name or how to reach him, as I don't plan on seeing him again. If you have further questions, please direct them to my attorney, Mr. Hinkley. You can ask him anything you like when he contacts you about suing both of you and the police station for false arrest."

"I accept full responsibility for that," I said.

"I'll be sure and let Mr. Hinkley know that." She pushed the elevator call button again, this time repeatedly. "Where is that elevator?" She sounded most exasperated.

"It's just that it seemed so odd Mr. Ricci was found murdered outside the bar you just happened to be in that day," Riker said.

She gave Riker a frustrated look. "I was sorry to hear about Mr. Ricci, I really was. It was quite a shock."

"You've no idea why he was in that alley?" I said.

"No, I do not."

"Just a coincidence, then?" I said.

"I told you I don't know. He obviously found me attractive from the way he was flirting with me at the cocktail party. Perhaps he followed me. I really can't say, nor do I care to."

"All right, fair enough. Are you attending the séance?" Riker said.

She rolled her eyes at him this time. "Yes, I am. I told you that before. Idiots. What else would I be doing here at this time of night?" She glanced at her wristwatch once more. "And thanks to the two of you, I'm late. It's already after seven."

"Again our apologies, Miss Lufkin," I said. "We're going to the séance as well, as I believe we mentioned yesterday morning."

"Yes, you did mention that, but I was hoping you'd changed your mind under the circumstances," she said. "Twice yesterday was twice too much of the two of you. I could go the whole rest of my life without seeing either of you again," she said as the elevator finally arrived and the attendant opened the door and grill. The three of us stepped in, and Riker and I removed our hats. "And now I have to endure sitting through a séance with you," she said.

"Four, please," I said to the operator.

"Yes, sir." He closed the door and grill and started the cab lurching upward.

"We'll be on our best behavior, Miss Lufkin," I said.

"Which isn't saying much, coming from you."

When we reached the fourth floor the operator opened the doors and grate again, and we all stepped out. "404 is to the right, Miss Lufkin," I said, as the elevator headed back down.

"I know that. I've been here before." If words could freeze, I'd be slipping on solid ice. She strode purposely away from us down the hall as Riker and I trailed behind like scolded puppies. She knocked upon the door, opened by Mr. Goodacre, who was wearing a green suit with cream pinstripes, and an expertly knotted red and cream tie about his neck.

"Good evening, Miss Lufkin, oh, and Mr. Barrington and Mr. Riker. Thank you all for coming. Won't you come in?"

"Thanks," Riker said. "I'm sorry we're a tad late."

"It's all right. We've just finished setting up. I didn't expect the three of you to all arrive together," he said.

"An unfortunate accident, in every sense of the word," Miss Lufkin said, glaring at me and Riker once more.

"Oh, I see," Mr. Goodacre said, though it was clear he didn't. "This is Mr. Nicholas Barnsby of the *Milwaukee Journal*," he said, nodding to a man standing nearby who was wearing an ill-fitting brown suit with a garish orange and blue tie. He appeared to be in his late fifties, with thin, graying hair. He was a bit on the jowly side, with large ears that gave him the appearance overall of an old hound dog.

"How do you do, Mr. Barnsby?" I said, shaking his hand.

"How do you do? Call me Nick. I was invited by Mr. Goodacre to do a story on the séance. Mrs. Firestone seems to think she can contact the spirit of her late husband."

"Yes, well, that remains to be seen," I said. "It should prove to be an interesting evening one way or the other, at least. I'm Detective Barrington of the Milwaukee police, this is Detective Riker, and this is

Miss Lufkin, president of the All-Seeing Almanzo's admirers here in Milwaukee."

"How do you do?" Mr. Barnsby said to each of us.

"I'm so sorry," Mr. Goodacre said. "I should have introduced you all."

"No harm done, buddy," Mr. Barnsby said, taking out his notebook. "How do you spell Lufkin, Miss?"

"Like it sounds, L-u-f-k-i-n."

"Thanks, and I think I got Barrington and Riker correct. Are the three of you believers in spiritualism?"

"I am," Miss Lufkin said, "These two are rather dense."

"Dense as we may be, we're trying to keep an open mind. Where should we put our hats?" I said.

"Please put your hats, gentlemen, and your handbag, Miss Lufkin, on the dresser between the lamps, next to Mr. Barnsby's hat," Mr. Goodacre said. "Mrs. Firestone wants the table and the area surrounding it completely free of obstruction."

"All right," I said. We did as instructed and then looked at Mr. Goodacre, who appeared unsettled and nervous, and Mr. Barnsby, who was still taking notes.

"Now then," Goodacre said, "I believe we're all here, so the séance shall begin shortly. Would you like anything to drink first, or perhaps a snack? We have some peanuts..."

"No, thank you," I said. "Miss Lufkin? Detective Riker?"

"No, thank you," Miss Lufkin said coldly. "I had dinner earlier."

"Nothing for me, either," Riker said.

"How about you, Mr. Barnsby?"

"I'd kill for a beer, if you'll excuse the expression, Detectives, but I'm on duty, so no thanks."

"Very well. I think I'll pass, also. Best to keep my mind clear, you know," Mr. Goodacre said.

"Where's Mrs. Firestone?" I said. "After all, she is the star of the show, so to speak."

"I'm right here," she said from behind me. I turned to see her standing in the now open doorway to the bedroom of the suite. She was resplendent in a floor-length black satin gown with silvery sleeves that billowed out from the elbows. She wore a sparkling silver turban, and just visible beneath the hem of the gown were silver slippers bedecked with rubies and emeralds, and metal tips on the toes. She reminded me of a glamorous movie star.

"Oh, good evening, Mrs. Firestone," Riker and I both said, almost simultaneously.

"Yes, good evening," Miss Lufkin said, her tone softer. "Nice to see you again."

"Thank you, dear. I'm so glad you could come," she said, smiling at Miss Lufkin. "And Mr. Barrington and Mr. Riker, I see you both made it."

"Wouldn't have missed it," Riker said.

"And you must be Mr. Barnsby of the *Gazette*," Mrs. Firestone said, looking at the man in the ill-fitting suit.

"The *Journal*, ma'am, the *Milwaukee Journal*. Can't say I've ever covered a séance before."

Mrs. Firestone glanced about. "Well, I'll do my best to make it interesting for you. No photographer? No photos for your article?"

"My editor didn't feel it warranted photos, ma'am," Mr. Barnsby said.

"I see. Well, I can provide you some headshots of myself or some with my husband and me together, if you like. I have a few of them lying about here somewhere."

"Thanks, but I think all they'll want is the article."

"Oh. Regardless, I'm sure it will be a good story. Thank you all for coming." She strode toward each of us and extended her right hand, palm down, which we each took in turn. After giving it a gentle shake, I perused the room. Six chairs and a round table had been set up in the center. The table was covered with a thin white cloth, and upon the cloth was a strange-looking small metal object in the shape of an arrow, surrounded by unlit red, green, and blue candles, all in ceramic holders. The only light in the room came from the two lamps on the dresser.

"Before we begin, you should know that we ask all attendees to contribute a small amount to the organization. Five dollars per person will suffice," she said, looking at each of us in turn. "Mr. Barnsby, you're excluded, of course, since you're here on business."

"Five dollars?" I said, taken aback. "Your husband was only going to charge me three dollars."

"That was for a crystal ball sitting, I believe. Séances are more complex. Regardless, it's for the organization."

"And what organization would we be contributing to exactly, Mrs. Firestone?"

A quick look of annoyance crossed her face. "The Organization for Spiritual Guidance, of course. Research into the paranormal. It all costs money."

"Research, right." I suppressed the urge to roll my eyes, opened my wallet, and took out a twenty, which I handed to her. This is for Detective Riker, Miss Lufkin, and myself."

"I can pay my own way," Miss Lufkin said. "I don't need your handouts."

"It's the least I can do, please," I said.

"Have it your way," she said. "But you're still an idiot."

Mrs. Firestone took the bill and folded it expertly into the palm of her hand. "I'm afraid I don't have change."

"Consider the other five dollars a donation," I said.

"The chief will kill you for that one," Riker whispered aside to me.

"Thank you, Mr. Barrington," Mrs. Firestone said.

"Of course," I said, ignoring Riker for the moment. "Do you mind if I examine the table and objects?"

"If it will allay your suspicions, by all means. I'm confident you'll find nothing out of the ordinary."

Mr. Barnsby, I noticed, had taken out his notebook and pencil and was jotting a few things down as he watched me. "Are you here on official business, Mr. Barrington?" he said.

"Detective Riker and I are investigating the murders of Almanzo Firestone and Lorenzo Ricci, so yes."

"How fascinating," he said, making a few quick scribbles. "So, you're trying to track down the Alley Cat Killer. Any leads yet?"

"A few, perhaps, but we're not at liberty to discuss that, Mr. Barnsby. The case is ongoing."

"And you're not here to do a story on the murders, Mr. Barnsby," Mrs. Firestone said, still somewhat annoyed. "You're here to do a story on the séance."

"Yes, of course, ma'am, but they are somewhat related, don't you think? I mean, you are trying to summon the spirit of your dead husband," Mr. Barnsby said. "And he was murdered by the Alley Cat Killer."

"Be that as it may, please direct your questions to me. Now, then, Mr. Barrington, if you will look at whatever it is you wish to examine so that we can move things along…"

"Right," I said. I moved over to the table and picked up the metal arrow first. It was solid, probably some kind of iron, and not attached by any wires or string that I could see. The candles and ceramic holders were heavier, but also apparently free of any encumbrances. A look under the small table yielded nothing except four legs holding it up around the perimeter. I walked around the room, opening doors, peeking behind the curtains and under the other furniture, as everyone watched, but came away with nothing out of the ordinary. "Okay," I said. "Everything seems satisfactory."

"Naturally," Mrs. Firestone said moving behind one of the chairs at the table. "I've no need to rely on tricks. Now then, shall we be seated? Mr. Barrington, you're to my left. Mr. Riker may sit next to him. Mr. Goodacre, you'll be to Mr. Riker's left, Miss Lufkin across from me, and finally Mr. Barnsby. I know it's a bit tight, but do squeeze in as best you can."

Mrs. Firestone didn't sit at first but stood behind her chair, making sure everyone else sat in the proper place.

"Good, good," she said when we were all in our seats except for her. "Now, feet flat on the floor, both hands on the table at all times." She picked up a large box of matches, struck one, and lit the three candles. I watched as each flame took hold, wondering what would happen next.

She looked about at each of us and started speaking softly and rhythmically. "The flames of the night have been lit. And so I must cover a few guidelines. Once the séance has begun, please do not leave your seat, for your own safety. The room will be dark, and we don't want anyone injuring themselves. Also, please no talking unless directly asked to do so by myself or by the spirit, if he so chooses to speak. Lastly, please do not touch me once I am in my trance or attempt to communicate with me in any manner, as this may sever my connection with the spirit world and could put me in great peril. Is that quite clear? I need verbal confirmation that you all understand." She pointed at me first, and I replied yes, then Riker, Goodacre, Mr. Barnsby, and finally Miss Lufkin. I felt like I was a little kid back in school.

Mrs. Firestone smiled and nodded. "Excellent. I know it may seem silly, but the spirit world is a dangerous place even for me, experienced as I am, and your safety and mine is of the utmost importance. So, now that everyone understands the safety protocols, we may continue. You will notice three candles lit in the center of the table. The red candle indicates no. If the spirit directs the arrow to the red candle, his answer to my question is no. If he directs it to the green, his answer is yes. And if he directs it to the blue, he is undecided, or the question asked cannot be answered yes or no and a more direct question may be needed."

"Like the question *do you still cheat on your wife*," Mr. Barnsby said. "No one can answer that just yes or no without incriminating themselves one way or the other."

"Silence, Mr. Barnsby," Mrs. Firestone said in a mildly scolding tone. "I must insist on no further outbursts. But yes. Your crude example is correct. I'm glad you have grasped the concept."

Riker looked embarrassed, but Mr. Barnsby just shrugged. Mrs. Firestone would have made an excellent schoolmarm.

She raised both arms and pointed toward the flames, the sleeves of her gown hanging low as she spoke. "These candles possess abilities from the beyond. They are now prepared to answer a question of your deepest desires before the spirit is summoned. Stare into the flames, each of you, and focus on the candles to answer the question burning in your heart tonight. Focus deeply and concentrate on the flames and your question. Remember, it must be a yes or no question. I shall turn out the lights momentarily, and when we are in nothing but candlelight, the flame that appears to burn brightest to each of you will give you your answer. Focus, now, focus," she said, her voice growing softer yet still commanding as she slowly lowered her arms. "Stare deeply into the flames and concentrate."

As we all stared at the three candles, I felt slightly stupid, since I couldn't think of a single question. Then suddenly it came to me. *Will Alan move in with me into a two-bedroom?* I was only slightly aware of Mrs. Firestone moving away from the table and turning out the lamps on the dresser before returning to the table and taking her seat, placing both hands on the table also.

As the lights were extinguished, I could swear the green candle burned more brightly than the other two, and as silly as it was, it made me happy. I glanced sideways at Riker and wondered what his question was, and if he'd tell me later if I asked.

"Have you each gotten the answer to your question? The question of your heart's deepest desire?" she said, in that soft, rhythmic voice that was almost a whisper. "It may not be the answer you wanted, but it is the answer the spirit candles have provided you. It is a gift. A gift from beyond."

"I asked if the Brooklyn Dodgers were going to be in the World Series," Mr. Barnsby said. "The answer is yes!"

"How nice that baseball is among your deepest desires, Mr. Barnsby," she said sarcastically. "But please, as I told you before, I must ask that all of you refrain from any verbal outbursts, is that clear?"

"Yes, ma'am," he said, looking down at his hands. "But you did ask."

Mrs. Firestone looked annoyed once more. "I shall now attempt to contact Almanzo's spirit and, if successful, I will ask him a series of questions. His energy will direct the arrow on the table to the appropriate candle color for a response. If the connection is strong enough, he may even speak through me, but that is not guaranteed. If he does so choose to, you may notice his ectoplasm spew forth from my lips, but do not be alarmed. He will not harm you. Now then, let us all join hands, and remember, silence, please."

I took Riker's hand in my left and Mrs. Firestone's in my right. Hers was soft and cool. She began humming softly, a steady note broken only by the words "Almanzo, hear me" now and then.

As she hummed and chanted, I glanced about at the others around the table. Miss Lufkin and Mr. Goodacre had their eyes closed. Mrs. Firestone stared straight ahead, unblinking, trancelike. Riker and Barnsby looked uncomfortable.

Mrs. Firestone continued chanting. "Almanzo, beloved husband, also known as Alfred Firestone, this is Muriel, your wife. Are you there? Do you hear me?"

I stared at the tabletop now, watching for any sign of movement from the arrow, but there was none.

"Almanzo, you're among friends, my darling. You're safe. Are you there? Do you hear me?" Mrs. Firestone said again, this time slightly louder, slumping down low in her chair and leaning back. Suddenly the arrow on top of the table began to vibrate ever so slightly. "There!" Mrs. Firestone said, "Almanzo, is that you?"

Goodacre and Miss Lufkin opened their eyes and we all stared at the little arrow as it moved shakily toward the green candle and stopped.

"Yes! Yes, Almanzo, you are here. Welcome," she said, her face beaming in the candlelight. "We have gathered here this evening to speak with you. To learn the truth about what happened. Will you help us, my dear?"

The arrow moved away from the green candle slightly, and then back. "Thank you, Almanzo. You have unfinished business in this world, don't you?"

Once again we all watched as the arrow moved away and then back, pointing straight at the green arrow for yes.

"Of course you do. Your murderer is at large, as is Mr. Ricci's. Will you be able to transition to the afterlife if that person isn't caught?"

This time the arrow moved slowly away from the green candle and over to the red.

"I didn't think so, my poor dear. Let us help you rest now. Do you know who murdered you? Who took you from us?"

We all watched transfixed as the arrow moved away from the red candle and back again to the green.

"You do know!" She still stared straight ahead, but her eyes sparkled. "Oh, my darling Alfred, I'm so sorry. Who was it? Who killed you? Who took you from me? From all of us?"

The arrow moved violently toward the blue candle. Mrs. Firestone began to rock back and forth, her head moving all around as she slumped even further down in her chair. "Oh, oh! I'm so sorry, Almanzo. That was not a yes or no question. Forgive me. Do you forgive me?"

The arrow slid away from the blue candle and back to the green candle.

Mrs. Firestone looked relieved. "Oh, I'm so glad. Thank you, my darling. Now tell me, was it a man who killed you?"

The arrow jerked back toward the red candle.

"No. The answer is no, it wasn't a man. Then it was a woman, obviously," Mrs. Firestone said. "Was it a woman you know? Do you know the woman who killed you?"

The arrow moved back to the green candle and stopped.

"Ah, a woman you knew here in Milwaukee, certainly. But you didn't know many women here that I'm aware of, Alfred. I wonder. Is it a woman I also know?"

The metal arrow slid back and then forward.

"Hmm, so it was someone we both knew. A female here in Milwaukee. But who? Someone at the theater?"

Back the arrow went to the red candle.

"No. Someone who works here at the hotel, then?"

It moved slowly away from the red candle, and then back.

"Hmm, also no. All right, was it someone at this table?"

The arrow moved away from the red candle toward the center of the table, and then slid back once more to the green candle as Mrs. Firestone gasped. I stole a moment to look at Miss Lufkin. Even in the candlelight, I could see her eyes were like saucers, her complexion pale.

"Who was it, my darling? Point to the culprit now and free yourself."

I figured it wasn't going to point to Mrs. Firestone, so that really only left one possibility at the table, but still I watched, absolutely captivated. The arrow started slowly away from the green candle and toward Goodacre, but then moved sharply to his left, where Miss Lufkin sat. It stopped, pointing directly at her. Miss Lufkin stared at it in disbelief, her eyes wide.

"It's not true!" Florence Lufkin said. "It's not! He's lying. Why is he lying?"

Mrs. Firestone began rocking back and forth again, this time more animated, tossing her head about. I wondered what was holding her turban on. Her hands flew up to it and then she covered her mouth as she gasped. "Silence! He wishes to speak through me," she said, her voice deeper and raspier. "The candles and the arrow are not enough. Speak Almanzo, speak!"

I watched in amazement as Muriel Firestone rolled about in her seat, a strange greenish substance that glowed in the dark suddenly dripping from her lips. She started groaning and moaning and began shaking violently, her eyes rolling about in their sockets as words spewed forth from her mouth in a deep, distorted voice.

"I am Alfred Firestone, the All-Seeing Almanzo. You killed me, Florence Lufkin," the disembodied voice said.

"What? *No*! No, I didn't!"

"You shot me. You killed me in cold blood."

Miss Lufkin looked confused and frightened. "No! It was Ricci who shot you. I saw him follow you that night. I saw him shoot you! It wasn't me!"

"You also killed Ricci, my friend."

"No! No, I didn't kill him either! I swear to you, Mr. Firestone, to all of you." She had pulled her hands free and gotten shakily to her feet.

"You met him at that bar, and then you killed him in the alley."

"I didn't kill him! I lied about meeting a date at that awful bar. It *was* Mr. Ricci, but I wanted him to give me money in exchange for my silence. I didn't kill him, I didn't! I told him how much money I wanted, he agreed to get it for me, and I left him very much alive. Why are you saying this, Mr. Firestone?"

"He refused to give you any money, so you shot him," the voice said. "The gun she used to kill me and Ricci is in her handbag," the disembodied voice said.

"This is insane. He's lying!"

"Get the handbag, Riker," I said. "But be careful where you handle it. Pick it up from the sides only."

Riker got up from the table and went over to the dresser in the dark, retrieving her handbag as directed.

"Mind if we have a look inside, Miss Lufkin?" I said.

"What? No, go ahead. I don't have anything to hide," she said. She was nearly hysterical. "I didn't kill anyone!"

"Open it, Riker, but use your handkerchief. I don't want to disturb any prints on the clasp."

"Yes, sir." He returned to the table and opened the handbag carefully, dumping its contents out and sending the metal arrow clattering to the side. Amongst her compact, lipstick, gloves and other items was a small-caliber handgun. Miss Lufkin grasped at her bare throat as she stared at the tabletop. "It's not possible! I never saw that gun before."

"You killed us both, Florence Lufkin. Why? Why?" The voice got softer. "Ricci tried to fight you off. He grabbed your necklace with your initial on it, but you shot him dead."

"He's leaving me, he's leaving us," Mrs. Firestone said, her voice almost back to normal as she returned to a more upright position in her chair and straightened her turban. "He will be at peace now that we know the truth."

"But it's a lie! I didn't kill him or Mr. Ricci or anyone!" Miss Lufkin was in hysterics now.

I got up and turned on both of the dresser lamps and the overhead light. Mr. Barnsby, I noticed, was scribbling furiously in his notebook and had been using one of the candles for illumination.

"Didn't you, Miss Lufkin?" I said. "Mr. Firestone will be at peace now that we know who killed him. He'll be able to complete his transition to the other side, as you say. The gun in your purse was the final piece of the puzzle. Please, no one touch it. It all makes sense now."

"Please, you have to believe me," Miss Lufkin said. "Please!" She stood frozen in place, gripping the edges of the table, her fingers white. She seemed almost unable to move, and I thought perhaps she might faint, the color drained from her face.

"Riker, go stand next to Miss Lufkin. She doesn't appear at all well, and I don't want her to topple over or attempt to make a run for it."

"Yes, sir," he said, moving past Mr. Goodacre to stand just behind Miss Lufkin.

Mrs. Firestone's head came to rest, and she smiled ever so slightly at me. "So, you're a believer now, Mr. Barrington? I believe you have an arrest to make."

"Quite so. Nice theatrics, Mrs. Firestone. Good show. But after all, it is what you do best."

"Not theatrics, Mr. Barrington. Communicating with the dead is exhausting. It's physically and emotionally draining." She pulled a white handkerchief from her bosom and wiped the greenish substance from her lips and chin. "I'll let you attend to your business as I have attended to mine. If you'll excuse me, I'm going to lie down now." She got slowly to her feet.

"Of course you must be tired, Mrs. Firestone. Just one question before you go. Perhaps two. How did Almanzo know Ricci had supposedly grabbed Florence Lufkin's necklace? That wasn't in any of the newspaper or radio accounts, and you told me you don't read or listen to those anyway. No one alive outside of the police department would have known Mr. Ricci was found clutching it."

"Oh, I assume Mr. Ricci communicated with Alfred in the spirit world. Both their spirits were in transition, and Mr. Ricci simply told Almanzo what had happened."

"Convenient. Hard to cross-examine a ghost," I said.

"I'm afraid I have no other explanation. There are things mortals cannot understand. You heard Almanzo accuse her. He even called her out by name."

"Yes, but that could have easily been faked just by you changing your voice," Riker said.

"I told you both before I don't need to rely on tricks. Besides, you all also saw the arrow move. It pointed directly at Miss Lufkin when I asked Almanzo who murdered him."

"That's true, Mr. Barrington," Mr. Barnsby said, "I saw it with my own eyes. And you examined that arrow before we got started. You said everything appeared to be on the up-and-up."

"Correct. I saw no wires or strings," I said. I picked the arrow up off the table and looked at it once more. "And I still can't."

"So, it was obviously moved by the energy of Almanzo's spirit," Mrs. Firestone said. "There's no other explanation."

"The spirit of Almanzo. Truly amazing," I said. "He really is All-Seeing, and All-Telling."

"I'm very tired, Detective," Mrs. Firestone said. "You said you had another question before I go lie down?"

"Hmm? Ah, yes. May I please have one of your shoes?"

"What?" She took a step back, looking at me in surprise.

"One of the slippers you're wearing," I said. "Would you mind removing it for me?"

"Whatever for?"

"If you wouldn't mind. The right one, please. I noted earlier that you're right handed, and most people who are right handed are also right footed."

"I'm afraid I don't understand what you're getting at."

"If you've nothing to hide, Mrs. Firestone, I would very much appreciate you handing me your right shoe."

She looked at me crossly and suspiciously. "Of course I've nothing to hide." She slipped off the right slipper and handed it to me. "What are you going to do with it? Those are custom made."

"I'm sure they are. Bear with me, please." I crawled partly

beneath the table, holding the shoe, while keeping my eye on the metal arrow. "Oh great spirit," I said, "Please point to the real murderer." The arrow began to move once more, this time across the table toward Mrs. Firestone. As it did, she backed farther away. Everyone was watching with great attention.

"Do not mock the spirits, Mr. Barrington. You don't know what you're doing," she said angrily.

"I think I do, and I think you do, too."

"I did not murder my husband! Get out from under there and give me back my slipper!"

I got slowly to my feet. "I agree you didn't shoot your husband, but I'm afraid I'll still need this shoe for evidence, Mrs. Firestone. I assume you have another pair you can wear when we take you to the police station."

"This is ridiculous," she said angrily. "Why would you take me to the police station? You should be arresting Miss Lufkin."

"How, Heath?" Riker said, one of his hands on Miss Lufkin's shoulder to support her. "How did you know, and how did the arrow move?"

"Mrs. Firestone manipulated the metal arrow using a magnet in the tip of her shoe, moving it wherever she wanted. You may have noticed how she slumped down in her chair in order to raise her foot beneath the table surface."

"Ingenious!" Mr. Barnsby said. "No one could see her foot under the table moving the metal arrow around."

"Exactly. A simple trick she used multiple times in all her séances, I'm sure. The candle holders were ceramic as opposed to metal, so they wouldn't interfere with the magnet. That green ectoplasm coming out of your mouth was a nice touch, Mrs. Firestone. I noticed right before Almanzo 'spoke' that you reached up to your turban, where you probably extracted a hidden capsule of some sort with a luminous green gelatin inside it, and then to your mouth, where you put the capsule in your cheek to bite down on shortly after."

"But who killed Mr. Firestone? Miss Lufkin or Mrs. Firestone? Or someone else entirely? And what does this all have to do with the Alley Cat Killer?" Mr. Barnsby said.

"There are two Alley Cat Killers, Mr. Barnsby," I said. "Or perhaps three. Mr. Ricci is the one who murdered Almanzo Firestone, but he didn't act alone. I'm not sure when the actual planning of Mr. Firestone's murder began, but most probably the fact that he was murdered in Wisconsin had something to do with the death penalty."

"How's that?" Mr. Barnsby said.

"I'm guessing, but I imagine the guilty parties wanted to hedge their bets. The last two states the All-Seeing Almanzo performed in, Indiana and Missouri, still have the death penalty for murder, but Wisconsin abolished it in 1853. If by chance they were caught, at least they knew they wouldn't be executed," I said. "So they chose to kill Mr. Firestone in Wisconsin."

"Makes sense," Mr. Barnsby said.

"Yes, it does. And, again I'm guessing, but I suspect Milwaukee and Saturday night were chosen in part because of Miss Lufkin."

"Me? Why?" she said, still shaking and pale.

"Because you sent Mr. Firestone a fan letter, Miss Lufkin, and Mr. Goodacre invited you to a private cocktail party and dinner Saturday night in this very room," I said.

"Yes, that's right," Mr. Goodacre said. "So what?"

"Had she not been in attendance at the party and at dinner later, things may have turned out very differently. We have you to thank, Mr. Goodacre, for inviting her. If she hadn't been there, the murderer may have gotten off scot-free."

"I don't get what you're driving at, Detective," Mr. Goodacre said.

"Allow me to explain. The Saturday evening performance at the theater didn't go very well in part because you forgot the fictitious name you were supposed to use, Mrs. Firestone."

"It was a complicated name, that's all," Mrs. Firestone said.

"Possibly. Or possibly you were nervous about what was going to happen later. Even for the coldest heart, the idea of murdering someone must be nerve wracking."

"I simply forgot the name."

"After the show, you and Mr. Firestone came back here to the cocktail party. Then Mr. Ricci got your gun out of the desk drawer and started waving it about, causing Miss Lufkin to spill her drink. Was the gun spontaneous or part of your master plan? Had you arranged with him to ask for a cigarette, and you would then direct him to the desk drawer where the gun was and have him pick it up to show everyone?"

"What on earth are you talking about? Why would a drunkard waving a gun about be part of any plan?" Mrs. Firestone said.

"To indicate to the police that anyone at that cocktail party would have known where the gun was kept, and that anyone could have taken it."

"And clearly someone did take it, Detective. Miss Lufkin used it to kill my husband and Mr. Ricci."

"Yes, obviously," Mr. Goodacre said. "I'm sure if you'll just do your job properly and test that gun, you'll most likely find it is the murder weapon."

"I'm sure we will, Mr. Goodacre. But Miss Lufkin is not a murderer, though that's what you wanted us to think, Mrs. Firestone. That was your backup plan, once you found out about Miss Lufkin and the cocktail party. If the police didn't believe your husband's death was a robbery gone wrong, you figured you could always pin it on Miss Lufkin by planting the gun on her, a deranged fan, a perfect patsy. And you'd deny any involvement."

"Of course I'd deny involvement, because I wasn't involved," Mrs. Firestone said.

"But you were, and oh so cleverly. After the cocktail party, Mr. Firestone, Miss Lufkin, and Mr. Goodacre left the suite to go down to dinner, leaving you and Mr. Ricci alone here. You gave the gun to Ricci, who may not have been as drunk as he pretended to be. Then Ricci went downstairs, stopping briefly at the table, and then out into the night to wait by the flower shop for Firestone to arrive."

"How would this Ricci know Firestone was going to go to a flower shop after dinner?" the *Journal* reporter said. "And why a flower shop? That seems a queer thing to do on a Saturday night."

"Because Mr. Firestone was known for his clandestine affairs in every city they went to," I said, looking briefly at Mr. Barnsby, "Milwaukee being no exception. And he relied on Mr. Ricci to arrange them. Ricci set up a rendezvous for Firestone, letting him know to go to Birdwell's flower shop Saturday night, sometime before ten p.m. when it closed. The flower shop, you see, was a front for a prostitution ring. But Firestone had to attend the dinner first, and that didn't even start until nine. No wonder he was irritable and always looking at his watch. With just a few minutes to spare, he finally broke away and headed quickly to Birdwell's, where Mr. Ricci was waiting in the shadows. Firestone passed Miss Lufkin at the bus stop on the way, but he was so anxious to get to his destination, he didn't even notice her. Curious, she decided to follow him and see where he was headed in such a hurry."

"That's right," Miss Lufkin said, coming around a bit but still looking pale and aghast, her voice shaky. "That's exactly what happened."

"Yes, Miss Lufkin, and you followed him to Birdwell's and waited while he went in. You saw him come out with a green carnation in his lapel, a signal to the person he was to meet for illicit purposes. After ten or fifteen minutes, you saw him walk away, head back west on Wells Street, and then cross to the alley. And you saw Ricci, whom you recognized from the cocktail party, step out of the shadows and follow him."

Miss Lufkin nodded nervously.

"And then you saw Ricci shoot Mr. Firestone, didn't you?" I said. "Or at least, you saw him fire a gun into the alley where Mr. Firestone had just gone."

She nodded again, this time her lower lip quivering. She looked like she was about to cry.

"I know, Miss Lufkin, believe me. You saw Ricci fire the gun, you screamed, he saw you, you panicked. He ran one way, you ran the other. You went home. The next day you saw the newspaper article and discovered Firestone was indeed dead. At that point, you probably thought several times about calling the police. Maybe you even started to a few times. But then you hesitated. You were recently let go from your job at the bank, no prospects, no money, behind on your rent. What Ricci did was horribly wrong. He murdered someone you admired in cold blood. You probably thought, what harm would there be in asking him for money in exchange for your silence? After all, Mr. Firestone was already dead. Besides, I'm sure you figured you could always leave an anonymous tip with the police after you got your money."

Now Miss Lufkin did start to cry. Mr. Barnsby handed her his handkerchief before going back to his notebook. It looked like he'd filled several pages already.

"But I still don't understand," the reporter said, looking up at me. "You said there were two Alley Cat Killers, or even three."

I looked across the table at Mr. Barnsby. "Yes. You see, Mrs. Firestone and Mr. Ricci were having an affair, isn't that right, Mrs. Firestone?"

"I don't think that's really a secret, Detective. Yes, we were having an affair, but I wasn't in love with him. Besides, my husband had plenty of sordid encounters in every city we went to."

"Yes, and you found what your husband was doing to be disgusting."

"It *was* disgusting. Immoral and vile."

"What was he doing?" Miss Lufkin said, trembling.

I ignored her for the time being. "No more immoral than what you were doing with Mr. Ricci, in my opinion. I wonder if Ricci slept with you in part to get back at your husband."

"How dare you? He slept with me because he found me attractive, and he cared about me."

"Did he? Oh I'm sure he found you attractive, but I think you may be wrong that he cared for you, and I think eventually you realized that. I think he enjoyed sleeping with you, knowing it annoyed Almanzo."

"Why would he do that?" Mr. Barnsby said.

"Because Almanzo wouldn't let Ricci be a proper part of the show. In fact, he was talking about firing Ricci, in part to spite you, Mrs. Firestone, and in part because he felt Ricci was a better performer than he was, and he felt threatened."

"Ricci *was* better, in every sense of the word," Mrs. Firestone said.

"That's your opinion. But no matter how good he was, Almanzo wouldn't let him shine onstage, and that didn't help the sluggish ticket sales, but Almanzo refused to give up touring. You were afraid you were all going to be broke and out in the cold soon, so you needed a plan. Clearly you and Ricci didn't care much for Goodacre, and vice versa, but none of you liked Almanzo. In fact, you all despised him, so you came up with an idea. The three of you formed an uneasy alliance."

"Me? What are you saying? I had nothing to do with this," Mr. Goodacre said, looking alarmed.

"Oh, I beg to differ. You see," I said, turning back to Mrs. Firestone, "with your help and encouragement, Mr. Goodacre started siphoning off money from the shows in small amounts, dividing it up amongst you, Ricci, and himself. But that was a mere pittance. You all wanted more, and you knew how to get it, didn't you, Mrs. Firestone?"

"I was his wife. I was entitled to half of his earnings. He had no right to keep it from me."

"But he did keep it from you. I believe Mr. Goodacre said Almanzo felt you had no head for business, so he put the money in an account under his name only."

"That's no secret, obviously."

"Obviously. But what *was* a secret is that the three of you agreed to kill your husband, make it look like a robbery, and then split the insurance money three ways. And if the robbery angle didn't work, you would pin it on Miss Lufkin. You and Ricci could go off on your own, perhaps forming a two-person show, and Goodacre could pocket a nice sum and go on to find a client more to his liking. A tale as old as time, or at least as old as insurance companies have been around."

"Insurance fraud, yes, fairly common," Mr. Barnsby said, still scribbling away.

"I don't know what you're talking about," Mr. Goodacre said, starting to sweat.

"Neither do I," Mrs. Firestone said. "But I think you're right about one thing. If you investigate the books, you'll find Clive was doing something underhanded. Alfred told me he suspected him."

"How dare you, Muriel?"

"Shut up, Clive."

"Dissent amongst the ranks. Tsk, tsk. Actually, it was a good plan overall. Most likely, Almanzo's body would have been found sometime the next morning, his wallet and watch missing, and it would have been deemed a robbery. But then little Miss Lufkin spoiled everything, didn't she? Then she decided to blackmail Ricci, complicating things even further. Detective Riker and I were in the room when the note was delivered. After getting it, Mr. Ricci mentioned needing to talk to you, Mrs. Firestone," I said. "But you were still out to lunch. I wondered why he wanted to talk to you suddenly. We now know it was because he wanted to tell you he was being blackmailed. Ricci was totally panicked, I imagine. He was terrified he was going to be arrested for your husband's murder, and you were worried that if that happened he'd rat you and Goodacre out. So, how to solve the problem of Miss Lufkin?"

"You're still just guessing," Mrs. Firestone said.

"I am, in part, I admit, but I think I'm a pretty good guesser.

Perhaps at that point you asked Ricci to kill Miss Lufkin, too, but he refused. Maybe he felt one person's blood on his hands was enough. I bet he wanted to just pay her off, but you weren't convinced that would be the end of it. Plus, she was probably asking for a substantial amount. So, on Monday morning you paid her a visit, perhaps with the thought of killing her yourself, or planting the gun in her apartment. But what if her apartment was never searched? What if the gun was never found? You couldn't risk her telling the police about Ricci."

"It was a social call, nothing else."

"Yes, a social call. So polite and cordial. And there the two of you sat, having tea, and you knowing she knew who killed your husband, but not knowing you knew, and the murder weapon probably in your purse the whole time."

"Say that again," Mr. Barnsby said, pausing briefly from his note taking.

"You see, Mr. Barnsby, Miss Lufkin spilled her tea during this little social visit, and when she left the room to change, Mrs. Firestone happened to see Miss Lufkin's necklace with the *F* on it that she was wearing the night of the cocktail party. It was on a table next to the sofa, and that's when she got the idea of how to deal with Miss Lufkin *and* Mr. Ricci. She took the necklace, and when she got back to the hotel she told Ricci Miss Lufkin was planning on going to the police even if he paid her off, and that the only way to be rid of her was for her to be dead. But I imagine he still didn't want to do the deed. Killing Almanzo was one thing. He was standing in Ricci's way and Ricci disliked him intently, but killing a pretty, young girl like Miss Lufkin was another."

"So, what happened?" Mr. Barnsby said. "Who killed Mr. Ricci? Mrs. Firestone?"

"Don't be absurd, Mr. Barnsby," Mrs. Firestone said. "As the good detectives know full well, I was in the lobby of this hotel all yesterday afternoon. Mr. Billings the desk clerk will testify to that in court, I'm sure."

"I'm sure he would," I said. "I'm sure you made sure of that, Mrs. Firestone. No, you didn't kill Ricci, but you had someone else do it."

"Who?" Barnsby said, scribbling way.

"The good Mr. Goodacre," I said, looking at the nondescript, pale little man.

"Me? That's ridiculous." He looked positively ill.

"Not really. How difficult was it for her to convince you to kill Ricci, Mr. Goodacre? I imagine she told you that you risked going to jail on fraud and accessory to murder charges if Ricci was arrested. And with Ricci out of the way, you could split the insurance money two ways instead of three. She gave you the gun and told you to go with Ricci to the bar on North Avenue, most likely in a cab. While he went in the front door, you'd go around to the alley and wait for him to exit out the back door with Miss Lufkin."

"We did go out the back way into the alley," Miss Lufkin said. "He seemed to want to keep me there. He kept talking to me, but finally I told him I had to leave, and I never looked back."

I looked at her now. "He was stalling, waiting for Goodacre to step out and shoot you, of course, probably wondering where he was. Why did you go out into a dark alley with someone you barely knew? Someone you were attempting to blackmail? That seems a risky thing to do."

"Mr. Ricci looked out the front window and said he saw cops waiting out front. He said they must have tailed me. I thought right away of the two of you. That's why I agreed to go out the back door with him."

"I figured, only I doubt he really saw us. It was just a ploy to get you to leave through the alley door with him. Once they were in the alley, Mr. Goodacre would step out from his hiding place and shoot Miss Lufkin, making it look like a robbery, as they had initially planned to do with Almanzo. I imagine Ricci agreed to it because he didn't have to do the actual killing, and he felt with her dead no one could pin Almanzo's murder on him. Except the *real* plan was to let Miss Lufkin leave. Once Ricci was by himself in the alley, Mr. Goodacre would shoot him, placing Miss Lufkin's necklace in his hand."

"And why, pray tell, would I do such a thing?"

"Because you and Mrs. Firestone figured Mr. Riker and I would question the bartender and determine Miss Lufkin had been there with Ricci, especially after finding the necklace clutched in his hand. The two of you probably figured we'd arrest her for Ricci's murder, she'd tell us Ricci killed Firestone, and that would be that. Even if she didn't go to prison for Ricci's murder, it would seem pretty obvious she was the one that killed him, and you'd be done with both of them. With Ricci dead, there would be absolutely no way to connect either of you to Firestone's death, and no blackmail money would have to be paid. And I'm sure you felt, Mrs. Firestone, that since you got Goodacre to kill Ricci, he certainly wasn't about to talk."

"That's absurd. And slanderous," Mrs. Firestone said. "I'll sue you."

"Be my guest," I replied. "I believe Miss Lufkin has the name of a good criminal attorney, a Mr. Hinkley, if I'm not mistaken."

"This is ridiculous," Mrs. Firestone said, her voice rising in anger, her lips pursed and tight.

"Tragic, certainly, but not ridiculous," I said. "Tragic that you fell in love with Ricci and roped him and Goodacre into your little scheme. Tragic that two lives were lost and two more ruined because of it."

"I already admitted Ricci and I were having an affair, but I told you we weren't in love. It was strictly physical."

"Perhaps, but still, you must have felt something for him. Certainly you must have felt rejected when you found him in bed Sunday night with Dolly."

"How did you know about that?" She looked like she'd been slapped across the face.

"I had a chat with Dolly. And I'm sure she would be able to identify you, if asked."

"It doesn't matter. Mr. Ricci was a womanizer," Mrs. Firestone said.

"Yes, indeed he was. A fact you learned maybe a little too late. You say you weren't in love with him, but after finding him and Dolly together you still sent him an envelope containing the six of hearts, torn in two, and the king of spades. Theatrical, of course, but that's what you know."

"What's the significance of the cards, Mr. Barrington?" the reporter said.

"In a standard tarot deck, the six is the card of love, the lovers, now torn in half, if I remember correctly from the books I studied. The king is the thirteenth card in a standard deck, and the thirteenth card in a tarot deck indicates death. Nice little message you sent him, Mrs. Firestone," I said.

"I could care less who he sleeps with, or slept with. Why would I send him those cards?"

"Actually, you *couldn't* care less, but you sent them because you wanted him to know you were angry and hurt. At that point, he disgusted you almost as much as your husband did, only in a different way."

"Men in general are disgusting."

"Again, your opinion, Mrs. Firestone. I think maybe you cared for Ricci more than even you realized. When you found him and Dolly in bed together, that somehow made it easier to pull the trigger the next day, or at least to have Mr. Goodacre do it."

"You've no proof I did anything of the kind. No proof I stole that necklace, no proof I sent those cards, or that Mr. Goodacre shot Mr. Ricci in that alley."

"Don't we?" I said. I pointed to the revolver still on the table. "After Miss Lufkin was arrested for the murder of Mr. Ricci, you probably thought your troubles were over. But then she was released from jail. You didn't know what she and Ricci had talked about in the bar, what he had told her, or what she would say to the police once she calmed down and had time to think. You knew she was coming to the séance tonight because you invited her, probably as a backup plan. A perfect opportunity to plant the murder weapon on her and have two police detectives witness it."

"I may be good at sleight of hand, Detective Barrington, but how could I possibly have planted that gun in Miss Lufkin's purse? I never went near it. She obviously brought the gun with her tonight, intending to use it against one or all of us if it was pointed out by my husband's spirit that she is the killer, which the spirit did."

"It is your gun, isn't it? You lied about it being missing, of course. You gave it to Ricci to kill your husband, and then you gave it to Goodacre to kill Ricci. You put the gun in the top dresser drawer before we all arrived and directed Mr. Goodacre to tell us to put our hats on top of the dresser, along with Miss Lufkin's handbag. Then, while you had us all staring at the candle flames and concentrating on our questions, you took the gun out of the drawer and slipped it into Miss Lufkin's purse, while also turning out the lamps on the dresser. Then, with all of us as witnesses, the murder weapon was found in Miss Lufkin's possession. Devilishly clever."

"You can't prove that," Mrs. Firestone said. "You can't prove any of it."

"But I can," I said, staring at her. "You were the only one to go near the dresser after we were all seated this evening."

"So what? Miss Lufkin stole the gun from me. It was in her purse, and she's the murderer."

"No, she isn't," I said. "You see, unbeknownst to you, Miss Lufkin dropped her handbag in the lobby when we bumped into her tonight, scattering the contents all over the floor. Detective Riker and I helped her pick her belongings back up. There was no gun in sight."

Goodacre looked like he suddenly recalled something important. "Say, you're forgetting, Detective, that I was in my room all yesterday afternoon. You can verify that with room service. I had a terrible stomachache. There's no way I could have gotten to that alley and back in that amount of time."

I looked over at him. "Ah yes, that. It took me a while to figure that one out. As we know, Mrs. Firestone was in the lobby. She made sure Mr. Billings not only saw her but chatted with her frequently. Of course she also made a couple trips upstairs to her suite. Nothing unusual about that."

"Of course not, I had to powder my nose."

"But while you were up there, you went into Clive's room using the key he'd given you, and disguising your voice, called for room service. You then pulled the drapes, turned out most of the lights, and got into his bed, or perhaps the bathroom. When room service arrived, you told them to come in and to leave the tray on the table. When they left, you went back downstairs. A while later, you went back up, called room service again and told them to pick the tray up, having disposed of the contents down the toilet, most likely. I remember you saying you started out in show business as a child with your parents, doing impressions and voices. I imagine you're quite good at it. Besides, no one in room service would be able to identify Mr. Goodacre by his voice, most likely."

"Once again, guesses. Unless you have any real evidence, I'm going to have to ask you to leave now."

"But I'm not quite ready to go, Mrs. Firestone. You know, it shouldn't be hard to find the cab driver who took Goodacre and Ricci to that bar on North Avenue, and I'm sure he'll be able to identify Goodacre in a lineup." I turned to Clive. "How did you get back here to the hotel after shooting Ricci, Mr. Goodacre?"

"I walked quite a ways, then hitched a ride with a fella."

"Clive, shut up!" Mrs. Firestone said.

"I…I didn't mean to say that, you tricked me!" Goodacre said, his face now purple.

"I want to call my lawyer," Mrs. Firestone said.

"Riker, call for a black-and-white. You can make your call at the police station, Mrs. Firestone. You too, Mr. Goodacre."

"Boy, you were right about one thing, lady," Mr. Barnsby said to Mrs. Firestone, tucking his notebook back in his pocket. "You certainly made the séance interesting. Now I wish I'd pushed my editor for that photographer. Could I still get one of those headshots of you and your husband? The ones you mentioned earlier?"

"Drop dead," she said, glaring at him.

"Riker, take custody of that gun and Miss Lufkin's handbag, but handle them delicately. I suspect both of them will show Mrs. Firestone's prints."

"Sure thing, Heath," Riker said.

"I…I suppose I should thank you, Detective, both of you, or at least apologize," Miss Lufkin said, a little color returning to her face.

"The best thanks you could give me, Miss Lufkin, is to straighten up and fly right, as the song says."

I turned to Mrs. Firestone and Mr. Goodacre once more, who were both looking defeated, angry, and frightened. "The squad car should be here soon. Let's get you a fresh pair of shoes, Mrs. Firestone, and wait in the other room along with Detective Riker and Mr. Goodacre. Miss Lufkin and Mr. Barnsby, you're free to go for now."

CHAPTER TWENTY-TWO

Evening, Wednesday, September 17, 1947

I'd been putting in some long hours the last few days, so after finishing up my final paperwork at my desk on the Firestone/Ricci murder case and going over it all with the chief, I called it a day just before noon and headed home, making a few stops along the way. Since Alan had the day off, I'd invited him to my place for drinks and dinner at six, and I wanted to buy a few things to prepare for that.

He knocked on my door promptly at six, looking dapper in a brown tweed suit with a blue and red tie.

"Good evening, sir," I said, ushering him in and closing the door behind him. "You look handsome as always. Put your hat on the table, the usual place."

"Hiya," he said, setting his hat down. "And thanks, but you're always nattily dressed. You even wear an apron well."

I glanced down at the basic white apron tied about my waist and smiled. "Well, you know, gotta keep the clothes clean while I'm working in the kitchen."

"Speaking of working in the kitchen, wowzer. Something smells terrific."

"I'm trying my hand at roast turkey with my special dressing, cranberry sauce, and giblet gravy, with broccoli and hollandaise sauce, and for dessert, I made a chocolate layer cake."

Alan whistled. "I'm impressed, but it's too early for Thanksgiving."

"Just feeling thankful, I guess."

"Because you solved another case?"

"Well, yes, and Riker and I both seem to be back in the chief's good graces. But for other things, too. I'm thankful and hopeful, I suppose I should say. Hold on, I just need to baste the turkey and get us some martinis."

"Need help?"

"Thanks, but I've got this under control. Make yourself comfortable, handsome. Take off your suit coat and shoes, and put some music on."

"Okay, I can do that."

I basted the turkey, made the martinis, his with olives and mine with a pickle, and took off the apron before returning to the living room with the cocktails. I noticed he'd tuned my console radio to a soft, romantic station.

"Nice choice on the music," I said. "Here's your drink."

"Thanks and thanks. What should we drink to?"

"To being thankful," I said. "And hopeful."

"Hear, hear."

We clinked glasses and made ourselves comfortable on the sofa, side by side, our knees touching. "Dinner will be about another hour or so," I said.

"No rush, I had a big lunch. So tell me, how did you and Riker solve the Firestone case? I've been dying to know, if you'll excuse the expression. And more importantly, how did you manage to solve it without me?"

"Honestly? I don't know how I manage to do anything without you, and you did help solve it. How else would I have known about myomancy, and the fact that Firestone had a roving eye for attractive young men such as yourself?"

"Well, I don't know about that, but I'm glad I could be of some assistance anyway."

"You always are."

"But you said Riker was a big help in many ways, too. The handsome Detective Grant Riker."

"He was indeed a big help, but it was strictly professional, Alan. No need to be jealous. He actually reminds me a lot of you, smart, quick-witted, and savvy. It was definitely a team effort, a three-way team. You, me, and him."

"I like the sound of that."

"Me too. Teamwork. Together we determined that the four of them—Almanzo, his wife, Mr. Ricci, and Mr. Goodacre—were in trouble financially. Ticket sales were drying up, and touring costs were beginning to be more than they were making, but still Almanzo refused to concede. Mrs. Firestone and Ricci had begun an affair, and Ricci had plans to go off on his own, thinking he could do better, but he needed money to do it. The two of them decided they could siphon off some money from the shows with Goodacre's help, so they formed an alliance. But all three soon realized it wasn't enough, and one of them, probably Mrs. Firestone, decided that it would be best to eliminate her husband altogether and cash in on the insurance money. She got Ricci to actually pull the trigger, and then she turned the tables on Ricci, getting Goodacre to kill him but attempting to frame Florence Lufkin for it."

"Cold and vicious. But if she and Ricci were having an affair, why would she want him dead?"

"Because she discovered he was a womanizing drunkard, and she also didn't want him spilling the beans to the police once she found out Miss Lufkin saw him kill Firestone. With him dead, she and Goodacre would be in the clear. Bonus points if Miss Lufkin was arrested for his murder."

"So Mrs. Firestone decided to eliminate Ricci and frame Miss Lufkin, thereby killing the proverbial two birds with one stone," Alan said, sipping on his martini.

"Correct. As I said, Ricci had fallen out of favor with Mrs. Firestone recently anyway, with his constant womanizing, especially when she walked in on him and Miss Dolly Sinclair in bed, so I don't think she felt too badly about getting Goodacre to pull that trigger. She had a few slip-ups along the way, though, the biggest one being when she put the gun into Miss Lufkin's handbag during the beginning of the séance, not knowing Miss Lufkin had spilled her handbag all over the floor in front of us earlier. The lab results came back this morning, confirming Clive Goodacre's prints were on the gun, and that it was the gun used in both killings. Careless of Mr. Goodacre to leave his prints on the gun, but I supposed he never thought about it. There was also still one print of Ricci's on the barrel, and Mrs. Firestone's, but that's only natural since it was her gun. I imagine she didn't have to worry about that. But Mrs. Firestone's prints were also on Miss Lufkin's handbag, proving she handled it, and her prints were on the playing cards I told you about that we found in Ricci's room."

"Cold, vicious, *and* devious."

"And without a conscience, as murderers often are. I don't know how much she stood to collect from that life insurance policy, maybe around ten or fifteen grand, originally intended to be split three ways. That's hardly worth taking someone's life over, let alone two."

"And framing someone else for it," Alan said. "Two lives lost, another nearly destroyed, and two in prison. But didn't you say they were all pointing fingers at each other? Why would they do that if they were all in on it together? Wouldn't they want to give each other alibis?"

"I'm not sure exactly, but I have a feeling that was Mrs. Firestone's idea. Make it seem like each one suspected the others, so that no one person stood out. And they all kept trying to steer us back onto the idea of a robber or mugger, or Miss Lufkin. Each of them made a point of telling us how unstable she was."

"Poor Miss Lufkin," Alan said.

"Yes. And don't forget, Mrs. Firestone did provide Goodacre with an alibi when it came time to kill Ricci. She is the one who probably suggested she pretend to be him in his room, calling down for room service."

"Yeah, that's right. How did you ever figure that one out?"

"Lucky guess, partly. I remembered Mrs. Firestone said she did voices and impressions in her youth as part of her parents' vaudeville group, the DeLario Trio. And then when I impersonated Ricci on the phone to Dolly, I got the idea that perhaps that's what Mrs. Firestone did, too, except she impersonated Goodacre."

"Yikes. So, what will happen now?"

"Mr. Goodacre will stand trial for the murder of Lawrence Lorenzo Ricci and as an accessory to the murder of Alfred Almanzo Firestone. Mrs. Firestone will be charged as an accessory to both murders and in the attempt to frame Miss Lufkin, as well as the theft of her necklace. As for Miss Lufkin herself, she admitted during the séance that she blackmailed Ricci, but he's dead and unable to testify against her, and no money ever changed hands, so I'm honestly not sure what will happen to her legally. In any case, her faith in spiritualism has certainly been shaken, if not broken."

"I imagine so. I have to admit I'm a little deflated myself after hearing how Mrs. Firestone rigged that séance you went to," Alan said, taking another sip of his martini.

"She was clever. If I hadn't seen her metal-tipped slippers and noticed the arrow was made of metal, I might not have figured it out." I took a drink of my own martini and then set the glass down, careful to use a coaster. "And as for Leslie Birdwell, Birdy's flower shop is closed for good, out of business, and Mr. Birdwell is awaiting trial."

"How about that young fellow you told me about? The one at the boardinghouse?"

"Scotty? Riker followed up with Mrs. Webster and found out he did make the call to that doctor I referred him to, and she'll do her best to make sure he keeps the appointment. After that, it's really all up to him, but it won't be easy, and I'm afraid the odds are against him. As for Mrs. Webster, she's made it this far in the world, and I admire her greatly. She's someone I think I'd like to know better."

"I'd like to meet her."

"She'd like you, Alan. Maybe we can pay her a social call some afternoon. And maybe someday the world will be a better, more accepting place for everyone."

"I sure hope so. Say, I wonder why Ricci didn't tell you how to find Scotty. You said he was hinting around that the fellow Firestone met in the alley was the one who killed him. That's what he wanted you to think."

"Yes, but I imagine he didn't know for sure what Scotty witnessed. Perhaps he thought Scotty could identify him, so best to leave it as an unknown, and hopefully case closed."

"Except you and Riker figure it all out. What about Riker, by the way?"

I looked at Alan. "What about him?"

"Just wondering what will become of him and his wife. From what you've told me, their marriage is kinda rocky."

"Oh, yes, right. I honestly don't know what he'll decide in regard to his marriage. Maybe Mary Jane will decide it for him. I hope he'll do the right thing, and I've tried to steer him toward that, but as he explained, the right thing is not always black and white. He did tell me he's taking Mary Jane to meet Mrs. Webster next weekend. Regardless, he'll make a fine detective. He is a fine detective."

"So, the case of Firestone's and Ricci's murders has been solved."

"Yeah, another one for the books. Say, I better check on my hollandaise sauce for the broccoli," I said, getting up from the sofa.

Alan wandered into the kitchen as I stirred the contents of the pot simmering on the stove, my apron on once more. "Sure I can't help?" he said.

I glanced over at him. "You can open the wine if you like. I picked up a nice bottle of red. Oh, and light the candles on the table, if you would. There's some matches on the counter next to the breadbox, and the wine opener is in the drawer to the left of the sink."

"Jeepers, Heath, you went all out. Even candles and red tulips for the table, my favorite. Where did you ever find tulips in September?"

"At a florist's, but not Birdwell's, of course."

"Of course. Flowers from a florist cost a lot of money, though."

I looked over at him and smiled. "You're worth it."

"Gee, this isn't like you, Heath. A Wednesday evening, fancy dinner, flowers, candles, music. You even made a chocolate layer cake. And you're wearing your gray suit with the lavender tie that I like so much. Why?"

"Do I have to have a reason? Besides, the layer cake kinda fell."

"I'm sure it will still taste wonderful."

"Thanks. I'll whip up some cream for it later."

"I do love whipped cream. So no special occasion?"

I stopped stirring the pot and turned to look at him again. "No special occasion, but a special question I have to ask you, one I've asked you before but not in the right way."

"Oh? What?"

"Let's eat first. I want everything to be just right when I ask."

"Okay, but I can already tell you, with all my heart, that everything *is* just right."

MYSTERY HISTORY

1. Spiritualism still exists today, though it was at its height of popularity in the 1920s. By the 1940s interest in it had waned considerably. Harry Houdini was a famous skeptic, often attending séances in disguise in an attempt to expose fraudulent spiritualists.
2. The Blatz Hotel was a real place, but all the characters and events in my novel are fiction, and the interior descriptions are strictly from my imagination. It was originally an office building on the corner of Water and Wells in Milwaukee. It became the Grand Central Hotel in 1872. It was then enlarged and a mansard roof was added when it became the Blatz in 1897. It was demolished in 1968.
3. Valentin Blatz founded the Blatz brewery after purchasing the brewery owned by John Braun after Braun died. Blatz also married Braun's widow. Blatz produced beer in Milwaukee until 1959.
4. WBSM radio is a fictitious Milwaukee radio station I first created for my book *Death Takes a Bow*. It's made up of the initials of my friends, who called themselves the WB.
5. Myomancy actually is a method of divination involving mice, and stercomancy involves using bird excrement or seeds found in it, and both are used by some to predict omens. Cartomancy uses a regular deck of cards for divination.
6. Banana slugs do exist, and are often bright yellow, hence the name. They are simultaneous hermaphrodites.
7. Mozart's opera *The Marriage Of Figaro* continues to be performed. The Florentine Opera Company of Milwaukee was founded in 1933, and in 1942 changed its name from The Italian Opera

Chorus to The Florentine Opera Chorus. They first performed at Lincoln High School but moved to the Pabst Theater in the later 1940s.

8. Ezio Pinza was a well-known Italian opera singer, born in 1892. He performed for twenty-two seasons at the New York Metropolitan Opera. According to an article in the March 28, 1948, Pictorial Review section of the *Milwaukee Sentinel*, Mr. Pinza actually did perform in Milwaukee in real life in April of 1948. He was considered one of the greatest Figaros and Don Giovannis in Mozart's operas. He died in 1957.

9. Boston Store was a major Milwaukee Department Store, with its flagship store located downtown. It closed its doors in 2018 and today operates an online presence only. Gimbels Department Store operated from 1887 to 1987, with a large store located in Milwaukee.

10. Like WBSM radio, the Circle Room at the Hotel LaSalle was first mentioned in my book *Death Takes a Bow*, but unlike WBSM, the Circle Room really existed and was a popular dinner and nightclub location, and even hosted Nat King Cole, who produced a live record album recorded there, *Live at the Circle Room*.

11. Woolworth's was a popular nationwide five-and-dime store chain, opening its first store in 1879.

12. Hot potato salad and frankfurters was a popular low-cost dish in the 1940s, made with potatoes, bacon, wieners, onion, and hardboiled eggs, along with a little vinegar, salt, and pepper.

13. Florence Lufkin's last name came from a tape measure I possess, a Lufkin.

14. *Golf World* magazine was first published in 1947, so it's very likely the publisher would have sent sample issues out to various libraries to hopefully be included in their monthly periodicals.

15. The State Theater in Minneapolis opened in 1921, and still stands to this day on Hennepin Avenue.

16. Soundies were three-minute musical films played on coin-operated movie jukeboxes called Panarams. They could be found in nightclubs, bars, and restaurants, among other places, and each film cost ten cents to view. They lasted from 1940 until 1947, the year this story takes place, at which time commercial television began developing rapidly.

17. *Bib and tucker* is an old expression referring to one's finest, nicest clothes.

18. The Broadway Hotel in Gary, Indiana, was built in 1908 and burned down in 1952.

19. The Chicken Dinner candy bar really existed, made by Sperry's of Milwaukee. It consisted of chocolate with crisp, crunchy peanuts. Production ended in 1962, after forty years.

20. The movie *The Ghost and Mrs. Muir*, about a young widow and the ghost of a sea captain who haunts her seaside cottage, was released in 1947 and starred Gene Tierney and Rex Harrison. It was later made into a television series.

21. The green carnation was first popularized by Oscar Wilde in the 1890s. In nineteenth-century England, gay men often wore green carnations as a signal to other gay men.

22. The post–World War II housing shortage was very real, caused by returning veterans starting families, as well as mass immigration and the War Production Board order L-41, which stopped all non-war-related housing construction in 1942. The Veterans' Emergency Housing Program built 2.5 million homes from 1946 to 1948, but still there were wait lists for apartments and homes.

23. Wisconsin abolished the death penalty in 1853, making it the first state to permanently do away with it for all crimes. Missouri and Indiana still have the death penalty as of this writing.

24. Christine Jorgensen was a transgender woman in the United States. She became widely known in the 1950s for having sex reassignment surgery. She was born in 1926 and actually served in World War II in the Army.

About the Author

David S. Pederson was born in Leadville, Colorado, where his father was a miner. Soon after, the family relocated to Wisconsin, where David grew up, attending high school and university, majoring in business and creative writing. Landing a job in retail, he found himself relocating to New York, Massachusetts, and eventually back to Wisconsin. He and his husband now reside in the sunny Southwest.

His third book, *Death Checks In*, was a finalist for the 2019 Lambda Literary Awards. His fourth book, *Death Takes a Bow*, was a finalist for the 2020 Lambda Literary Awards.

He has written many short stories and poetry and is passionate about mysteries, old movies, and crime novels. When not reading, writing, or working in the furniture business, David also enjoys working out, and studying classic ocean liners, floor plans, and historic homes.

David can be contacted at davidspederson@gmail.com or via his website, www.davidspederson.com.

Books Available From Bold Strokes Books

Busy Ain't the Half of It by Frederick Smith and Chaz Lamar Cruz. Elijah and Justin seek happily-ever-afters in LA, but are they too busy to notice happiness when it's there? (978-1-63555-944-6)

Pursuit: A Victorian Entertainment by Felice Picano. An intelligent, handsome, ruthlessly ambitious young man who rose from the slums to become the right-hand man of the Lord Exchequer of England will stop at nothing as he pursues his Lord's vanished wife across Continental Europe. (978-1-63555-870-8)

Best of the Wrong Reasons by Sander Santiago. For Fin Ness and Orion Starr, it takes a funeral to remind them that love is worth living for. (978-1-63555-867-8)

Coming to Life on South High by Lee Patton. Twenty-one-year-old gay virgin Gabe Rafferty's first adult decade unfolds as an unpredictable journey into sex, love, and livelihood. (978-1-63555-906-4)

Death's Prelude by David S. Pederson. In this prequel to the Detective Heath Barrington Mystery series, Heath discovers that first love changes you forever and drives you to become the person you're destined to be. (978-1-63555-786-2)

His Brother's Viscount by Stephanie Lake. Hector Somerville wants to rekindle his illicit love affair with Viscount Wentworth, but he must overcome one problem: Wentworth still loves Hector's brother. (978-1-63555-805-0)

The Dubious Gift of Dragon Blood by J. Marshall Freeman. One day Crispin is a lonely high school student—the next he is fighting a war in a land ruled by dragons, his otherworldly boyfriend at his side. (978-1-63555-725-1)

Quake City by St John Karp. Can Andre find his best friend Amy before the night devolves into a nightmare of broken hearts, malevolent drag queens, and spontaneous human combustion? Or has it always happened this way, every night, at Aunty Bob's Quake City Club? (978-1-63555-723-7)

Death Overdue by David S. Pederson. Did Heath turn to murder in an alcohol-induced haze to solve the problem of his blackmailer, or was it someone else who brought about a death overdue? (978-1-63555-711-4)

Every Summer Day by Lee Patton. Meant to celebrate every summer day, Luke's journal instead chronicles a love affair as fast-moving and possibly as fatal as his brother's brain tumor. (978-1-63555-706-0)

Everyday People by Louis Barr. When film star Diana Danning hires private eye Clint Steele to find her son, Clint turns to his former West Point barracks mate, and ex-buddy with benefits, Mars Hauser to lend his cyber espionage and digital black ops skills to the case.(978-1-63555-698-8)

Cirque des Freaks and Other Tales of Horror by Julian Lopez. Explore the pleasure of horror in this compilation that delivers like the horror classics…good ole tales of terror. (978-1-63555-689-6)

Royal Street Reveillon by Greg Herren. In this Scotty Bradley mystery, someone is killing the stars of a reality show, and it's up to Scotty Bradley and the boys to find out who. (978-1-63555-545-5)

Death Takes a Bow by David S. Pederson. Alan Keys takes part in a local stage production, but when the leading man is murdered, his partner Detective Heath Barrington is thrust into the limelight to find the killer. (978-1-63555-472-4)

Accidental Prophet by Bud Gundy. Days after his grandmother dies, Drew Morten learns his true identity and finds himself racing against time to save civilization from the apocalypse. (978-1-63555-452-6)

Counting for Thunder by Phillip Irwin Cooper. A struggling actor returns to the Deep South to manage a family crisis but finds love and ultimately his own voice as his mother is regaining hers for possibly the last time. (978-1-63555-450-2)

Of Echoes Born by 'Nathan Burgoine. A collection of queer fantasy short stories set in Canada from Lambda Literary Award finalist 'Nathan Burgoine. (978-1-63555-096-2)